CHRISTMAS ESCAPE TO ARRAN

A heart-warming and uplifting novel set in Scotland

ELLIE HENDERSON

Scottish Romances Book 2

Choc Lit
A JOFFE BOOKS COMPANY

Choc Lit
A Joffe Books company
www.choc-lit.com

This edition first published in Great Britain in 2023

© Ellie Henderson 2023

This book is a work of fiction. Names, characters, businesses, organizations, places and events are either the product of the author's imagination or are used fictitiously. Any resemblance to actual persons, living or dead, events or locales is entirely coincidental. The spelling used is British English except where fidelity to the author's rendering of accent or dialect supersedes this. The right of Ellie Henderson to be identified as author of this work has been asserted in accordance with the Copyright, Designs and Patents Act 1988.

Cover art by Jarmila Takač

ISBN: 978-1-78189-634-1

PROLOGUE

Two months previously

Amelia walked out of the meeting and threw the box of homemade muffins in the bin. She always made them for these last-Friday-of-the-month meetings. But she had kept her hands gripped on the lid throughout. She didn't wish to share them after what they had just told her.

She knew redundancies were a possibility, but hadn't actually expected to lose *her* job. She'd been with the drinks company for five years and things had changed. Rising overheads and lower profit margins meant they'd had to streamline the business and outsource their marketing budget. Her job as marketing manager was obsolete with immediate effect. Standing by her desk though it was all hot-desking these days she cast a glance around the office. Her colleague and manager, Cara, coughed behind her.

'Sorry, Amelia. Please don't take it personally.' Her face was flushed and she did at least look slightly awkward.

Amelia sat down, twisting her platinum wedding band. What would Declan say? How would they ever be able to afford to buy their own home if they were going to need to survive on one income?

She glanced over at her best friend, Suna, who was the receptionist and sat at the top of the open-plan office. Suna winked at her and smiled, which made her feel slightly better.

'The thing is, Amelia . . .'

Amelia swivelled her chair around to look at Cara, who stood behind her.

'Well, we need you to leave now.'

Amelia burst out laughing. 'You're joking, right?'

Cara hopped from one foot to the other. 'No, I'm not . . . it's company policy.'

Amelia shook her head in disbelief. Standing up, she pulled on her blazer and swept the few possessions she had on the desk into her handbag. She strode defiantly towards the kitchen.

'Um, where are you going?'

'Well, you told me to take all my belongings. I think that includes my things in the kitchen.' Amelia marched in, opened a cupboard door and retrieved a box of peppermint tea. 'I might have left them for you if I felt a bit more generous — I know how much you like to help yourself to them.' With a toss of her ponytail, she reached for her mug on the draining board and threw it in her bag. It said *Newly Married* in bright-pink lettering. 'I'm going, Cara. You don't need to escort me off the premises.'

Cara smiled tightly as she continued to hover next to Amelia until they reached the lifts.

'Bye, Suna,' Amelia said. 'I'm leaving, as you can probably tell.'

'I'll give you a call, Amelia. Keep smiling, my love, and go and see that gorgeous husband of yours.'

Cara was still lingering. 'I hope we can still be friends,' she said as an afterthought.

Amelia stepped into the lift and turned around. 'Sure,' she said. 'Besties.'

Somehow, she managed to hold her emotions in until she reached the front door of their shoebox flat. At least Declan was working from home today. Things could always be worse. So much for upsizing, she thought, as she spotted the piles of wedding presents dominating the living room.

'Declan,' she called, walking into the bedroom and kicking off her shoes. She went into the kitchen, noticing how tidy it was, and filled the kettle. How good of him to clear up and declutter the surfaces. She momentarily wondered where he had put the coffee maker they'd been given as a gift, then saw the white envelope propped up against the toaster with her name on the front.

Strange. Had she missed something? A special date? She scanned her brain and realised it was their three-month anniversary. How sweet of him to remember. She ran her finger under the rim of the envelope and opened it in anticipation. Declan used to write her poems when they'd first got together. Maybe he'd written her an ode? She unfolded the paper and began to read.

Dear Amelia,

I'm so very sorry to be doing this. But I don't know what else to do. I have tried. But married life isn't for me. Please don't think you have done anything wrong. You are amazing and wonderful. I want you to be happy. You deserve someone who loves you one hundred per cent.

I've taken my stuff and am staying with a friend. The rent is paid for the next two months, so I hope that's one less thing to worry about. Please don't try to change my mind. I can't go on like this. I am so sorry.

Declan

The paper fluttered from her hands onto the floor. Amelia collapsed into a chair and sat in silent disbelief. Then the tears finally came and her whole body shuddered as she sobbed.

CHAPTER ONE

Describe yourself in ten words:
 Sad, hurt, confused, anxious, worried, lost, unloved, betrayed, broken-hearted, humiliated, alone, shattered, unlovable, unanchored...

Amelia stopped writing and closed her notebook. She could describe herself in far more than just ten words. All this journal exercise was doing was reminding her what a mess her life was.

CHAPTER TWO

The November air was sharp and stung Amelia's cheeks. She swayed outside on the deck of the ferry, looking to the island in front of her. Nausea bubbled in the pit of her stomach, and she took a deep breath, hoping to stop herself from vomiting. Throwing up en route to her new life wouldn't exactly be a great start. She gulped in a huge breath of air and the sensation passed. For the first time in weeks, Amelia allowed herself a wry smile. Trust her to forget she was prone to being seasick.

The boat created white foamy trails as it sliced through the dark green waves towards its destination: Arran, a small island in the Firth of Clyde. The sea journey lasted just under an hour — time enough to allow her to feel as though she was escaping. Despite the chill in the air, she had spent most of the crossing outside admiring the stunning scenery. She looked across the water to the Ailsa Craig, a seabird colony, which sat on its own and rose proudly from the water. The island was also where the granite for curling stones came from. Licking the saltwater from her lips, she jumped when the horn blasted. She focused her gaze ahead on Arran, trying to spot the castle. The hills were a patchwork of different shades of green and she could just about make out the slash of yellow beach. The buildings looked like dots. For the twentieth time that day she pinched herself. She couldn't believe she was really doing this.

Pulling her hat down over her ears, she pushed her hands deep into her coat pockets. She had always wanted to visit Arran as her parents had spent their honeymoon there. In fact, she had harboured dreams to perhaps have her own wedding there. But Declan insisted it would probably rain, the midges would bite all the guests and it was too far away from civilisation.

Looking around she watched an older couple on the other side of the deck, holding hands and admiring the view. Amelia's rucksack, stuffed with all the possessions she needed, toppled over and banged her foot. She wiped away a tear and reminded herself, again, life wasn't over. Things had merely taken an unexpected turn.

Covering her mouth, she stifled a yawn. After leaving London at the crack of dawn, she couldn't quite believe she was nearing the end of the long journey. Her friends all thought she was having some sort of breakdown when she'd announced she was quitting London to go and work on an island she had never been to. Not only that, but in the middle of nowhere and in winter. She'd tried to argue that technically it was still autumn, but her protests had been ignored.

Amelia had spotted the advert for the job online a few weeks after Declan had left.

TOURISM OFFICER WANTED FOR A BRILLIANT PROJECT!

I am looking for a temporary tourism officer to work on a secret new project on the beautiful island of Arran. The job will involve research, copywriting and marketing and a few other things. The successful applicant will be friendly, enthusiastic, open and flexible. They must also have a sense of humour! Pay will depend on experience, however the position also comes with free accommodation. Please email me and tell me why you think you're the person for the job! Edie@Coorie.com

Amelia had quickly emailed Edie telling her why she was the perfect person for the job. If she got the job, surely that was a sign it was meant to be? The old Amelia had always believed in serendipity. This job offered a glimmer of hope and at the very least would be a distraction from her broken heart.

'I can't believe you're actually going to do this,' Suna had said last night as Amelia had finished packing. 'This is so not you. I mean, an island in the middle of nowhere. Seriously?'

'I want a change. I don't want to be here anymore. I want to go somewhere quiet and have some solitude.'

Suna narrowed her eyes. 'You could do that in London. You don't need to go hundreds of miles away. Anyway, how will you cope? You're a city girl.'

Amelia laughed at her and tried batting away her concerns. 'I need to give it a go. This is something I must do for me. I need to try and make the most out of a crappy year.'

'Promise me if it doesn't work out, you'll come back?' Suna said. 'You'll always be welcome here.'

'Thanks.' Amelia looked around Suna's tiny bedroom, which had doubled as her room too for the past few nights. She hoped she wouldn't have to return with her tail between her legs and sleep on this floor again. This was meant to be all about positive thinking, new adventures and a fresh start.

As the ferry neared the harbour, Amelia began to wonder if she had made the right decision. It was freezing, growing dark, and she pulled up her hood as fat raindrops started to fall on her head. Hauling her bag onto her shoulders, she joined the line of passengers waiting to disembark.

She wasn't sure if it was the smell of diesel or her nerves making her feel sick again. Her new employer, Edie McMillan, had promised to collect her off the boat and Amelia prayed she would be waiting. Edie had 'interviewed' her over the phone, a loose description of what had ended up being an informal conversation about everything and anything including the island's historic buildings. Amelia was still unsure what the actual job entailed as Edie hadn't got down to specifics, other than to mention that she would be tasked with bringing more visitors to a specific tourist site, which she'd assumed was the castle. When she'd told Edie about her parents' connection with Arran, and that they had spent their honeymoon there, Edie had decided Amelia was perfect for the job. Especially when she'd heard about her work background.

Amelia had asked how many people had applied for the role, but Edie had remained vague and changed the subject. Amelia wondered if she should have asked more questions before uprooting herself and coming all this way. But it was too late now.

A gust of wind blew her hood down as she stepped off the gangplank and searched for Edie. As she waited by the bus stop as agreed, she felt very alone. So much for the new life she'd planned. Her friends were right: she was clearly having some kind of breakdown. With a sigh she pulled out her mobile, squinting to find out if she had reception. Edging nearer the car park, she was almost blinded by the approaching headlights of a van, which sailed through a massive puddle and drenched her.

She gasped, not quite believing it, but also totally believing it. Both her gasp and muttered, 'Brilliant,' were swallowed by the wind. She was now soaked, cross and ready to take the ferry back to the mainland. Why on earth had she thought this was a sensible plan?

'I'm *so* sorry,' said a voice behind her. 'I didn't see you.'

She turned around to see a man with an apologetic expression on his face.

'Are you the guy who just soaked me?'

'Yes. That was me. I totally didn't mean to do that.'

'Well,' she said, 'at least you're apologising.'

He shrugged. 'It's the least I can do.' His wet hair glistened and the rainwater ran off his jacket in huge droplets.

She bit her lip in case she said something she regretted. Having a tantrum was not the best idea, given she had been on the island for less than ten minutes.

'Look, can I help you?' he said, his voice softening. 'You seem lost.'

'I'm fine.'

'You sure?'

She nodded.

'All right, if you insist.' He sauntered off in the direction of the terminal.

Meanwhile, Amelia almost punched the air when she saw her phone finally had a signal.

'Hello, is that Edie?'

'It is.'

'Hi. This is Amelia . . . erm, I'm here.'

'That's wonderful news,' Edie said warmly.

'Are you still able to meet me?'

'Oh dear. No, I'm afraid not. Car trouble . . .'

Super, thought Amelia. *Now what?*

'He should be waiting for you.'

'Who?'

'Fergus.'

'Who's Fergus?'

'A friend. He said he would come and get you and bring you to the village. He'll be there any minute. You can't miss him. I told him to check inside.'

Amelia turned to watch the man she had just exchanged cross words with walking back towards her.

'He's quite easy on the eye, if you know what I mean.' Edie chuckled. 'He drives a van. An orange camper van. You can't miss him.'

Amelia's cheeks flushed. *Could this day get any better?*

CHAPTER THREE

'You must be Fergus?' said Amelia.

'And you're Amelia?' He raised an eyebrow. 'Though I must say you don't quite fit Edie's description.'

'Oh. Why, who were you looking for?'

'Hmm, going by what she said, an older woman who may look slightly knackered and in need of a holiday.'

Amelia couldn't help laughing. Her new employer was certainly correct with her comment. 'Well . . . I'm not quite sure what to say. She might be right.' Just at that moment another drop of water ran across her forehead and down her nose.

He chuckled. 'Don't worry, Edie never has been good on details. She tends to make things up as she goes along. I'm Fergus. Nice to meet you.'

'Amelia,' she said. Should she try to shake his hand? She couldn't help but notice his dark eyes and strong stubble-covered jaw.

'Come on, we're over here.' He pointed at the VW van. 'Can I help you with your things?'

'No, thank you. I'll manage.'

He shrugged and walked towards the car park. Hesitating, she wondered if she should forget all this. There was still time to catch the ferry back to Ardrossan and a train to Glasgow. Though then where would she go? She didn't really belong anywhere anymore.

'Problem?' He frowned when he realised she wasn't moving.

She gave herself a shake. 'No, no. I'm coming.'

He opened the passenger side so she could jump in and took her bag. 'So, you're here from London?' He slotted the keys into the ignition and started the engine.

'Yes.' Amelia yawned. The last thing she wanted was to make polite small talk with a stranger. Even a good-looking one.

'You're here to work with Edie?' He glanced across at her.

'Yes,' she said, suddenly lost for words. 'Should be fun, I hope.' What did that even mean? She was hardly going to be working at a theme park. 'I haven't worked in a castle before.'

He nodded and cleared his throat as though about to speak but stopped. Instead, he flicked on the radio and she rested her head against the window. Fergus turned up the volume and she smiled when she realised it was her favourite song, 'I'm A Cuckoo'. 'I love Belle and Sebastian.'

'Oh.' His tone indicated he was clearly surprised she knew them.

'I saw them in London a few times.'

'Right.'

Amelia closed her eyes, and the combination of the music and the hypnotic sound of the windscreen wipers lulled her to a happy place several years ago, when her brother, Jack, had come over to visit. They rarely managed to spend time together due to his busy career as a doctor in Boston. They maximised their time together, out most nights at the theatre or pubs and gigs. The concert at the Roundhouse had been extra special, and not only because they'd laughed so much together and danced, carefree and without a worry in the world. It had been the night he'd told her he was in love with his new boyfriend, Ray. His eyes had shone and Amelia had been so glad to see him smitten again after being miserable and broken-hearted after several bad break-ups.

Jack and Ray had come over for her wedding, and her brother had been a rock ever since Declan walked out. He'd never tried to talk her out of moving to Arran or accused her of being ridiculous. He'd listened to her crying across the Atlantic at different times of the day. They were close and had been for a long time. Jack might only have been two years older but he'd assumed a bit of a father role after their own dad passed away ten years ago. Their mother had decided to return to her roots in New Zealand and now lived in Auckland, where she'd remarried. Aside from her brief visit back to the UK for Amelia's wedding, Auckland was now her home and she didn't like to travel too far unless necessary. If it hadn't been for Jack and Suna, she didn't know how she would have coped the past couple of months . . .

Amelia woke to the sound of tyres moving across gravel. Fergus had pulled into . . . a driveway? A light came on, illuminating the outside of a cottage.

'We're here.' Fergus gently patted her shoulder. 'Welcome to Lamlash.'

She became aware of the drool sliding down the corner of her chin. Wiping it away, she turned to him, her voice groggy. 'Sorry. I must have dozed off.'

'Well, it sounds like you've had a long journey.' He jumped out and went into the back to retrieve her bag. 'Though you're quite a loud snorer.'

Amelia's face flushed.

'Just joking.'

A small woman, with grey bobbed hair and cerise lipstick, opened the front door of the whitewashed house and beamed. Two large pieces of driftwood framed the door and above it hung a little sign: *Welcome to Coorie Cottage*. 'Hello, dear. Great to meet you!' She stepped forward to hug Amelia.

'Hi.' Amelia was unexpectedly overcome with emotion. 'I'm glad to finally be here.' In a bid to stem the tears threatening to start, she focused her eyes on Edie's bright pink dungarees covered in tiny sunflowers.

'Do you like them?' She noticed Amelia staring.

'Yes. They're very . . . colourful.'

'My way of adding a splash of cheer to a drab day. Anyway, come on in, out the cold. What a long day. I know you had an early start.'

'Here's your stuff.' Fergus walked in behind her and put the rucksack on the hall floor.

'Thanks for that, my love. You're a wee superstar.'

He smiled fondly at Edie. 'Always pleased to help.'

'Thank you for the lift. I appreciate it.' Amelia smiled at him.

'No bother.'

There was a sudden patter of paws, which skidded across the hallway.

'Well, hello, gorgeous girl.' Fergus knelt to tickle the ears of a spaniel, which started licking his face.

Edie laughed. 'I think that is the most enthused I have ever heard you around a female. Amelia, meet Molly.'

Molly wagged her tail so vigorously that her whole bottom moved back and forth. She looked up at Fergus in adoration, then barked softly when she spotted Amelia and ran over.

Amelia reached forward to stroke her silky head. 'Aren't you lovely?'

'She's a real sook,' said Edie. 'And she likes to pretend that she's never ever fed. Don't be fooled. Come on, Molly, come over here.' Molly obediently trotted over and sat at Edie's feet, looking in turn at Fergus and Amelia. 'Do you want to stay and have a cuppa with us, dear?'

'No, Edie. Much as I'd love to stay, I best be off. I've got a bit of work to get on with. I'll see you later.' He waved and turned to go.

Edie closed the door behind him and ushered Amelia through into the living room at the back of the house. The cottage was as homely as Amelia had imagined it would be — she had looked it up on Google Maps before her arrival — with its cushions and throws and the log burner ablaze in the centre of the room. The wooden floors were shiny and the walls tastefully decorated with bright canvas pictures of wildflowers.

'What did I tell you?' Edie winked at her. 'He's rather handsome, isn't he?'

'Erm, it was really kind of him to pick me up . . . although I got a bit wet.' She looked down at her trousers, which stuck to her legs.

'Oh, I didn't realise your clothes were all wet. Come on. Let me show you upstairs to your room and you can sort yourself out.' She reached under the sink and gave Amelia an old towel to dry her hair with. 'This way.' Amelia followed her upstairs and Edie showed her into a cosy bedroom with a huge en-suite.

'I'll quickly change and then come down.'

Edie waved her hand. 'Take your time.'

Although part of Amelia wanted to throw herself onto the very comfortable-looking bed, she knew she couldn't hide out for long. Instead, she put on some dry clothes and looked around, wondering what to do with the damp pile. She folded them up and placed them by the door. She would ask Edie about using her washing machine later.

'Does that feel better, dear?' Edie looked up as Amelia walked into the room. 'Take a seat and I'll make you something warm to drink. I'm not sure about you but I'm gasping for a cuppa.'

'Thank you. That sounds nice.' She sighed. 'I can't believe I'm actually here.'

'Well, that's all that matters. Sit yourself down and I'll be back in a minute.'

Amelia sank into one of the large easy chairs and Molly immediately sat down beside her on the floor. It felt surreal to be so far away from home and from Declan. This was a million miles away from what her life had been only a few months ago. Yet she was comfortable sitting in this stranger's house with a dog at her side.

Although she knew Edie was in her seventies, you would never have thought it. Her bright clothes, high cheekbones and clear, unwrinkled skin gave her a youthful look. Her brown eyes were kind and observant, and she moved with an effortless grace, which was down to years of yoga. Amelia knew this, as yoga and age had cropped up in the 'interview'.

'This is a lovely room,' said Amelia as Edie walked back in with a tray.

'I'm glad you think so,' she said, setting the tray down. 'What do you take in your tea?'

'Oh, I take it black, please.'

'Here you go.' Edie poured her a cup. 'Are you hungry?'

Amelia's stomach rumbled.

Edie laughed. 'Perfect timing. I've a pot of soup on the stove and some fresh bread from the bakery. Travelling can take a lot out of you so you'll be tired and a bit out of sorts.'

Amelia stifled a yawn. 'Yes, I am. And thank you, that sounds lovely.' This was perfect and exactly what she needed. She took a sip of the tea and closed her eyes, just enjoying the moment.

'Miserable weather for your arrival. But don't worry. Things can only get better. The spare room is made up for you tonight as it's so dark. There's no point in faffing about outside now.'

Amelia opened her eyes to look at Edie. 'Oh, okay.' She thought she would be lodging with Edie for the duration of the job. Free accommodation was part of the contract. What did she mean outside?

Edie burst out laughing. 'Don't look so worried, dear. It will all be fine. You'll see the surprise tomorrow.'

Amelia's heart sank. She hated surprises.

CHAPTER FOUR

Edie's hands clasped the letter a bit tighter as she sat on the edge of her bed and read the contents over for the umpteenth time. It had arrived earlier that day with a pile of bills and leaflets, so she hadn't immediately noticed it. Instead, she'd popped the mail on the small hallway table and carried on with the hoovering. If she had known what the letter contained, would she have opened it earlier?

When she'd stopped for a coffee, she'd remembered there were bills to attend to. Shuffling through the envelopes as she'd walked back into the kitchen, she'd frowned when she'd clocked the thick white envelope with a printed label. Perhaps an invitation to an exhibition on the mainland? Receiving something that wasn't a bill or a discount coupon for the supermarket was such a rare pleasure these days. The simple act of sliding a knife along the rim of the envelope had had a magic effect, and she'd smiled when she'd seen a folded piece of paper inside. When had she last received a handwritten letter? She'd placed it on the kitchen table and busied herself making coffee. Then she'd sat down, put on her glasses, unfolded the paper and started to read.

Dear Edie,

Please don't throw this away. I need you to read what I am about to tell you. I am sorry I am telling you my news in this way. I wish I could speak to you in person. This may be the coward's approach but as you are well aware by now, that is what I am. There is no simple way to tell you I am dying. Even writing the actual words feels strange. I'm not sure if you ever get used to the idea your life is drawing to a close. Yet I am still here, and I am still me. I'm not dead quite yet.

This is not an easy letter to write. Especially after all these years. What can I say, Edie? Other than I am sorry. I can't rewrite history. How I wish I could. But I need you to know that I am so truly sorry for what happened and for what I did. I can never forgive myself, but I hope you are able to forgive me before I go.

I've got cancer. The doctors won't tell me how long I have — they're vague about the prognosis. But they have told me that this Christmas will almost definitely be my last. I think I'll be lucky if I am still here by the end of the year. I'm at the Beatson in Glasgow having treatment and I'm finding it tough. I know I don't have to tell you how cruel life is. But this has made me realise that I have to speak to you and hug you one last time. That thought is what's keeping me going. I'm hanging on for you, my beautiful little sister.

I know I don't deserve you, but I wondered if you could find it in your heart to come and visit me one last time? Please don't let's leave things like this. Give me the chance to say sorry again. And to say goodbye. Please?

With all my love,
Christine x

Edie had blinked as she'd read the words, clasping her hand over her mouth in shock. She'd sat in stunned silence until the light had started to fade, and finally, her legs stiff, had shakily stood and gone straight to the cupboard to pour herself a whisky. She'd swallowed it quickly, enjoying the burning sensation in the back of her throat. All she'd wanted to do was watch some mindless TV to distract her racing thoughts. But that couldn't happen because she was due to collect Amelia from the ferry terminal. So she'd called Fergus and claimed car trouble and politely asked him to go instead.

Now, as she sat on her bed going over the words again, they were like bullets in her stomach. It still hadn't sunk in, though she had read the letter several times. She could scarcely believe it. And the onus was on her to decide what to do. Her sister, who she hadn't spoken to for almost twenty years, was dying. She opened the top drawer of her bedside table and tucked the letter into her diary. In the meantime, she would focus on Amelia and the job she would be tasking her to do. That had to take priority for the moment, regardless of Christine's news. She could not and would not just go to pieces. She climbed into bed and pulled the covers up tightly, Molly grunting in annoyance that her sleeping position was being disturbed.

Edie thought about Amelia for a moment. She always believed things happened for a reason and she believed fate had brought Amelia here. Despite her perfect appearance — groomed hair and French manicure — and her polite ways, she could sense sadness in Amelia. She looked frail and forlorn, and Edie could see the anguish and hurt in her eyes. Something must have happened to make her come here on her own. Yet experience had taught Edie that Amelia wouldn't welcome any prying questions. She would tell her story when she was ready. In the same way that she would share her story about Christine when she was ready to do so. Except Edie wasn't quite sure if she ever would be.

She reached out and ruffled Molly's ears and the dog sighed deeply, as though she'd spent the day racing up and down Goatfell several times rather than the reality of a day lying dreaming by the fire. 'Oh, Molly,' she said. 'What should I do?' The dog seemed to sense Edie's anguish and moved even closer to her owner, licking her hand when she settled.

Edie slept restlessly as broken images of her and Christine as children came back into her mind. They'd been inseparable, always finishing each other's sentences and somehow picking up on what each other thought without needing any words. She thought about the time they'd spent playing in their Wendy house at the bottom of the garden, lying on the grass and making daisy chains and holding tea parties for their dolls with homemade lemonade. She thought of how much of a rock Christine had been to her so many times in her life. Then when Jim died suddenly, they'd supported each other through a hideous time of grief and shock. She couldn't allow her mind to dwell on what had caused their fall-out. The sad thing was that they'd never been the type of siblings to compete for attention from their parents or hold grudges. They really had always been the best of friends.

The move to Arran had saved Edie when life had almost overwhelmed her. She'd built a new life for herself in this wonderful community and felt safe and supported.

As day dawned, she dragged herself from her bed and rolled out her yoga mat, falling into her daily gentle routine of asanas to stretch, lengthen and balance her system. Christine's news had shaken her to her core and her mind was a whirl of emotions. She tried her best to focus on her breathing and counted slowly in and out. But this morning it didn't help her let go of her worry and fear. When she opened her eyes, nothing had changed. The letter was still there and she had no idea what to do.

CHAPTER FIVE

The following morning, Amelia crept out of the cottage, admiring the burnt orange leaves scattered over the grass. She walked down the path towards the gate opening onto the beach. Pink clouds streaked the pale blue sky and she gasped at the stunning view. The sea was as still as a pond and the Holy Isle, a small rocky island across the bay, looked so beautiful. Mainly a nature reserve, it was also home to a community of Buddhist monks.

Clambering over the pebbles, she began walking along the shoreline, taking huge gulps of the clean, fresh air. She couldn't believe she had the whole beach to herself. What a contrast to her usual London morning walk and Tube journey to work. She wasn't complaining though, she could easily adjust to this. She pulled her phone from her pocket, snapped some shots and sent them to Suna.

Good morning! Welcome to my world and my new favourite place xx

She looked at the three dots moving and waited for Suna to reply.

Wow. Looks amazing. But is there a Costa? Call me later. Some of us have to go to work! X

She smiled and realised for the first time since losing her job she was actually okay. Redundancy had come completely out of the blue and she had taken it very personally, particularly when their sales had reached an all-time high. She had worked for a trendy boutique drinks company selling vodka and rum, and which, according to Suna, was now expanding its line to include gin and whisky. Over the past five years she'd implemented a successful brand strategy that had over-delivered on all its forecasts and budgets, and its online presence had won loads of awards. She'd thrown herself into the role and worked tirelessly over the years. That was why she had been so gutted to lose it. Apparently, she was dispensable.

As she continued to walk, looking around in awe, the job stuff no longer mattered. She felt completely refreshed this morning after a very comfortable sleep. Last night, Edie had fed her delicious soup and amazing bread from the bakery. Amelia had laughed at Edie's reaction when she'd told her how much she used to pay for a cup of soup and a piece of baguette from the deli by her office. Afterwards she'd retreated back to the lovely guest room. The bed had a thick, white, puffy duvet and more pillows than she knew what to do with. The en-suite bathroom looked as though it belonged in a boutique hotel with its underfloor heating, huge bathtub and piles of freshly laundered, fluffy white towels. After a relaxing soak she'd climbed into bed, rolled herself up in the quilt and fallen asleep almost immediately. When she'd woken up, a few moments passed before she realised that her first thought wasn't worry or a sense of heaviness descending on her. For once she hadn't thought of her broken heart. Instead, she'd focused on the excitement of being somewhere new.

Standing on the beach, she watched the diving gannets swoop in and out of the water and listened to the gentle lap of the waves. What an invigorating way to start the day. She hoped her time on this island would help her untangle the jumble of thoughts in her mind and maybe help her to heal.

She clicked a few more images and sent them to Jack, so he would see them when he woke up. Then, turning, she continued her journey along the beach, smiling as she passed a dog-walker whose puppy strained at the lead. A bolt of grief hit her. *They'd* always planned to get a dog. Declan had promised her that when they moved from the city, they would definitely buy a puppy. She could picture him, his face earnest, as he nodded and said it was also his dream to have a cockapoo. Another promise in the pack of cards that had tumbled down in the wake of his departure.

She stared out at the sea and tried to forget. Come on, Amelia, you can't let a memory like that ruin your day. Not when you woke up feeling optimistic. *You have to let it go.* She was tired of all the questions and memories that kept bouncing around her head. As she stood there, intent on regaining the sense of peace and composure that she'd started the day with, she realised something was moving in the water. It had a smooth head and she narrowed her gaze. This was all just getting better. It had to be a seal. Loads of them lived in these waters. Wait until she told Suna and Jack! She pulled her phone back out and was about to take another shot when she zoomed in. Since when did seals wave? Or swim directly towards people, smiling? Slipping her phone in her pocket, she waited, bemused, as the bobbing head got closer and the person emerged from the water in a wetsuit, hood and gloves.

'Good morning,' said Fergus cheerily, pulling off the hood and raking his fingers through his hair.

'Oh. Hello,' she stammered.

'Hello! Lovely morning, isn't it?'

She nodded. 'What were you doing?' *Oh, for goodness' sake? What did she think he was doing? Playing the violin.* How she wished she could stuff the words back inside her mouth and move away as swiftly as possible.

'Erm, swimming.' His dark brown eyes crinkled in amusement.

Amelia couldn't help staring at him as he stood there like some sort of action hero, clad from head to foot in neoprene. 'Isn't it cold?'

'Well, it is at first but you soon warm up. The wetsuit helps. You should try it sometime.'

She giggled. *Swimming? In Scotland? In the sea? In November? Never.* 'Yes, I should,' she said casually, as though it was the sort of thing she did all the time.

He gestured at his van parked up on the road. 'I'd better go and warm up. I'll catch you later.' Then he reached a hand towards her cheek.

Amelia felt herself start to wobble. What was he doing? Wasn't it a bit early for this kind of thing? He barely even knew her. She involuntarily started to tilt her head up toward his hand. *What was she doing?*

'You've got a feather in your hair.' He pulled it from her head and blew it away.

Oh, dear God. 'Clearly I didn't look at a mirror before I left the house this morning.' Her cheeks turned bright red and she managed to laugh. 'It will probably be from one of Edie's many pillows. Thanks. Again.'

'No bother.' He jerked his head towards his van. 'I'd better go get some clothes on. I'm a bit chilly.'

She smiled and said, 'Bye for now,' then turned and retraced her steps back along the beach, forcing herself to keep her eyes ahead and not turn back. As she walked, she mulled over the interaction again and again. What on earth was wrong with her? She'd known him for approximately five minutes and had turned into a quivering wreck. It wasn't exactly how newly separated women were supposed to behave, was it? Shouldn't she be broken-hearted? At that moment all she could think about was what was underneath that wetsuit and the annoying way she kept blushing whenever he happened to glance her way.

CHAPTER SIX

Fergus watched Amelia make her way back along the beach, unable to pull his eyes away. He sighed softly. It had been a long time since he had felt drawn to a woman in the way he was to her. She was pretty, with her dark hair and huge smile that lit up her face. But she was funny and real, which attracted him even more. Plus, there was something about her that intrigued him. He could sense sadness in her eyes, yet a glimmer of something else, and the fact she had come here alone in the middle of winter meant she was plucky. Inhaling a deep breath of the crisp morning, he felt invigorated, and not just because of his cold swim.

Smiling, he headed back up to the van, parked on his usual patch of grass. He quickly dressed and then made his way towards Cèic, the café, to pick up his usual coffee.

* * *

When Amelia arrived back at the cottage, she walked through the garden, admiring the view of the rolling hills in the distance. She let herself in and crouched to tickle Molly, who greeted her happily.

Edie was bustling around the bright kitchen making tea and toast. 'Good morning, dear. Enjoy your walk?'

'It was lovely, thanks. I love that beach . . . and I saw Fergus.'

'Let me guess . . . was he swimming?' asked Edie.

Amelia nodded.

'That would be a sight for sore eyes,' she said, erupting into a deep throaty chuckle. This morning, Edie wore slim-fit jeans with a navy sweater and a necklace made from huge mustard-yellow beads. She leaned against the worktop and crossed her arms. 'Well, you've got some colour about your cheeks. You must be hungry. Sit down and help yourself.'

Amelia realised she was ravenous and took a seat at the table, which had a large vase of white roses placed in the middle. She tucked into several slices of toast with Edie's homemade marmalade. 'This is delicious,' she said, allowing her eyes to close as she appreciated the flavours of lemon and lime. 'And your coffee is too.' The smell of vanilla-scented coffee was divine.

Edie laughed. 'I decided it was time for an upgrade and to move on from the instant. These pods are quite the thing, you know.' She patted the coffee machine.

'You have everything you need. Fancy coffee, artisan bread and delicious homemade soup. Can I stay here for ever?' She traced her finger across the red-spotted oilcloth that covered the table. 'It's so peaceful.'

'Is there anything in particular you would like to do today?' asked Edie.

'Well, I'm happy for you to show me the ropes at work and tell me what I need to do.'

Edie shrugged. 'Of course. But don't worry too much about that. Let yourself settle in and have a look around the village. Lamlash is just one of the villages on the island. There is so much to see. What can I tell you about it?'

'I've done some research,' said Amelia. 'I'd love to have a look around Brodick and check out the castle. Then there's the King's Caves, Blackwaterfoot and the cheese company and Arran Aromatics . . .'

'You certainly have done your homework. That's what I like to hear.'

'But I'm here to work, Edie. Honestly, I am more than happy just to get started.' When Edie didn't say anything, Amelia quickly filled the silence. 'Or let me know if there is anything I can help you with here? I don't want you to think that I'm taking advantage.'

'There will be plenty for you to do but, in the meantime, just humour me. Think of the next couple of days as staff training or something like that.'

A few minutes passed as the women sat in comfortable silence sipping their mugs of coffee. 'You mentioned that your parents spent their honeymoon here?'

Amelia nodded. 'Yes, they stayed in a B&B in Brodick. Though I can't remember the name.'

'Can you ask them?'

'Well, my father is dead . . . and my mother has since remarried. I don't really want to bring it up in case it upsets her.'

'Does she know you're here?' Edie asked softly.

Amelia nodded, though she could feel the tears that never seemed to be far away threatening to appear. 'Yes. She lives in New Zealand now. But I let her know about my plans.'

The truth was that Amelia and her mother weren't close, and when she'd mentioned her plans to visit Arran, her mother hadn't really said much at all, other than, 'I'm sure you'll enjoy it.'

She swallowed hard to stop herself from crying. 'I'm just keen to explore and have some time on my own.'

Edie drained her mug and stood up. 'Okay, well, don't worry about that. I don't think that will be a problem. First things first. I need to show you your new staff quarters.'

'Oh, okay,' said Amelia uncertainly.

'Come on, you'll need your jacket, and slip your shoes back on.'

Amelia followed her to the shoe rack by the front door where she'd left her trainers. She reached up to the peg and pulled off her jacket. She didn't want to leave this cosy cottage. Where on earth was Edie, who had pulled on her wellies and raincoat, going to take her?

'Come on, follow me.'

Amelia did as she was told and walked behind Edie, who marched down the path. But instead of opening the gate, she suddenly veered to the left and down towards a large grassy area which was tucked away and which Amelia hadn't noticed earlier.

'Well,' said Edie excitedly. 'What do you think?'

Amelia gasped in astonishment. This was not at all what she'd been expecting.

CHAPTER SEVEN

'So . . . what do you think?' Edie said again, twirling around in excitement.

'Well, erm, I think it's . . . lovely?' Amelia said, completely taken aback.

'You're my first guest!' Edie's eyes shone and she clapped her hands together.

'Oh, okay.' Amelia managed to squeeze out a smile. In front of her were steps leading up to a veranda and a small oak cabin.

'Do you want to look inside?' Edie didn't wait for a reply, instead turning to walk up the steps. 'It's a shepherd's hut. Luxury and handcrafted with love.' Edie giggled. 'I think it's quite cosy and I hope you'll enjoy staying here. I'm quite tempted to move in myself.'

Amelia tried to seem enthusiastic but inwardly she grimaced. This would be like camping . . . which she didn't mind in the summer somewhere like France when it was warm and dry. But the thought of roughing it in Scotland in winter didn't inspire her at all. Especially if she was going to have to swaddle herself in a sleeping bag and hundreds of blankets. Not to mention the lack of facilities. Was she going to have to get up in the night to go back inside the cottage to use the loo? Or, worse still, squat in the corner of the garden?

'Come on and see inside,' Edie said, gesturing to Amelia. 'And don't worry, there's an en-suite shower room, in case you were wondering.' She opened the door and Amelia's eyes widened in surprise when she looked inside, blinking wildly as she took it all in. The hut was painted white and had watercolours in pale, chalky blue frames artfully hung on the walls. The solid oak flooring shone in the early morning sunlight. At one end of the hut was a small double bed with built-in storage underneath. The bed had a thick white duvet, lots of pillows and several scatter cushions in a duck-egg blue along with a chenille throw. The large windows, with pale blue curtains, were at the end of the bed and looked right out onto the beach.

'Look — you can leave the curtains open at night if you want and let the sunrise wake you naturally.'

'Wow,' said Amelia, her feelings of doubt evaporating. Just along from the bed was a small wooden breakfast bar, with a jug of yellow roses, and another window looking out on the same view over the beach. A couple of stools were tucked below. Along from the bar and by the door were pale blue wooden coat pegs. At the other end of the cabin was a tiny but well-equipped kitchen with oven, hob, fridge and small Belfast sink with a large wooden chopping board on top. Next to the kitchen area was a log-burning stove and a comfy tub chair.

'It is beautiful, Edie. So cosy and welcoming,' she said, turning around in awe. 'Just incredible.'

Edie beamed. 'You could be in the middle of nowhere and you're only a stone's throw from the beach.'

Amelia looked out of the window at the multicoloured leaves on the hedge, which lined the front of the garden. 'And it is so peaceful.'

'Imagine what it will look like in spring and summer!' Edie quickly rattled off a list of summer activities that she was sure Amelia would enjoy.

Amelia watched Edie's face. She was clearly thrilled with the arrangement and Amelia didn't want to remind her that the job had been advertised as temporary. She had no idea if she would still be here by Christmas, never mind spring or summer, though she couldn't stop herself from imagining the pale pink blossom on the trees and the snowdrops and daffodils, which would surely be resplendent in Edie's garden.

'I know you will be very happy here, my dear.'

Amelia nodded. 'I think you're right.' She looked at the stools and imagined herself sitting there warm and relaxed, with the heat from the stove and a glass of red wine. That would be the perfect place to write in her journal or read a good book. She smiled.

'Oh, and I decided to go for solar power, so there is electricity.' Edie pointed at the USB ports. 'And those. I know they're a necessity for you young ones. Have a look around, take your time, and come over and get your stuff when you're ready,' she called over her shoulder as she opened the door.

'Thanks, Edie. I will.' Amelia gently shut the door and turned round, leaning against it. This all seemed too good to be true. She walked back over towards the bed, tentatively sitting down. She stared out of the window at the blue sky and the dark sea ahead. What a different world this was to the grey life in London she had just left. Leaning back against the soft pillows, all she saw was sky. It would be magical to wake up to this. For a brief moment a buzz of excitement fluttered in her stomach as she focused on the view in front of her. Then she leaped off the bed and went to look at the en-suite facilities at the other end of the cabin.

She unlatched the door and peeked inside — a small but perfect shower room with a gas-shower, sink and toilet. It had all that she needed. It was the perfect romantic hideaway, she thought. It really was idyllic, but her smile disappeared when she thought of Declan and her impending isolation here. How she wished they were enjoying this together. *If he hadn't left you, you wouldn't even be here*, a voice reminded her.

A memory of putting on her wedding dress popped back into her head. She had tried the gown on so many times in the run-up to the big day, but there was something extra special about slipping into it on the morning of the wedding. Fitted at the waist and made from satin and lace, it fell straight to the floor below her hips. Amelia had wanted something simple, which moved easily yet was also flattering. When she'd worn it, she'd felt amazing, and as she'd walked down the aisle towards Declan, gripping Jack's arm, she'd known from the way Declan had looked at her that he'd been bowled over too.

Or had he been? Maybe he hadn't and she'd just imagined it. Perhaps she should have paid more attention and been less self-absorbed.

She slipped her hand into her pocket and found her phone, suddenly desperate to talk to him. She hadn't seen him in person since he'd walked out, and although she had tried calling him a couple of times and left voicemails, he had only responded with the briefest of texts.

Before she changed her mind, she pressed call and waited. It didn't go straight to voicemail, but this time rang out several times. Her heart skipped a beat as she realised that he might actually pick up the phone. But then he must have ended the call because, again, she was directed to voicemail. This time, she didn't leave a message. Instead, she tapped out a quick text.

I miss you. Please call me. x

She pressed send before she changed her mind.

CHAPTER EIGHT

Edie walked towards the main street to post a letter and let Molly stretch her legs. Amelia hadn't wanted to come with her and had made an excuse about needing to unpack and settle into the hut. Edie had a sense that it was best not to push her at the moment. She would give her a day to acclimatise and then try again tomorrow. There was no point in prying into the young woman's business. That wasn't at all Edie's style anyway. She knew people here would be curious about Amelia's background and story, and hoped they wouldn't be too nosy. Everyone had baggage but that didn't necessarily mean they wanted to unpack it. She sighed and brushed away a stray coil of hair from her face.

As she wandered along the road, she looked appreciatively at the seascape, which never failed to calm or inspire her. The palette of colours was so varied. Some days the water was a vivid, fresh blue which merged with the bright sky, other days an olive green topped with grey-and-white clouds. Every day was different, which she absolutely loved. How she adored this place that was now her home. She waved at Davey, the lollipop man, who stood waiting at his usual spot, and smiled at Cano in the window of Cèic, the bakery and café where she was a regular visitor. His face brightened when he saw her and he grinned.

Most of the shops on the island, aside from the large Co-op, were independent retailers, and social enterprises which reinvested back into the local community. It had a vibrant tourism industry, and during the summer months the ferries were usually packed with holidaymakers who always spent their holidays on the island and the day-trippers who fancied a quick escape. Although in recent times the unreliable ferry service had put a lot of the day-trippers off visiting.

Edie and Christine used to spend summer holidays here as children and she loved it. Her parents had always taken a cottage round at Kildonan, a small village on the south coast of the island. They'd spent many a happy day exploring the rock pools, fishing, crabbing, learning to swim and enjoying picnics at the beach. They'd been outside all day, come rain or shine. She often smiled when she thought back to those special days. Little did she know she would end up moving here permanently.

She kept walking past the small pier and Molly wagged her tail, sniffing the ground closely as though it was covered in gourmet treats. Someone had crammed their fish-and-chip containers in the bin and a seagull determinedly tapped at it with its beak, almost disappearing inside the rubbish to try and prise it open. Molly lifted her head and barked and it eyed her lazily, before eventually flapping away.

Edie had lived in Edinburgh for years, where she'd been rather anonymous, and had always longed to be part of a community where she would say hello to familiar faces and people stopped to have a chat. There were of course lots of positives about living in the capital though. She loved how dynamic and vibrant it was, and the way that the ancient and modern blended so seamlessly. She could walk from the New Town, where they'd lived in a huge apartment, and be at Princes Street Gardens in a brisk ten-minute walk. She never tired of the walk past the castle or visiting the Scottish National Gallery, where she would often stop for a coffee and stare out at the view of the gardens. It was a wonderful city to explore on foot, and throughout the year there were festivals and cultural productions that ensured she and Jim had been frequent visitors to the theatres.

Jim had been a finance broker for one of the banks and had spent much of his time travelling between Edinburgh and London. Although Edie had worked at Edinburgh University as an English Literature lecturer, and had plenty of friends, she'd been particularly lonely when Jim had been away and she'd always looked forward to his return. They'd been happily married and had decided not to have children as they were so focused on their careers. Edie had often been asked why she never had children and her answer created mixed reactions. But even now she stuck by her decision and her choice not to become a mother.

Being in Arran had given her a sense of belonging and purpose. Not only that but the chaos and sadness of her life had begun to dissipate and she'd been able to slowly rebuild a life for herself. It was there that she'd rediscovered her creative side and her love of pottery. She'd decided to try out the class at the local hall, and there'd been something healing about having the time and space to use her hands to create and make while allowing her head to process all the thoughts that had been stuck.

She'd spent several years enjoying it as a hobby, then, realising she was actually quite good, had started selling pieces in the local craft shop. She made bowls and mugs capturing the rich textures and colours from the island that inspired her. Each creation was unique and sold quickly, and her career continued to flourish. She'd even won an award from a creative organisation that supported older people in pursuing their art, which had raised her profile and made her work even more in demand.

She was often asked to give demonstrations and classes on the island, and on the mainland too. Her warm and engaging personality meant she was popular with everyone and she had a real knack for helping people to regain their confidence. These days she preferred to stay local and had started to scale back her commitments on the mainland, preferring to go into her workshop at home and focus on her own things.

She paused to look in the window of The Wee Trove and smiled when she noticed two of her mugs set against a backdrop of aqua-coloured silk scarves and on a base of crushed shells. Somehow the owner, Thea, managed to dress the window in an enticing way that attracted customers who then bought lots. It was a shop Edie was drawn to frequently. It was indeed a treasure trove. Edie posted the letter in the post box outside the shop then turned and retraced her steps back along the road and past Cèic. Cano stood at the door.

'Hey, Edie.'

'Hello, you,' she said.

'Did your visitor arrive?'

She nodded and smiled. 'Yes, she's here.'

'Oh good. That's great.'

Edie felt a wave of affection for the gentle man who had been through so much yet always took time to ask after others. Cano and his family were Kurdish asylum seekers who had settled in Glasgow. They had always wanted to move to Arran, after spending many happy holidays on it with their children. Their two daughters were now grown up with families of their own on the mainland. But they came over regularly to see their parents.

'Wait here.' He disappeared into the back of the shop and a few moments later reappeared with a paper bag. 'For you and your friend.'

'Oh, Cano, that is so kind of you. Thank you.'

He beamed with pleasure.

'See you soon,' she said and walked on, Molly tugging at her lead. The sun had started to set and she admired the twinkling lights that hung around the shop windows, making the street look quite magical. She took her time to walk back, enjoying taking a peek inside other worlds. Sighing, she wondered if *he* would have loved it here as much as she did. She still missed him terribly. Edie's heart had swelled when she was with him and she'd radiated with happiness.

He really had been the love of her life. But there was no point in dwelling on the past. She knew she needed to move on and thought she had. But the arrival of the letter had thrown her. She'd tried to ignore it and distract herself with Amelia's arrival and making sure the hut was perfect. But the letter's contents kept popping up in her mind along with the question, what if?

As she reached Coorie Cottage she felt a sense of relief. She would always be grateful that she'd made this little house her home. She hoped Amelia would find some solace and respite here too from whatever she was running away from.

CHAPTER NINE

The next morning, Amelia woke up in the cosiest of beds and for a couple of blissful, suspended moments had no idea where she was. Then she remembered and she stretched, enjoying the sensation of not having to rush to get up and off to work. Leaning forward, she opened the curtains and smiled at the sea and clear blue sky in front of her. She spotted a lone paddle-boarder in the distance and fleetingly wondered if it might be Fergus. She fell back into the pillows and lay there watching, the duvet tucked around her. It was as though she was staring at a painting and she marvelled at the stunning view. The sun was waking up and she spotted a robin, watching from a branch. Something was missing though, and she realised she was waiting for the familiar feeling of dread to arrive. This morning the sinking sensation in her stomach took slightly longer to appear. But once again she was reminded why she was lying in this bed alone and the circumstances that had brought her to this place.

Staring up at the ceiling, she studied the wooden grooves and wondered for the umpteenth time how she was going to get through this and move on. She reached for the phone on the ledge behind her. He hadn't replied to her text. Though should she really be surprised?

She sat up and swung her legs round, stretching her arms up. Then she looked at her hand for a moment and decided it was time to remove her wedding ring. She slipped it off decisively and tucked it away in a zipped pocket in her handbag. Padding through to the en-suite, she hesitated for a moment as she felt her bare finger and then she turned the shower on, turning the dial to blue. Apparently cold water was good for the soul and the circulation. Stripping off, she gingerly stepped into the cubicle. She closed her eyes and squealed as the force of the icy water shocked her. It was hard to stand there comfortably under the freezing water but she quickly washed. She could stand it no more, so turned it off. Her skin was tingling, her heart beating faster as she reached for a fluffy white towel.

Catching her reflection in the mirror, she saw some colour that hadn't been there for a long time. She had a pale complexion anyway but her skin had looked sallow for the past couple of months. At least now she looked a bit healthier. Though maybe that was more to do with the shock of the cold water. It must have done something for her circulation as her veins tingled. She smiled at herself. Maybe a daily cold shower would help get her through this.

Hearing a gentle tap at the front door, she slipped into her bathrobe and unlocked the bathroom door.

'Just me,' called Edie. 'Are you okay? I heard you squealing.'

Amelia opened the door. 'Good morning,' she said, and laughed.

'Now, don't worry, I won't make a habit of this. You need your space. But I thought seeing as you've just had your first night in the hut, I should check on you.'

Amelia looked fondly at Edie who this morning wore dark green jeans, wellies and a mustard rain jacket.

'I slept so well,' she said, pulling the robe tighter around her. She smiled at the robin that had landed on the end of the veranda.

'Oh, that's Johnny, our resident robin. Looks like he's found a new friend.' Edie tilted her head to one side. 'Your cheeks are glowing this morning, dear. The sea air must agree with you.'

'Well, that or the cold shower I had, which caused the squealing.'

Edie groaned. 'You've got to be joking?'

'No. The water was absolutely freezing.'

Edie's face fell. 'Och, I am so sorry, Amelia. That is not good at all. I will need to call Fergus and see if he can fix it.'

'No need to do that, Edie . . . I had a cold shower on purpose.' Now Edie looked confused.

'But why would you do that?'

'Because cold water is meant to be good for you.' Amelia burst out laughing. 'Sorry, Edie. Everything is perfect and the shower is fine. But I decided I would start the day with a cold blast to get me going. And it definitely did.'

'Ah, I see,' she said, clearly baffled as to why anyone would want to do that. 'Well, here you go,' she said, placing a paper bag on the counter. 'A wee treat from the bakery to enjoy with your coffee. Cano, the owner, is really looking forward to meeting you . . . when you're up to visiting.'

Amelia smiled appreciatively. 'That is so kind of you. Thank you. I will go and see him soon, I promise.'

'Well, look, why don't you come over to the house later and we can have a chat about the job, if you'd like? I can take you and show you around?'

* * *

Amelia filled the kettle at the tiny sink and lit a gas ring on the stove. While she was waiting for the water to boil, she reached for the cafetière and spooned in some coffee. Edie had kindly left the kitchen well stocked with granola, oatcakes and home-made marmalade and jam in the cupboard, and milk, yogurt and — in case she was vegan — coconut milk in the fridge, along with some fresh pasta and sauce. There was salad, berries and a packed fruit bowl, and a jar with herbal teabags. Beside the kettle was a square tin box, with a picture of a Highland cow on the front, and when she prised the lid off she discovered homemade shortbread dusted with sugar, which smelt heavenly. She was looking forward to tasting it later.

She poured the water into the cafetière, allowing the coffee to brew for a minute or two before pushing down the plunger. Pulling on her jeans and a sweater, she scraped her dark hair into a ponytail and applied some moisturiser to her face. She peeked inside the paper bag Edie had brought to find a croissant. Placing the pastry on a plate, she took it over to the breakfast bar by the window with her coffee and just sat for a minute, savouring the view.

She poured the coffee into a pottery mug in shades of green and blue and inhaled the bitter scent before taking a sip. Bliss. The croissant was huge and covered in flaked almonds, and Amelia picked one off and popped it in her mouth. She couldn't remember the last time she'd had a croissant. Declan said they were far too calorific and high in fat and so she never bought them. Taking a bite, she closed her eyes, enjoying the buttery sensation of the pastry and the rich, smooth almond filling.

She sat for a while, thinking, before clearing the dishes away. Then she grabbed her jacket from the peg by the door and ran down the steps onto the grass. Stepping stones had been laid, which wound over to the path from the house. She jumped from stone to stone, enjoying the sound of the birds chirping and the tang of the salty air. She took a deep breath and felt the air cleanse her body inside. When she got to the door of Coorie Cottage she hesitated, then knocked. Edie had told her to make herself at home but, still, she wanted to respect her privacy. Wandering straight in would be strange.

'Come on in,' said Edie, opening the door and ushering her through to the kitchen. She had a rag in her hands. 'I've been doing a bit of cleaning. It is never-ending.' She threw the cloth under the sink and turned to wash her hands. 'Now, please, dear, do let yourself in the next time.'

'You're very trusting,' Amelia said as she slipped her jacket off and hung it over the back of the chair. She sat down at the table across from Edie.

Edie shrugged. 'There's no other way to be.'

Amelia begged to differ but knew this wasn't the time or place to say anything. 'The croissant was delicious. Thank you. I honestly don't think I've ever tasted such a perfect pastry.'

'They're amazing. We are so lucky to have such a brilliant bakery. I'll take you up later and show you around. There is a wee café to sit in too if you fancy a change of scene. And sometimes, when the weather is warmer, they put chairs and tables outside and you can just watch the world go by. In fact, I've asked Cano to put some seats out for the dog walkers like me, all year round.'

Amelia learned that the café was more of a social drop-in zone and where Edie picked up most of her gossip. Cano and his wife, Naza had taught themselves how to do everything, and were also responsible for baking many of the island's birthday cakes.

'Then there's the gift shop, The Wee Trove, run by Thea. Her partner, Grant, also works with Fergus at the outdoors centre. Did he tell you about that?'

'No,' said Amelia, though that made sense as he was obviously a fan of the outdoors.

'Well, as you may have noticed from his athletic physique,' Edie said, knowingly, 'he's keen on outdoor sports.'

Amelia stifled a laugh. She hadn't failed to notice the number of compliments that Edie paid Fergus, and the way she said them with such a mischievous grin. She wondered what Edie was up to and tilted her head to the side to listen to what she would say next.

'In fact, when he was younger he was quite the expert skier, apparently.' She waved her hand. 'Now he and Grant are busy organising kayak adventures and paddle-boarding and trekking and whatever else you fancy. What else can I tell you? Oh, the fishmonger and the butcher, and the beauty salon.' She paused for a moment to think. 'Oh, the newsagent, which also doubles as a bookshop, and they'll order you in any books you want. The fish-and-chip shop . . . the distillery, oh, and the deli. And the hotel — where the bar is. How could I have forgotten!'

Amelia's head had started to spin. 'Sounds like a busy place that has everything you need.'

Edie nodded. 'Yes, well, we're quite proud of what we've got, and things get even better with the Christmas fair — we have stalls which have loads of local produce for sale . . . that should definitely be an essential part of your visit. But you can explore everything for yourself soon.'

'I'm looking forward to having a wander. Is the bus service good?'

'Yes, not too bad at all and will take you all over the island. Though you're also very welcome to use my car. There are some wee nooks and crannies which I'm sure you'll want to go to, and having the car may make things a bit easier.'

'Ah. Thanks, Edie, you're very kind.' Amelia frowned. 'Well, I suppose that would take me on to why I'm here. You were going to tell me a bit more about the job?' She glanced over at Molly who had slumped in a heap on the floor beside the stove. She lazily opened her eyes then thumped her tail a couple of times.

'Right . . . well, as you know, the role is for a tourism officer . . . of sorts.'

'Of sorts?' Amelia tried to relax her clenched jaw. What was she going to say next?

'Yes. I suppose that is a bit of a loose description.'

'Uh-huh,' said Amelia, unsure where this conversation was going. 'What do you mean?'

Edie clasped her hands together and rested them on the table. 'Well, yes, tourism will play a big part. But why don't we make things less restrictive . . . and you design the role as you want to. I mean, your background is in marketing? So, you know, all about selling something.'

Amelia raised an eyebrow. 'Vodka. I know how to sell vodka.'

Edie waved her hands dismissively and laughed loudly. '*Pffft*. Vodka, gin, perfume, chocolate, cruises. Doesn't matter. The bottom line is you can sell something.'

Amelia nodded in agreement. 'But you don't need to try to sell this place,' she said. 'I thought tourism was thriving?'

'Well, yes, generally things are busy. But . . . well, I need to sell something more specific.'

Amelia waited for her to continue. She was fairly confident she was able to turn her hand to most things, as long as the product could be photographed and packaged as something people *needed* in their life.

'I need you to sell the shepherd's hut.'

'Oh . . . okay. I wasn't expecting you to say that.' A wave of panic made her blurt out, 'Are you throwing me out already?'

'No, dear, the opposite. Don't you see? I want you to live here in the hut like a tourist and tell me what you like about it and what you don't. Imagine you are here on holiday and this is the first time you have visited.' Edie closed her eyes but continued to talk. 'You are here to escape and are doing a travel review for a magazine about finding yourself again . . . perhaps your life has been lacking in purpose or focus and you've been struggling to find a clear sense of direction. Your time in the hut reconnecting with yourself and nature will help to clarify your goals and where you are going next, and you will leave with a sense of . . . calm, hope and joy.'

She snapped her eyes open.

Amelia couldn't help feeling as though Edie's words were aimed at her in particular. It was almost as though she could read her mind and knew what had happened in London, which left her slightly perturbed.

Edie rubbed her palms together. 'But for the moment you're telling me directly from your own lived experience what works and what doesn't. Do you need any other items in the hut? Is it too hot or too cold? What would you like to do as a visitor? That way, with your help and feedback, I can make things perfect before its proper launch.'

Amelia tucked a strand of hair behind her ear. 'Okay, so what you're saying is that you want me to be part of your soft launch?'

Edie's brow furrowed in confusion. 'What's that?'

'It's what the big hotels and holiday resorts do. They do a trial run with guests to gain feedback about what the food is like or how soft the beds are, so that when it comes to the real launch they have ironed out any of the teething problems that may potentially create negative publicity. It's usually done when a business doesn't want to draw a great deal of attention to a product right away.'

'Oh,' said Edie in surprise. 'Well, that is exactly what your job is here. A soft launcher . . . or something like that. I need your first-hand thoughts and your tourist perspective. Oh, and I could also do with a new website to advertise. And how do I advertise? And where do I advertise? I believe it's all about being on social media these days?'

Edie exhaled a huge sigh of relief.

A buzz of excitement rippled through Amelia as she thought about how she could help Edie. Lots of ideas were already starting to take shape in her mind and she was desperate to write them down.

'What do you say? Do you think you are up for the job?'

'Yes!' said Amelia. 'The only problem I think you will have is getting people to leave the hut. It is blooming wonderful.'

'Oh, good! That is what I like to hear.'

'You can maybe tell me a bit about why you decided to buy it and why you chose a shepherd's hut in particular.'

Edie sighed. 'Well, I'm trying to plan for the future. My pension isn't that great thanks to me being a woman of a certain age and I was looking on this as an investment. I know how quickly everything gets booked up over here during the school holidays. Even the campsites can be full. I saw it and, well, to be honest it was a bit of a spur-of-the-moment purchase. Initially I had actually been looking to have some sort of pottery studio put in the garden, and then while I was browsing it popped up and before I knew it I had kind of bought it.'

Amelia laughed. 'That is one impressive random purchase.' Glancing over at the window, she gasped. A man's face was pressed up against the glass. 'Edie, erm, stay exactly where you are and don't turn round — but there's a man outside and he's staring at us. What will I do? Should I call the police?'

CHAPTER TEN

'You can if you want. But they'll take ages to get here,' Edie said dismissively, turning round and clocking the man staring in. 'Let's go and confront him.' She pointed to the back door. 'Grab the broom over there . . . and be ready.'

Amelia followed Edie's instructions and clasped her hands around the broom, ready to attack. Not that she really knew how to use a broom as a weapon. 'Are you sure this is a good idea?'

Edie unlocked the door. 'There's only one way to find out.'

The door handle turned and Amelia paled. How could Edie be so calm when a weirdo was hanging around her garden? Maybe all that yoga she said she did helped keep her calm? The door opened and standing there, in his overalls and a woolly hat pulled down over his ears, was Fergus. The hat must have been obscuring his face when he was at the window. No wonder she didn't recognise him, he looked completely different.

'Ah, hello, ladies.' He nodded at Amelia. 'Edie, I'm doing a quick trip to the tip and I know you had something you wanted me to take away?'

'Oh, Fergus, you are a treasure. That pile of cuttings in the corner.'

Amelia's cheeks flushed when she saw Edie wink at her.

'Are you going somewhere?' Fergus asked Amelia.

'What do you mean?'

He tipped his head to the broom she was gripping. 'Um . . .'

'She's about to brush up those crumbs for me.' Edie laughed. 'Must be my age. Sometimes it's a bit of a struggle trying to bend down to reach them.'

Amelia giggled and Fergus looked on in bemusement. Although she was mortified that she'd thought he was an intruder, she wasn't too embarrassed to notice the triangle of skin where his shirt was unbuttoned. *Oh God.* She couldn't stop herself from staring at him.

'Hey, why don't you tag along with Fergus and he can show you some of the island's hotspots?'

That was the last thing Amelia wanted to do, especially as she seemed unable to string a coherent sentence together in his presence, but she wasn't able to think of an excuse quickly enough.

Fergus shrugged. 'Sure.'

'Okay. I'll go and grab my jacket,' she said, hoping she could at least go and check her hair.

'It's here, dear.' Edie unhooked Amelia's jacket from the back of the chair.

'Thanks.' She attempted to give Edie a bit of a look but Edie grinned mischievously at her.

Amelia took a deep breath and stepped outside, waiting for Fergus to load the garden cuttings into the back of the van. She felt a bit childlike as she stood waiting and Edie fussed around her, giving her a list of things she should look out for.

'I'll leave you young ones to get on with things,' said Edie, waving and disappearing back inside the cottage.

'Jump in.' Fergus opened the passenger door for her.

The pair drove in silence for a while, back along the road which took them to the ferry terminal. Amelia stared out at the CalMac brick-built ferry terminal and people milling around waiting for the arrival of a boat. Was it really only a couple of days ago that she had arrived here with all her belongings in one bag? It felt like such a long time ago.

'So how are you getting on so far? What do you think of Arran?'

'It's beautiful, although to be honest I haven't seen much so far . . . and Edie has moved me into the shepherd's hut, which is amazing.'

'She was so excited about making it a complete surprise.'

'It wasn't what I was expecting at all. It is even better.'

'Yeah, she was pretty chuffed when she got it. Though it didn't look anything like it does now. She has added her own creative twist.'

'She's got amazing taste.'

'Yes, she does. I bet she's put some of her own mugs in there too?'

Amelia thought about the lovely stoneware cup she'd drunk her coffee from that morning. 'Wow. I didn't realise that Edie had made them.'

Fergus laughed. 'Yes. She's made some amazing things and she sells them in The Wee Trove, the shop in the high street. She's actually quite a well-known artist, although I would imagine she hasn't told you that.'

She shook her head. 'No, she hasn't.' Mind you, there was so much to learn about Edie. Amelia was intrigued to learn more about the woman she was becoming really fond of.

Amelia could sense Fergus's gaze on her but couldn't quite bring herself to turn and make eye contact. She was slightly embarrassed to admit to him that she hadn't ventured out other than to walk on the beach. 'That's my plan tomorrow. The high street. Edie has told me all about it. The bakery and café and fishmonger and butcher. Sounds like you have everything you need.'

'We're lucky,' he said with a shrug. 'We do quite well with what we've got here. Some people hate the thought of island life and being away from the hustle and bustle of the city. Whereas others are quite content and the thought of the city brings them out in a cold sweat.'

Amelia knew he was talking about himself. 'How long have you lived here?'

'I came back two years ago.'

'Did you grow up here?'

He nodded. 'Yes. Then I left and went to explore the world.'

'Oh, where did you go and what did you do?'

'I spent some time in South America, then the States, and worked in a ski resort in Canada then went to New Zealand.'

'Wow, that sounds amazing. My brother lives in Boston and he loves skiing in Canada. Where were you?'

'Whistler, you know the ski resort over in British Columbia?'

'Yes, I know Whistler. It's Jack's favourite place to snowboard.' She paused. 'My mum actually lives in New Zealand now. How funny that you lived there too.'

He didn't say anything.

'How long were you away?' she asked.

'A few years.'

'What made you come back?'

He didn't answer immediately and Amelia wondered if she had said something to offend him.

'It was just time.' He flicked on the radio, clearly signalling that the conversation was over.

Amelia glanced sideways and could see the sadness on his face. 'Where are we going first?' she asked, trying to lighten the mood.

'Well, in my capacity as your tour guide, I thought we would check out the castle first.'

Amelia admired the scenery as he drove up the winding drive to the castle, where he parked and insisted she walk around the grounds.

'I used to play hide and seek here all the time as a kid,' he said as they walked through the walled garden.

'Is that a palm tree?' Amelia looked in disbelief as she spotted one in the corner of the grounds.

'It is indeed.'

'But . . . how?'

'Well, Arran is one of the few places in Scotland to have a climate that is temperate enough for palm trees to grow.'

Amelia was impressed. 'You learn something new every day. Any other interesting facts?'

'A person belonging to the island is known as an Arranach,' he said, chuckling.

'Not quite so impressive.'

'Hey, I think that is pretty good for a random bit of information.'

'I can tell you one.'

'Oh, what's that?'

'Arran is described as Scotland in miniature.'

He nodded. 'Very good. But do you know why?'

'Erm, because it's Scotland in miniature . . .'

'Well, yes, but technically it's because the island is divided into Highland and Lowland areas by the Highland Boundary Fault.'

Amelia sniggered. 'You certainly know your stuff.'

'It helps to when you're mostly working with tourists during the summer.'

'That's true.' Her face fell as she was reminded that he probably felt obliged to be doing this.

'But you're not a tourist. I can tell you're here to stay.'

'Well . . . for a bit anyway. I guess until my work with Edie comes to an end. It's a temporary post.'

As they continued walking in a comfortable silence, everything seemed simple and uncomplicated.

'When we were kids we would sit here for hours counting the ferries.' He pointed over at the Firth of Clyde. 'Sometimes you can see the submarines coming in and out.' He looked at his watch. 'Oh, didn't realise that was the time already. I'd better finish these errands and get you back. I'm taking some more kids out kayaking later.'

'Tourists?' She twisted to look at him.

'No. Arranachers. Kids from the secondary.'

'You're quite the multitasker with all that you do,' she said as they walked back to the van.

'What do you mean?'

'Well, with the outdoor sports and helping Edie and then your wild swimming . . .'

He laughed. 'Edie's always been very good to me.' His eyes briefly clouded over. 'I don't have family here anymore. My parents are both dead and my brother lives in Aberdeen . . . She's always been a good friend to me and I like to help her when I can. She's independent as you will have gathered. But I think she's starting to realise that asking for help is okay . . . which is good.'

When they got back to the van, Amelia found she had enjoyed listening to his stories, and she watched the scenery as he told another from his younger years. He took a quick detour past the large spa hotel, which sat in beautiful grounds. 'If you ever want to swim, in a heated pool, then this is the place you should come. Though I can highly recommend the wild option.'

Amelia shivered. 'Mmm, maybe.' The thought of it wasn't quite as horrifying as the first time he'd mentioned it.

All too quickly they were back at Edie's and Amelia reluctantly climbed out. 'Well, thanks again for looking after me and showing me the sights.'

'Any time. It's always good to show it off and we have only scratched the surface. There is loads more to see. Maybe another time?'

They looked at each other and Fergus flashed her a smile. 'Bye, Amelia.'

'Thanks again. Bye-bye.'

* * *

As Fergus drove away from Coorie Cottage he couldn't stop thinking about the woman who he'd just spent a thoroughly enjoyable couple of hours with. He usually steered well away from women as they were too much trouble. His last girlfriend, which was a very loose description of their relationship, was Kelly, who lived on the mainland. That had all been fairly relaxed and had quickly petered out as they only saw each other when Fergus was able to get over on the ferry. Kelly never wanted to come over to Arran to visit him and insisted that she was a city girl. As far as he was concerned, their arrangement suited them both, and everyone else presumed Fergus was single and avoiding women. Which officially he was.

But there was something quite captivating about Amelia. He wondered what her story was. Why on earth had she come here on her own? And why had she removed her wedding ring that she'd worn when he'd picked her up from the terminal the other night?

CHAPTER ELEVEN

The next day, inspired by her outing with Fergus, Amelia decided it was time to explore properly. She made the short walk down the path and onto the beach. There was a gentle breeze and, despite the sun, she shivered and dug her hands deep into her jacket pockets. A few clouds scudded across the sky and she enjoyed the fresh air, which she gulped in. When she reached the end of the bay, she ventured onto the high street. She was slightly apprehensive about having to make conversation with too many people she didn't know. But she also knew she couldn't hide out at Edie's forever. Especially as Edie was paying her to do a job. She needed to live like a tourist and that meant leaving her comfort zone of the cabin and Edie's beautiful garden. Although it had crossed her mind that a particularly romantic couple probably wouldn't bother setting foot over the threshold of the shepherd's hut at all during their stay. It had everything anyone could possibly wish for, and Edie had also suggested a barbecue for the summer. The thought of grilling sausages and sipping a cool beer or chilled wine while overlooking the sea was perfect. Although the hut was in Edie's garden, it had been positioned in a quiet corner so it appeared to be in its own grounds.

Amelia picked her way along the sandy bay then over a whitewashed wall and across the grassy verge towards the road. She clocked the hotel and the newsagent, and smiled at the elderly man who passed her, with a newspaper tucked under his arm. She continued along and spotted the bakery and café with its bright awning and huge windows. She could already smell the aroma of coffee and saw the door wide open. Hesitating for a moment, she deliberated over whether she should go in. That would be a first step. As she stood having an internal debate with herself, she read the slate chalkboard sign which said, 'Come in and start your day the Cèic way'.

Just then a woman, who looked about the same age as Amelia, with long, curly auburn hair and a huge smile, came out clutching a takeaway cup. She had bright eyes and wore navy jeans with a thick crimson sweater and red boots. She stepped aside to let Amelia pass.

'Good morning,' she said cheerily. 'Beautiful day, isn't it?'

'Yes, it is,' said Amelia shyly. 'The coffee smells bliss.'

The cheery woman paused. 'Now, wait a minute . . . you don't happen to be Amelia, do you?'

She nodded in surprise. 'Yes, I am. How did you know?'

'Edie told me you'd arrived and I've been looking out for you. I know everyone here and didn't recognise you so I figured it out. Plus, Edie gave an accurate description.' She smiled. 'Though you're even prettier than she said.'

Amelia blushed. She immediately liked this warm and friendly woman.

'Sorry, you must be wondering who I am. My name's Thea. I run The Wee Trove over there.' She flicked her spare hand to the shop on the other side of the road.

'Ah, yes, of course.' She was glad that the jigsaw pieces were slotting into place. 'Edie has told me about you too.'

'Oh, I hope it's all good stuff and nothing naughty.' Thea gave a huge laugh that came from deep inside.

Amelia couldn't help but chuckle along with her. 'Don't worry, all positive.'

'Well, look, it's fab to put a face to your name. I'd better go and open up. But please do pop in anytime. It would be great to see you.'

'That is so kind of you. I will do that.'

'Enjoy your coffee. Cano will look after you.'

Amelia turned and walked into the café, which only had a couple of customers. She noticed the older man she'd passed earlier now sat in the corner, at a small table, with his newspaper spread out and a pot of tea. She glanced around apprehensively, taking in the surroundings. A long wooden table ran along the front of the huge floor-to-ceiling windows, which looked out over the bay. The oak floors were lightly scuffed and plants were dotted around, offering bursts of vivid green. She breathed in scents of cinnamon and nutmeg, and listened to the whir of the coffee grinder. A man behind the counter, arranging pastries, glanced up and smiled when he saw her.

'Morning. What would you like today?'

'Hello. I would love a latte, please.'

'Okey-dokey,' he said in a soft accent.

He turned away to fill the portafilter with coffee grounds and slotted it into the machine. While the espresso trickled out into a mug, he busied himself with steaming the milk. The noise of it whooshing and hissing reminded her of her usual stop, at the shop next to where she used to work. This was so much better. Amelia's eyes roamed over the mouthwatering selection of goodies. There were croissants, muffins, huge slabs of fruitcake, brownies and scones, and her stomach rumbled, making her want to order one of each.

'Can I offer you something to go with your drink?' he asked over his shoulder.

She pulled a face, knowing she would give in to temptation. 'Well, okay, twist my arm. I will.'

Cano had tongs at the ready. 'What would you like?'

She pointed at a scone studded with blueberries.

'Superb choice,' he said, picking up a large one and placing it on a plate with a knife and butter. He spun round to reach for her coffee.

'Are you Cano?'

'Yes.' He grinned.

'I have heard about you. And sampled the lovely almond croissants.'

'Ah — you must be Miss Edie's friend?'

She nodded. 'Yes. I'm Amelia. Good to meet you.'

'You too,' he said. 'I hope you enjoy your stay on the island.'

'Thank you. I am enjoying it very much.' She was aware that a couple of people waited in line behind her and so she headed over to a table and sat down facing the window. She shook herself in disbelief that she was having her breakfast with such a stunning vista. Taking a picture of the cup with the scenic background, she sent it to Suna.

Having a latte and thinking of you.

She paused to see if she would reply. When she didn't, Amelia pulled out her notepad and began to write. Today's prompt started with the words, *What is the best way to get out of your head?* She smiled, clicked her pen and let the words flow.

> *The best way to get out of your head is to move to an island, live in a hut overlooking the sea and admire the amazing view. To think at the moment this is my life, compared to what it was like before. Only a couple of months ago, my life was in tatters. When Declan left I really didn't think I would smile again. I thought my life was over. And yes, I still miss him . . . but being here is reminding me that there is a world waiting to be discovered.*

She sat for a moment, remembering when she and Declan had met at a party her company had hosted to launch the latest brand of vodka. He'd tagged along with a friend and although it was cheesy, their eyes had connected across a crowded room. It had been an instant attraction. He was tall with cropped blond hair and a smile that lit up his face. They'd stood chatting and laughing at the bar, drinking free shots until Amelia's boss had tapped her on the shoulder and told her to work the room. They'd swapped numbers and the next day Declan texted her, asking her to go to dinner that weekend. He'd been funny, intelligent and self-assured, and Amelia had fallen head over heels in love with him very quickly. They'd both worked hard but had enjoyed weekends hopping onto the Eurostar for romantic breaks in Paris or eating out. They'd been happy, or so Amelia had thought. Now, as she took another sip of her coffee, she wondered if she had been naive or just completely stupid.

After a while Cano came over to clear away her dishes. 'Did you like the scone?' he asked as he wiped the table.

'Fabulous,' she said. 'The best I have ever tasted.'

He beamed with pride. 'I have been trying to make different flavours. That's the first time I have tried blueberry. Normally they are plain or have raisins.'

'Well, it was delicious,' she said. 'Thank you.'

'Would you like another coffee?'

She was about to say no and that she'd better be on her way when she realised that actually she didn't need to be anywhere. There was no deadline and no place to rush to. 'Yes, please, Cano. That would be nice.' She enjoyed watching the ebb and flow of the customers who came in and out. A few young mums came in with their babies in pushchairs, and an older couple who stopped to get a loaf. She said hello to some of the people who took a seat at the communal table. Everyone said 'good morning' at the very least.

Rob, who ran the local hotel, introduced himself. 'Pop in for a drink sometime,' he said.

Amelia wondered if he was being polite as he knew about Edie's tourist project, then started to realise people were genuine. A woman in her late forties rushed into the café in a whirlwind, speaking loudly into her phone. When she spotted Amelia, she paused her conversation briefly to say hello and introduced herself as Doris, owner of the gin distillery. Amelia thought about mentioning her work background to her at some point. For now, she would take her time getting to know folk. Keeping herself under the radar was probably for the best as her time here might be limited.

She kept expecting her phone to ping with a message from Suna. It was strange that she hadn't yet replied as she tended to be such a rapid responder. However, she was likely to be in a meeting. Sometimes Amelia had to remind herself how lucky she was not to be in an office routine. Being her own boss and in charge of her own time was certainly liberating. She lingered for a couple of minutes making some notes about the shepherd's hut, and pencilled out a basic marketing strategy which would help Edie to boost its profile to potential holidaymakers.

She imagined how she would describe it on a postcard.

Nestled by the water overlooking the Holy Isle, this shepherd's hut is the perfect peaceful escape. Cosy yet stylish with wonderful sea views. The comfiest of beds, a tiny but superb kitchen, a small shower room and a wood-burning stove. It has everything that I need.

When she realised the time, she packed her notepads away and pulled on her coat. Then she went to the counter and bought a loaf of brown, nutty bread.

Cano popped it in a paper bag. 'Please come again.'

'I will. Thank you so much. I really enjoyed that.'

He waved and smiled, and Amelia left feeling full, happy and content.

CHAPTER TWELVE

After leaving the café, she stopped by the deli to buy some more provisions. That huge scone had filled her up but she knew she would need to eat later and probably wouldn't want to come out again. She bought some more salad, fruit and cold meat, and a pint of milk. Then she spotted some locally made chocolate and decided to slip a bar of that into her basket. At least she had regained her appetite, which was something of a surprise. She had been picking at food since Declan left. When she saw the box of mince pies, she was almost tempted to add that to her shopping too. However, it was only the start of November — still plenty of time to indulge in festive treats. The items she'd picked up would keep her going for a few days until she did a proper grocery shop.

She walked back down the high street and towards the beach. Coorie Cottage could also be accessed via the road, but walking on sand was a bit of a novelty, and one she didn't think she would ever grow tired of. Making her way along the shoreline, she admired the boats bobbing about in the bay and stopped to take yet another photo. She sat down on a bench to admire the view and listen to the gentle sound of the waves. Declan loved sailing and her happy mood dipped as her thoughts turned to him again and how much he would love it here. Or would he?

She reminded herself how scathing he had been when she'd suggested a trip to Arran. He'd claimed it would be far too cold and miserable. She and Declan hadn't had the kind of relationship where they'd argued. Except when it had come to holidays or weekends away. Amelia loved exploring and didn't care so much for fancy hotels, whereas Declan insisted on the best and he liked his locations warm. The arrival of their credit card bills reminded her how much they spent on frivolous things when they were supposed to be saving a deposit for their first home together.

'Penny for them?' a voice said.

Amelia turned to find Edie and Molly. 'Oh, hello. I'm admiring the view,' she said.

'Do you mind if we join you?'

'Of course not.' Amelia slid her bags onto the ground to make more room.

'How has your morning been?'

'Lovely, thank you. I met Thea, then Cano at the café . . . Rob and Doris.'

Edie laughed. 'Sounds like it has been busy.'

'This is not a bad job at all,' she said.

The wind had started to whip up and Edie pulled her hat over her ears. 'It's getting a bit chilly, isn't it? Sometimes when the sun is out you forget that we're getting into winter.'

'How are you?'

'I'm fine, thanks, dear,' she said. 'Just thought I should take this one out for a walk and I needed to stretch my legs too.'

'It's peaceful here.'

She nodded. 'Yes. This is a good place to come and think and just be.'

Amelia sensed the woman wasn't her usual cheery self, which seemed to be reflected in her choice of grey clothes. 'You're subdued this morning. Is everything okay?'

She didn't answer immediately and then let a sigh escape. 'I've got a few things on my mind.'

'Anything that I can help with?'

Edie glanced over at her and shook her head. 'No, but thank you for asking. This is one dilemma I need to try to figure out by myself.'

She stood up, tugging at Molly's lead, before Amelia could ask anything else. 'Right, we'll leave you in peace and be on our way. Come on, my pup, let's go and find some rabbits.' Molly's ears pricked up and she wagged her tail excitedly. 'See you later.'

'Bye.' Amelia watched the woman continue to make her way along the shore, Molly at her heels.

Amelia's phone pinged and she pulled it from her pocket, smiling when she realised it was a WhatsApp voice message from Suna. She pressed play and listened.

'Hi honey, I am so sorry it's taken an age to call back. Work's been so busy . . . and, well, no excuses, I should have replied by now. How are you? By the looks of all the pictures you are sending you're having an amazing time, which I am so glad about. You deserve to. I hope you've found somewhere that sells decent coffee!' Suna sighed. *'You aren't missing anything here. Same old, same old. Work is manic but not in a good way . . . it's cold and raining. But I expect it's the same with you in the middle of nowhere.'* Amelia could hear the sound of some muffled talking. *'Sorry about that. Another crisis. I'd better go. Let's talk soon. Miss you. Bye.'*

Amelia shook her head as she looked at the blue sky and enjoyed the sunshine on her face, once again relieved not to be in damp London. The thought did not appeal. Mind you, even if the sun wasn't shining she had no desire to go back anytime soon. She couldn't help but be disappointed by Suna's hurried words and her slightly off tone. She had to remember Suna was at work and life was hectic and very different for her. And she was calling from the office.

Yet something about her message niggled at Amelia and left her feeling deflated. She frowned and looked ahead at the horizon. The wind had picked up and the sun disappeared behind a cloud. Suddenly she wanted to be back in the comfort of the hut. She tucked her phone away and stood up, gathered her things and slowly made her way rather forlornly back to Edie's garden.

CHAPTER THIRTEEN

The next day Fergus woke early again. He had actually always slept well until . . . *it* had happened. The seagulls swooped and screeched outside, and he threw the covers back, stood up and stretched. Once awake, just lying there wasn't an option, otherwise his thoughts became overwhelming.

He vaguely wondered if Amelia was up and walking along the beach. Pulling open the curtains to let the morning light seep in, he looked out and narrowed his eyes. A solitary figure stood in the distance watching the waves. Could that be her? He shook his head, wondering why he even cared.

He made himself a mug of tea and walked to the window seat, one of his favourite spots to sit and watch the sun rise. This time of year, the days only got shorter, and as a guy who loved being outside he sometimes found the lack of daylight hard.

Winter was the time he found most challenging, with the countdown to the festive fair and then Christmas itself. But he would never admit that. Plastering on a smile and mustering up as much enthusiasm as he could was easier.

He frowned as a memory of Ellen floated into his mind. She no longer constantly dominated his thoughts, though she was never far from them. They'd met when they'd both worked as ski instructors in the lively resort of Whistler. It was one of the most popular resorts in the world, with a small-town vibe and loads of events and festivals over winter. The staff came from all over the world — Australia, Europe and New Zealand, where Ellen hailed from. One morning Fergus had gone heli-skiing with a group of mates and she'd joined when someone had dropped out at the last minute.

Heli-skiing wasn't for the faint-hearted and his interest had been immediately piqued when he'd set eyes on her. As she'd overtaken him on her snowboard, carving tracks in the snow ahead, he'd been smitten. Later, when they'd been out at a bar celebrating their day, they'd struck up a conversation, which had led to a kiss and then him falling head over heels in love. Ellen had loved extreme sports and hadn't been afraid of a challenge. But she'd also had a sensitive side, which not many other people had experienced aside from Fergus.

Christmas had always been her favourite time of year and she'd embraced every aspect. The shopping, careful wrapping of presents, decorating the tree, cooking and all the chaos that went with it. A wave of grief hit him. How he missed her.

Four years had passed since she died, yet the pain of her loss could be so visceral and raw, there were days it felt like yesterday. At times he wondered how he'd managed to rebuild his life here. Sometimes it felt like he had sleepwalked through the past couple of years. Keeping busy was the key to coping. That was why he always kept active and on the move, working or helping Edie or anyone else. He'd also joined the local RNLI crew last year. That made him feel useful, especially when he felt so utterly responsible and guilty about Ellen's death. They should have been married now and maybe have started the family they'd always planned to. Feeling the horrible, unsettling emotions that still visited him regularly descending, he drained his tea and glanced out at the figure now making her way along the shore.

Moving was the best way of making sure his mind was distracted, and there was no shortage of things to do.

CHAPTER FOURTEEN

Later that day, Edie and Thea sat at the long table at Cèic waiting for Doris to arrive. Even though Doris ran a successful gin distillery on the island, exporting its brand around the world, her timekeeping skills were terrible. How she ever managed to get anything done, Edie had no idea. Thea, who had put a *'Closed for 20 minutes'* sign across her shop door, kept checking the time and muttering that she couldn't hang around much longer.

'Sorry I'm late.' Doris ran in, letting a cold rush of air whoosh through the door. Her cheeks were flushed pink and she pulled off her pale green hat. Dumping a pile of papers on the table, she asked if anyone would like a drink and dashed to the counter before they had the chance to answer.

Edie gave a nod in Cano's direction and he mouthed, 'Same again,' to her. She nodded her thanks.

The women were gathering to discuss the Christmas fair, which kicked off at the start of December with the switch-on of the festive lights. All the local traders played their role in making sure the event went smoothly. But Edie, Thea and Doris were the regulars at the meetings and executed the plan. Although things were mainly sorted, there were still plenty of details to take care of and discussions as to whether it would snow or not. This happened every year. Doris was a tremendous organiser, although Edie thought 'control freak' a more accurate description. She was far too controlling and spent too much time worrying over tiny issues like the size of the cups for hot chocolate and how much they should charge for a visit to Santa's Grotto.

Doris finally sat down at the table with her mug of peppermint tea. She avoided caffeine as it 'played havoc with her nervous system' though she didn't have any problem with alcohol. She browsed through her notes. 'How are we getting on with this? Thea, do you have the checklist?'

'Yes,' said Thea, listing all that had been done and the few things that needed to be finalised, including who would be Santa.

'Davey, as always.' Edie saw a look flit between Thea and Doris.

'I did mention it to him the other day, but he was a bit non-committal,' said Thea.

'Oh, I wonder why that is?' Edie looked thoughtful. 'I'll speak to him.'

Edie's mind was heavy with thoughts and her focus began drifting off from the discussions about the fair. She knew all about how easy it was to try to plan everything in life, only for it all to be upended and turned inside out. Look what had happened to Jim. If only he hadn't been on the train that day. If only he'd sat in a different carriage. If only . . . and so on. If only he had or hadn't done something, perhaps he would still be here with her today. Or would he? Would their life together have carried on as normal? Edie now doubted that would have been the case.

Everything that was familiar to her had disappeared in a flash and she had had to get on with life without him. Afterwards she'd sunk into a depression, which followed her around. Her grief had overwhelmed her and more often than not she had woken up in the middle of the night struggling to breathe. After she'd had bereavement counselling, which had helped her adjust and adapt to the monumental life changes, the panic attacks had subsided. She'd come to the conclusion that she owed it to her memory of Jim to try to make the most of her life and seize the moment. She'd let go of the past and tried her best to keep moving forward.

Being open-minded had brought her to Arran to embrace a new future, and she'd done so with the tiniest glimmer of excitement and hope. Edie had eventually unfurled from a dark place to flourish through her creative work and by connecting with nature around her. A few years ago, she'd even briefly found love again with George, an artist who'd visited the island for a summer. Then she frowned as she thought about the letter, and its contents flitted around her head.

'The ceilidh, what about the ceilidh? Edie? Earth to Edie,' Doris called.

'Sorry.' A frown knitted Edie's brows together.

'The band for the ceilidh for Christmas Eve — are they booked?'

'Erm, yes, they are.'

'Are you okay? You're not your usual self. You're looking a bit peaky.' Thea's voice was kind.

'Sorry, I'm just tired.'

'How about getting your visitor involved in all of this?' suggested Doris, suddenly. 'Didn't you say something about her having a marketing background?'

Edie couldn't remember what she'd told Doris. 'Yes, she used to sell vodka.'

'Ideal.' She clapped her hands together. 'She can help run the bar and launch our special gin.'

'Don't you think we should ask her first?' Thea looked slightly concerned.

Doris shook her head. 'Not at all. This will be a wonderful way for her to meet people.'

Edie knew Amelia wanted to stay under the radar, but when she opened her mouth to protest, Doris cut in.

'Great. That's all settled.' Doris smiled. 'Edie, you can tell Amelia that we are thrilled to have her on board and that I will be in touch with instructions. In fact, why don't I ask her if she will come and taste the new Christmas gin. I bet she will be full of super ideas as to how to sell it. Brilliant.' She pulled on her coat and swept her papers into her huge bag. 'Right, I'd better be off. Things to do, people to see. Super seeing you, ladies.'

'Bye, Doris,' called Thea. But she was already out the door and marching across the road to her car.

'She's certainly a force of nature,' said a bemused Edie.

Her comment made Thea laugh. 'She is indeed.'

'Poor Amelia. I hope she won't be annoyed. I get the impression she is here for a quiet life.'

'I'm sure she won't be. Not when she realises how much fun she can have. Anyway,' Thea said, chuckling, 'I'm not sure if she's actually got a choice.' Glancing down at her watch, she stood up. 'I'd better go too.' She paused. 'Are you sure you're okay?'

Edie nodded. 'Yes, I'm sorry I've been so distracted this morning. I'm not entirely sure I heard everything that was being discussed.' She looked up at Thea, her eyes apologetic.

'Please don't worry. Grant says the lights team are all good to go and they'll start getting them up soonish; we can use the hall as usual for the grotto, and Grant and Fergus checked over the stands and the canopies and they all seem fine.'

Edie smiled at Thea. 'I'll need to get out all the chutneys and jams I made.' She scribbled that down on her notepad. 'You'd better head back to work.' She tried her best to sound bright. 'Off you go now, dear.'

Thea turned to walk away and Edie felt her smile falter. She was tired and aware she would need to do something sooner rather than later as she was up against a deadline that couldn't be changed.

CHAPTER FIFTEEN

When Amelia's mobile began ringing, she saw Jack's name flash up and grabbed it excitedly. 'Jack, how are you?'

'I'm fine, darling, but how are you? Where've you been? Why haven't you called?'

'I didn't want to wake you up. Every time I thought about calling, I realised you would either be at work or sleeping. Did you get the pictures?'

'Yes. Wow. What an amazing place. Looks like you've been strolling around taking in the scenery?'

'I've been quite busy. Seriously, relocation is an exhausting business.'

'Sure.' He laughed. 'But, honestly, how are you doing?'

Amelia sat down on the bed and started to tell Jack all about the hut.

'You have landed on your feet, sis. It sounds adorable.'

'It is. You and Ray would love the cabin. It's cosy and romantic . . .' She could feel her eyes welling up and had to choke back the emotion in her throat.

'Are you okay?'

She reached for a tissue and wiped away a few tears before steadying herself. The last thing she wanted to do was let her brother, on the other side of the Atlantic, know she was upset. 'Yes, I am fine. Maybe a bit emotional, and hearing your voice always brings on the waterworks.'

'Hey, it's okay,' said Jack softly. 'You don't have to put a brave face on things all the time.'

'I know.' She sighed. 'I suppose I've been trying to keep a lid on everything since I got here.'

'Have you told anyone about Declan?'

'No. There isn't anyone to tell yet. Well, other than Edie, who is a sweetheart, but I'd rather tell her in my own time.'

'Of course. Well, sis, I would say that you're stuck in one of the most awful places you could be. What with the beach right in front of you and your own shepherd's hut . . . all that fresh air and stunning scenery. I am so sorry for you. How on earth are you coping?'

That made Amelia laugh. 'It's terrible, Jack. I mean, there are seals and beautiful sunrises. The sound of the rain bouncing off the hut is soothing, especially when the log burner is on.' She sank back into the pillows on the bed and smiled. 'There's a lovely café and bakery which makes amazing pastries and coffee. People smile and stop to say hello when they pass you on the street.'

'Sounds absolutely hellish. Next you'll be telling me that the local hunk is in the lifeboat crew or mountain rescue team.'

Amelia laughed. 'No, not quite . . .' She hesitated, wondering if she should mention Fergus.

'Talking of men. Have you heard from Declan?'

'No. Which is part of the reason I haven't told anyone anything. I can't bear pity. Or questions. I still don't really understand why he left. How can I tell people what happened when I don't know myself?'

'You don't need to tell them he left. Just say you're separated.'

'It's never as simple as that, though, is it? People always want the details . . . and, to be honest, I feel ashamed.'

'Look, don't go there again. There is nothing for you to feel bad about. You didn't quit the marriage. He did. You didn't do anything wrong.'

'But I do. I keep thinking if I'd done more or been more . . .'

'Well, stop. You are amazing and this is his loss.'

'Sometimes I think it would be easier if he had died.' Amelia caught a sob at the back of her throat as the words tumbled out. The thought had been percolating in her mind for a while now but until this moment she hadn't had the courage to say the words out loud.

'That's totally understandable. In a way, that might have given you closure. This is a type of grief, Amelia. Except the love of your life is still very much alive and kicking.'

Amelia twirled a coil of hair as she listened. Having him acknowledge what she said, as normal, made her feel slightly less wretched.

'He hasn't replied to any of my messages either, if that makes you feel better.'

Amelia knew that would hurt Jack. The two of them had always got on so well. 'Oh, I wish you weren't so far away. I could do with a hug.'

'I want to give you the biggest cuddle ever.'

'Enough of me, though, and my woes. How are you? And how is Ray?'

'We are good, thanks. Work has been as hectic as ever, but then at least I get the weekends off. I keep hearing the horror stories about shifts at the hospital that go on and on and on. So, I can't complain.'

'And Ray?'

'He is great, too. I mean, busy with his patients as well, and always on at me to maintain my dental health. I swear, if his teeth become any whiter I'll need to start wearing my sunglasses to bed.'

Amelia laughed. Ray was a dentist, with the brightest, whitest smile she had ever seen. He was a walking advert for his practice and it was no wonder he was doing so well. 'Is he still enjoying his convertible?'

'Oh, yes. He loves nothing better than going for a spin . . . Look, sis, I should go now, but keep in touch and send me more pictures so I can live vicariously through you. And keep your eyes peeled for a nice Scottish hunk.'

'I will,' she said, laughing. 'And thank you. I love you, Jack.'

'Love you, too. Bye, sis. Call me soon.'

Amelia placed the phone on the breakfast bar and sat quietly for a moment. She was fine when her mind was occupied, but in the quiet moments her thoughts drifted back to Declan's letter. If only she'd picked up on how unhappy he'd been. How she wished he had spoken to her about their problems rather than running away. Then she thought about her journal prompt for the day: *Write about what you are most grateful for.* When she'd sat with her coffee this morning, she'd made a list: *a warm place to stay, good coffee, fresh air, the sea, the beach, happy dogs, this place.*

She had forgotten one of the most important things she was grateful for and that was her brother. She reached for her notebook, tucked underneath her pillow, and added: *Jack, laughter, conversation with someone who listens, and the shepherd's hut because it is what I need right now.* She was about to close the book when she added another word: *Edie.*

CHAPTER SIXTEEN

Amelia was starting to think it never rained on the island. Aside from the day she'd arrived and a couple of heavy showers during the night, when she was happily and cosily tucked up in bed, she enjoyed waking up to a view of the sparkling sea. If it wasn't for the cooling temperature, the scent of bonfires in the air and the red leaves now rapidly falling from the trees, it would be easy to think it was late summer. She loved the way a grey plume of smoke twisted from the chimney at Coorie Cottage. She saw Edie most days, though they didn't chat all the time. Mostly Edie gave her a wave and smile before disappearing back inside. Amelia made a note to knock on her door later.

She had grown quite used to her morning routine of having her icy shower, which seemed to be doing wonders for getting rid of her worries for a while. Afterwards she would pull on her clothes, which now included a hat, and stroll along the beach until she reached Cèic. She had since learned that was the Gaelic word for cake.

Cèic had some of the best views she had ever seen. She loved it, and not only for the stunning views, or the freshly baked scones, but because it was like the hub of the community, where people would talk about everything and anything or pass some time, in fact quite a lot of time, discussing the weather. Amelia realised that it gave them focus. The first man she had seen there, reading his newspaper in the corner, was called Ed and he came in every day. He told Amelia that his wife had dementia and had been moved into a care home. They'd been married for fifty years and he'd sounded devastated that he could no longer manage to look after her on his own. He visited her as much as he could but he missed her and struggled on his own. That was why he brought his paper into the café every morning, where he would distract himself in its pages for a while and eat his breakfast.

Doris always called in for her takeaway coffee, and whenever she saw Amelia would shout, 'Good morning!' She had already made sure to sign Amelia up for the fair, and had also asked if they could catch up to brainstorm the new festive gin. 'We'll meet at the bar and you can taste some and we can play with words,' said Doris. How could she refuse?

'How are you today, Amelia?' Cano asked.

'I'm well, thanks.' Amelia was growing fond of Cano and loved listening to him talk proudly about his children and grandchildren. If the café was quiet, he would whip out his phone and show the latest pictures of his two granddaughters and one grandson. In the New Year, a fourth baby was due, which he was excited about.

'Are you enjoying your time here?'

'Yes, I really am.'

'I make your coffee and bring it over for you. Please, take a seat.'

Amelia went over to her usual spot at the long table and mouthed, 'Hello,' at Ed, who briefly looked up before resuming reading. She glanced over, and when she saw Fergus coming through the door, her pulse started to race and her heart gave a little skitter. Trying not to stare, or let her jaw fall open, she busied herself with her notepad.

'Oh, Cano. I can't tell you how good that smells. I am so in need of my coffee this morning,' Fergus said.

'Of course. To go?'

As Fergus stood at the counter, Amelia glanced up and checked him out. He wore his usual outdoors gear black all-weather trousers, a dark red fleece and a black jacket. Fergus looked over and caught her staring. Their eyes locked.

'Amelia, hello. I didn't see you.' He clocked the empty chairs next to her. 'Want some company?'

She tried to shrug casually. 'Sure.'

'Well, if you don't mind, I'll join you. Cano, I will take it for here, please . . . Amelia, can I get you anything?'

'No, thanks. I've ordered.'

'Go sit down,' said Cano. 'I will bring your coffee over.'

Fergus strolled over and sat in the chair opposite her.

'I haven't seen you in here before,' Amelia said. 'Is it your regular stop-off?'

'Yes, every day. I'm a bit predictable. Although normally I'm in much earlier than this,' he said, checking the time. 'Which is why I'm crotchety this morning. I need my coffee.'

'Ah. That explains why I've not seen you. I've been coming in every morning but later than you. What an amazing spot. The views, the coffee, the aroma . . . and it's a million miles from London.'

'Yes, it is indeed.' He looked at her curiously. 'You're not missing the big smoke?'

'Not at all. This place has got under my skin.'

'Except you haven't tried out any of the water sports yet,' he said with a grin. 'You must do that.'

'Okay, well, what do you suggest first?'

'Either a wild swim or a spot of kayaking.'

Cano arrived with their coffees and a croissant for Fergus. 'There you go. Enjoy.'

'Thanks, Cano.'

Amelia couldn't help staring at Fergus's long fingers as he wrapped them around the mug and took a sip of his latte. 'Perfect. Just what I need.'

She had to pull her gaze away from him and took a gulp of her drink. 'I honestly think it's the best I've tasted.'

'So, what is it to be?' He was obviously trying to make sure she didn't dodge the conversation.

'I would quite like to do the wild swimming . . . but I don't have a wetsuit.' Her voice was a tad too triumphant.

'That's not a problem. I can sort that. We have a whole range at the centre.' He looked her over, assessing with a mischievous twinkle in his eyes. 'Say the day and in the meantime I'll drop one off.'

Amelia laughed. 'You're persuasive, aren't you?'

'Yip.' He looked at her intently.

'Busy day?' she managed.

'Yes. We're making the most of this dry weather and taking some of the high school kids out later.'

'Edie said you do a lot to help with their confidence.'

He broke off a piece of croissant and chewed thoughtfully. 'We try to give kids a chance who maybe aren't doing so well. The ones who find it harder to fit in. This can help bring them out of themselves.'

'That's brilliant.'

He shrugged and stifled a yawn. 'Sorry. Early start.' He ate another bit of his pastry, managing not to make a mess despite its flakiness.

A vision of Declan floated into Amelia's mind at that moment. There was no way he would have eaten a croissant on a weekday, or even on a weekend. It was all about the fat-to-carb ratio and that wouldn't have ticked the boxes. Having coffee and a croissant at 10 a.m. on a random Wednesday morning in November with a very handsome man was extremely liberating.

'So, you've been roped into the Christmas fair?'

'Yes . . .' She hesitated. 'Although it sounds like fun.' His eyes were on her, contemplative and curious. Something about the way he looked at her was unsettling.

'How long do you think you'll stay?'

She sighed. 'I don't know if I'm honest . . . I, well, let's just say I'm not in a hurry to return to London. I lost my job and . . . anyway, I don't have to be back anytime soon.' Her face coloured.

He tilted his head to the side. 'There's a lot that's great about this place. You should stick around.'

'Where do you live?' She was trying her best to prolong the conversation.

'I'm along from the hotel.'

'Have you known Edie for long?'

'Yes, she's fab. A true gem.'

'She's great,' agreed Amelia. 'Though she's been quiet the last couple of days. I'm worried something is on her mind.'

'Oh.' He looked concerned. 'I'll try to pop by soon and check up on her.'

'Has she ever been married?'

Fergus looked at her contemplatively. 'She's quite private but most folks know that yes and she was widowed.'

'Oh dear. I'm sorry to hear that.'

'It happened a while ago, before she came here. But I know she was devastated at the time. He died suddenly in an accident.'

'Poor Edie.' Amelia felt a wave of emotion and she clenched her fingers into her palms. When she heard a sad story, it unlocked something within her that made her want to cry.

Fergus was about to say something when his phone rang. He accepted the call instantly. 'Grant.' He pulled a face. 'Okay, I'll be there in five.' He drained the remainder of his coffee. 'I'd better go, otherwise Grant won't be happy at being left to handle a bunch of teenagers on his own.'

'Oh.' She was surprised at just how disappointed she was that he was leaving. 'Well, it was good to see you.'

He stood up, his hands on the back of the chair, and once again her eyes were drawn to those hands, then his fingers, and she couldn't help noticing his nails. 'Sorry to scoot off. Enjoy your day.' He started walking away and stopped. 'We didn't make a plan to go for a swim. When do you fancy?'

'Um . . . just whenever works for you?'

'Perfect. What's your number and I'll text you.' He punched the digits into his phone as Amelia recited them to him, and immediately sent her a message. 'That's so you've got my details now too.' He grinned. 'There's no escape.'

CHAPTER SEVENTEEN

Amelia sat for a while looking out after Fergus and wondering what his story was. Why hadn't he settled down with anyone? He seemed too good to be true. Then she felt a hand on her shoulder. She looked up to find Ed smiling down at her. His white fluffy hair was thin across his scalp and he wore slightly too big glasses, which he kept having to push up his nose. 'I think he's got a soft spot for you, dear.'

Feeling flustered, Amelia had no idea what to say. 'Oh, I don't think so . . .'

'Trust me,' he said. 'I know these things. My Daphne always did say I had an instinct for spotting true love. See you tomorrow.' Off he sauntered, with his newspaper rolled up and tucked under his arm.

Just then her mobile started to ring from the depths of her bag. By the time she fished it out and saw Declan's name, it was too late. She had missed his call. She was stunned that he had actually bothered to call. Then her voicemail pinged. Hesitating, she lifted her mobile to her ear and played the message.

'Amelia. It's me. I'm sorry that I haven't called. I needed some space. I'll maybe try later.'

The sound of his voice, flat and quite matter of fact, had a strange effect on her. *I'll maybe try later.* He didn't sound at all bothered that he'd not been in touch and had ignored her calls and messages for so long. She stared at her phone, not sure whether to stamp on it or throw it in the sea.

'Try this.' Cano put a plate in front of her. 'It's a new Christmas shortbread I am testing. Cinnamon and nutmeg. Let me know what you think.'

Amelia wiped away a tear and tried to compose herself.

'Oh, I'm sorry. You are upset.'

'I'm okay,' she said, annoyed at herself.

'Man worries?' His voice was knowing.

Amelia laughed in surprise. 'How did you know?'

'I have two daughters. If they cried it was generally over two things.'

'And what were they?' she asked.

'Sore feet when they insisted on wearing those silly high heels. Stilettoes?'

'Yes, stilettoes.' She smiled. 'And what was the other thing?'

'Men.' He glanced down at her trainers. 'You have nice sensible shoes on and so your feet look okay to me. I can only assume it must be the other thing. A man.'

She exhaled loudly. 'Yes, you are right. But I am trying not to think about him.'

He eyed her for a moment. 'You are a beautiful young lady, Amelia. A man who makes you cry is not worth anything.' He gestured to the bay outside, which was glittering in the sunshine. 'Focus on the positive things in your life and do what you enjoy. Life is too short to waste.' His face clouded over briefly as his mind went elsewhere. It brightened when he looked back at her. 'I would like very much if you tried this. That is sure to cheer you up.'

Amelia smiled gratefully at him for dispensing wise advice and festive treats.

'You tuck in and I will get you another coffee, if you would like?'

'I would love that. Thank you.' She took a bite of the sweet, buttery, crumbly biscuit and closed her eyes. It was delicious. She opened her eyes to see Cano looking at her nervously. She gave him a thumbs-up. 'Wonderful.'

He beamed with delight.

Amelia once again said a silent prayer of thanks for circumstances bringing her to this place, and the kindness of strangers who were helping her realise she *could* rebuild her life.

CHAPTER EIGHTEEN

Edie usually loved the weeks leading up to the Christmas fair, and she had a long-held tradition of counting down the days with her creative calendar pinned to the back of the kitchen door. On it she had an intricately detailed plan of what needed to be done and when. She would busy herself for hours making small clay Christmas trinket dishes shaped like leaves of holly. Then she would leave them to dry for a few days before painting or varnishing them in shades of rich green. Sometimes she made beautiful star-shaped Christmas tree decorations, which were painted bright gold and studded with costume jewels. Thea would sell them in her shop and they sold very quickly. However, this year things had not gone to her usual plan. To start with, her regular clay supplier hadn't been able to fulfil her order so she'd bought a different type.

She based herself in the kitchen, cosy, thanks to the wood-burning stove, and spread old newspaper all over the table. She gathered everything she required to get going. She placed a sharp knife next to her along with a damp cloth for her sticky hands. Having Classic FM on quietly in the background always set the scene, and as soon as she put on her old, oversized shirt to protect her clothes she was ready to begin. She loved the process of picking up the clay and getting started, losing herself in shaping and moulding it. Today, however, the scissors kept snagging on the packet, which was a real nuisance to open. When she did start warming it in her hand, it was rock solid and non-malleable. She reached for the knife and cut a small chunk off, focusing on exploring its consistency and temperature, and she closed her eyes, using her fingers to press and manipulate. As her thumbs pressed down and explored the texture, her mind wandered once again to her sister.

Christine had been married once, long before Edie had met Jim, but the wedding had been short-lived and she'd moved to London to pursue her career as a lawyer. She'd lived in a lovely apartment in Bloomsbury and had led a busy and full life. She'd travelled extensively with her work and loved exploring different parts of the world. After her brief marriage, she'd always vowed she would never wed again and, true to her word, had never shown any signs of settling down with anyone, despite Edie's protests that she should give love another chance.

Noticing the clay becoming dry in her hands, Edie gently dipped her fingers into the small cup of water on the table and rubbed it into the clay to moisten it. But she added too much and it soon became sticky. Frustrated, Edie threw it down, cut off another piece from the block and started again.

Her mind flitted back to Jim and she glanced over at the framed picture that sat on the window ledge. It had been taken in the Botanic Gardens in Edinburgh, one of their favourite places to visit, on a sunny summer's day. Jim stood beside the glasshouses, beaming at the camera. That day had been glorious. She remembered how they'd strolled around the beautiful, landscaped grounds, stopping to admire the city skyline and the castle. She'd laughed at Jim as they'd wandered through the steamy palm houses and he'd kept mopping his brow. They'd admired the tree collection before having vanilla ice cream at the café. Looking at Jim in that photo was exactly how she wanted to remember him and their marriage. In the weeks and months after his death, she'd spent a lot of time there because she'd felt most connected to him in that very spot. She hadn't been able to bring herself to put the photo away, despite all these years passing. Some days, Jim's death felt like yesterday and she could still feel the physical pain of her shattering into millions of pieces. She'd visited a counsellor afterwards who'd reassured her that her grief was hugely complex due to the circumstances surrounding his death and the way in which he'd died.

Rolling the clay around in her hands, she wondered if she should be more open to seeing her sister now that Christine's life was drawing to an end. Was she a bad person for not immediately wanting to rush to her bedside? She certainly felt guilty although technically she knew she had no reason to. Focusing on her breath, she tried her best to work out how she felt about Christine right at this moment in time. Sorrow? Hurt? Pain? Loss? But it was a futile exercise as the same thoughts came back into her head and feelings of resentment and anger started to surface.

She looked down when she realised that she had balled the clay up in her hands. It looked nothing like it was supposed to and she attempted to flatten it out by pulling and folding it. But it was no use, it just didn't want to be shaped the way she wanted to mould it and she threw it down in yet more frustration. Her sister made her cross. She was angry that the onus was now on her to do something about their relationship, and if she didn't she would have another burden to live with. Standing up, she gathered up the remaining clay, walked over to the bin and dumped it in. She slammed the lid shut.

Molly barked.

'Sorry, Molly,' she said. 'I didn't mean to scare you.'

The dog jumped up and came over and sat at Edie's feet. 'What would I do without you, my precious girl?'

Molly wagged her tail and licked her owner's hand.

'Right, well, this isn't working out so good for me today, Molly. Which is most annoying. How about we sort the labels on the jars?'

She pulled off the shirt and went to the sink to scrub her hands, which were chalky and sticky. She knew the best thing to do at the moment was to distract herself with a simple task, which would allow her to feel a sense of achievement. The mundane job of labelling all the jars seemed to calm her mind, and after an hour or so, all were boxed and ready to deliver to Doris. She smiled and ticked it off her list.

She turned and started pulling out ingredients for her famous festive tablet, a Scottish version of fudge. She needed condensed milk, butter, milk and sugar, cranberries, ginger, orange zest and red and green sprinkles. Opening the cupboard, she took out her large heavy-based saucepan and the sugar thermometer from the drawer.

She started melting the butter with the milk and slowly added the sugar, bringing it to the boil. Then she stirred in the condensed milk, mixing it so it wouldn't stick to the bottom of the pan. As she brought it back to the boil, she kept the wooden spoon swirling through the mixture until it turned thick and honey-coloured. It was her mother's recipe and she could vividly remember the days when she and Christine would sit in the kitchen, on high stools, watching their mother stir and stir. It had taken around twenty minutes until they could help with the best and most magical bit of all. Edie would hold the bowl of ice-cold water at the ready and Mother would drop a small amount of the hot mixture in.

As the older of the two, Christine would get to pick it up and try to form a soft ball with it in her fingers. If she could, then it was ready. They would leave it to cool and her mother would beat it again before pouring it into the tin and leaving it to set.

Checking it with the thermometer was much easier, though not quite as much fun. After Edie poured it into the prepared trays, studding each one with the festive ingredients, she put them aside to cool.

This was just getting silly, she told herself. There was no option other than to call the hospital and find out the truth. She washed her hands at the sink, glancing at Jim again, and went to the hall. She picked up the phone.

CHAPTER NINETEEN

Amelia opened her eyes. It was 2 a.m. and the temperature in the hut felt as though it had dropped below zero. She heard a rustling noise at the door . . . Her heart raced as she gingerly sat up, pulling the covers around her. *What on earth was that?* She shivered as she watched the handle turn. *Oh God* — had she locked it? She couldn't remember. Her imagination started to work overtime and her eyes flicked from left to right as she wondered what to do. Thank God she'd had the sense to draw the curtains last night. At least nobody could see in. Whoever was behind the door depressed the handle and tried again. She sighed in relief. But the locked door didn't make her feel much better. Reaching for her phone, she wondered whether to dial 999. It was hardly an emergency, was it? She also couldn't alert Edie in case that panicked her. She had two choices. She needed to go and confront the person attempting to break in. Or she could call Fergus. She was more concerned about Edie and hoped that she had locked her door last night. She tapped out a text.

Someone is trying to break into the hut. I am worried about Edie!

She tried to settle her breathing while she waited for a reply. What if Fergus was a deep sleeper? She didn't dare move out of the bed in case the floor creaked. Her heart thudded and she stuffed her fist into her mouth at the loud bang against the door. As her eyes accustomed to the dark, she wondered what she could use as a weapon. A mop? A knife? But would she actually be able to use it?

She steeled herself to move and then blinked when her phone screen lit up.

On my way.

Amelia was tempted to peek out of the window but didn't want to risk it in case they saw her. Strange noises in the night didn't really feature in her marketing plan for this place. Could it be haunted? Though did shepherd's huts even have ghosts? She wondered if she had pulled the latch properly on the bathroom window. She thought her heart was about to explode with worry as she weighed up her options once again. The window was tiny and it was therefore highly unlikely anyone or anything could squeeze through. Unless they were rabbit-sized.

Her imagination raced as she sat there looking at shapes in the dark. Realising everything had gone quiet outside, she knelt forward on the bed and tried to look out the side of the curtain. She screamed. A face stared in.

Amelia didn't know who was more scared, Edie or her. They looked at each other and Amelia moved off the bed. When she opened the door, Edie remained at the window.

'Edie,' she said gently, noticing she wore just her pyjamas. Amelia put her hand on Edie's arm. The woman turned but stared straight through her. 'Are you okay, Edie?' Edie remained rooted to the spot and Amelia looked down to see her bare, muddy feet. She ran back inside to grab a jacket to slip round the woman's shoulders. The best thing was to try to get her back safely to the house and into her bed.

She turned Edie in the direction of the steps and carefully helped her down. Then she tried to keep her distance as much as possible as Edie walked slowly back across the grass and towards the house. Amelia shivered, glad she had pulled on a hoody over her own pyjamas.

Just then she heard a car crunch over the gravel. Fergus. She hoped his arrival wouldn't startle Edie. The door slammed and the torchlight flashed around the corner of the house. Fortunately, he dipped the beam when he saw them and ran over.

'She's sleepwalking?'

'Yes,' whispered Amelia.

'I thought this had all stopped. You know to leave her to get back into her bed?'

She nodded and the pair followed behind and through the front door. Amelia jumped when she felt something brush against her legs. Molly. Edie wiped her grubby feet on the front mat and started climbing the stairs. Molly scampered up beside her.

'I need to go and put some warm socks on her at the very least.'

Fergus nodded and said he would wait downstairs.

Amelia made sure Edie got into bed and then Molly jumped up and curled in a ball next to her. Amelia opened a drawer, hoping she wouldn't need to root around looking for socks. Beginner's luck. She immediately found a pair of thick, fleecy socks and quietly slipped her hands under the duvet, managing to put them on Edie's feet. Molly opened one eye curiously and thumped her tail a few times. Amelia tucked Edie in and pulled the blanket from the end of the bed up and over her.

'Is she okay?' asked Fergus.

'Sound asleep,' said Amelia, self-conscious that she stood there with her pyjamas on and bed-head hair. She didn't even want to begin to think what she must look like. 'Thanks for coming. I got a fright when I thought someone was trying to break into the hut.'

'I'm not surprised.' He raked his fingers through his hair. 'You're cold,' he said, noticing her shiver.

'A bit.' She pulled the hoody tighter around her shoulders and stifled a yawn.

'Come on. Let's get you back to your own bed now.'

'Will she be okay though?'

'Yes, she should sleep now and hopefully not move.'

'Has she done this before?'

He frowned, clearly thinking about what to say. 'Yes, she has mentioned to me before that she used to be a sleepwalker. I had a spell of insomnia and that's why it came up in conversation. Though I didn't realise she had started again . . . there must be something on her mind.'

'She hasn't said anything to me,' said Amelia.

He shrugged. 'She wouldn't. She plays her cards close to her chest. Come on, she'll be okay now and you can check in on her again in the morning.'

Amelia was grateful Fergus insisted on chumming her back to the cabin. She shivered as she walked up the steps.

'Let me come in and make you a cup of tea.'

She didn't argue. She was frozen. She kicked off her shoes and reached under the bed for her own warm socks. Meanwhile Fergus filled the kettle.

'Get back into bed. I'll make it for you.'

'Thank you,' she said, climbing into the bed, trying desperately to warm up. Fergus handed her the tea and she took a sip. He brought another mug over and pulled out one of the stools from the bar.

Amelia frowned. 'I hope she's warm enough. Poor Edie.'

'You must have had a fright.'

She nodded and her face paled as she remembered waking up and seeing the handle move.

'It's quite safe around here. But I'm glad you locked the door. Imagine what would have happened if Edie had come in. You might have whacked her with a saucepan.' His eyes settled on the pot at the end of the bed.

Amelia laughed. 'It was the nearest thing I was able to reach and . . . I was scared. Look, thanks for coming to my rescue. I appreciate it. I didn't know what else to do. I gather people here don't just dial 999 at the first sign of trouble?'

His face lit up with a smile. 'No, they don't.' He finished the rest of his tea and stood up to take the mug over to the sink, washing it and stacking it on the rack.

'You'd better get back to your bed.' She stifled another yawn. Though if truth be told she didn't want him to leave. She had been a bit spooked and wondered if she should go and sleep inside the house in Edie's guest bedroom.

'Are you going to be all right?' He looked at her quizzically.

Amelia didn't want to act like some kind of damsel in distress but her throat constricted and she struggled to get her words out. 'Mmm.'

'You don't sound too sure about that.'

She could hardly beg him to stay. She didn't want him to take it the wrong way, so she didn't say anything. Feeling his gaze on her, she managed to mumble that she would be okay.

Fergus walked over to the door and pulled the latch, then settled himself in the chair next to the wood stove, which still gave off a gentle warmth from the night before. 'I'm going to sit here until you fall asleep. Would that help?'

She smiled gratefully and curled up under the covers. 'Only if you're sure?'

'Yip. I'm too tired to drive now anyway, so this works for me.'

'Thanks, Fergus,' she said softly, and turned off the lamp by her bed.

'Try not to snore.'

She shook her head and closed her eyes, reassured at his presence.

CHAPTER TWENTY

Amelia managed to fall into a brief deep sleep but spent the rest of the night tossing and turning, her head a jumble of thoughts. In her dreams she was being chased down a corridor and ran in to a bright white room. Declan sat waiting, annoyed she hadn't called him back and demanding an explanation. Amelia tried to talk but she couldn't get the words out. She turned away and ran and he chased after her. Then she suddenly stumbled and fell down a hole in the ground . . . She sat up with a gasp, her heart racing and tears rolling down her cheeks. As her eyes became accustomed to the dark, she realised where she was.

'Amelia,' said Fergus, jumping up from his chair. He sat down on the side of the bed. 'What is it?'

His voice was gentle and kind, which made her cry even more. Covering her eyes with her hands, she rubbed them and wiped away the tears. When Fergus handed her a tissue from the box on the bedside table, she dabbed at her face.

'Oh dear, sorry, I must have had a bad dream.'

He reached out to touch her arm. 'You okay?'

She nodded, hoping he would leave his hand there as it was soothing. 'I thought you were going to go as soon as I went to sleep.'

'Why would I want to go home to my own bed when I can sit in a chair all night?' he said mischievously.

'You tell me,' she teased, briefly managing to regain her composure. Her voice cracked with emotion. 'Thanks for being so nice and for coming to my rescue. Doesn't say much for me, does it? I'm a snowflake.'

'Ah, don't be daft, and you don't have to thank me. It's been a bit of a strange night, hasn't it? I'm sure you weren't expecting any of this when you came here. I get the feeling you were looking for some peace and quiet.'

That made her smile and she budged across the bed, making space for him. He sat beside her, which felt the most normal thing in the world. She leaned her head into his shoulder and he circled his arm round her. Amelia lifted her head for a moment and looked into his eyes. 'Thank you for being such a good friend,' she said, giving a contented sigh. Having him next to her was comforting and reminded her that she wasn't alone. For the first time in ages, she actually felt supported, and realised how much she had missed human contact. Closing her eyes, she felt his cheek press against her hair and she drifted off to sleep.

A bird gently tweeted outside when she opened her eyes. She could tell from the way the light sliced through the tiny gap in the curtains that it was morning. She sat up and stretched. Fergus had gone. Slipping out of bed, she saw the note on the worktop. *Sorry to dash. I need to get to work. I'll check in later. Fergus.*

She turned on the tap and poured herself a glass of water, taking a gulp. What a strange night. She just hoped Edie was okay. She would have a shower and then go over and say hello.

CHAPTER TWENTY-ONE

When Edie woke up, she stretched her arms above her head. Swinging her legs round and out of bed, she looked down at her feet, wondering why on earth she had thick, fleecy socks on. She didn't remember putting them on, unless she'd got up in the night to do so. Pulling on her dressing gown, she tightened the belt around her middle and padded downstairs to make her usual mug of warm water and lemon juice. Years ago, her mother had taught her that it was good for the digestive system and stimulated one's 'agni'. It was one of the few good habits that she had managed to keep up over the years. As she bustled around the kitchen, she found herself singing an island lullaby her mother used to sing to her.

'Coo roo koo, cooruku, coo ru ku, coo ku. Coo roo koo, cooruku, coo ru ku, coo ku.'

'Oh, Molly,' she said to her faithful pet who sat wagging her tail, clearly hoping for some breakfast. 'What's happening to me today? I've gone all melancholy.'

Glancing out of the window she was surprised to see Fergus walking up the path. Had she asked him to do some work in the garden? Then she narrowed her gaze when she noticed that he wasn't in his work gear. In fact, he seemed to be wearing pyjama bottoms. And he was coming from the direction of the shepherd's hut. 'Oh my. Well, he certainly didn't waste any time, did he? I hope she doesn't mention that he's a perk of the hut when she starts trying to market it.'

Fully expecting him to jump in his van and drive off, she was surprised when she heard the door.

'Hey, Edie,' he called. 'Just me. Are you up? Are you decent?'

'Am I decent?' She looked at Molly. What a cheek! 'Hi, Fergus. I'm here in the kitchen, come on through.' Molly's ears pricked up and she ran to greet him, hoping he might feed her.

'Good morning. You're up bright and early, aren't you? Did you have a *stopover?*'

Fergus frowned when he realised she was staring at his checked pyjama trousers. 'No!' he shouted, as it dawned on him what she was insinuating. 'Though, yes, kind of, but not in the way you think.'

'Are you sure about that?' Her eyes glinted with mischief. 'Now, Fergus, I don't mean to lecture you but I get the sense that Amelia isn't here for that kind of thing, if you catch my drift. She wants to be somewhere quiet and uncomplicated without any hassles.'

Fergus took a deep breath. 'Edie, I'm not quite sure what you're referring to, but Amelia and I are friends. She's a sweet girl but . . .'

Edie raised an eyebrow. 'Friends with benefits. Isn't that what you young folk are all into these days?'

'Edie.' His voice was gentle. 'Amelia actually messaged me in a bit of a panic last night. Someone was trying to break into her hut.'

'What do you mean?' Edie's eyes widened in shock.

'She woke in the middle of the night and someone was trying to open her door. Fortunately, she'd locked it, but she got an awful scare. Her first thought was of you and she asked me to come and check you were okay.'

'Oh.' Her face paled. 'Somebody tried to break in?'

Fergus pointed to the table. 'Let's sit down for a minute.'

Edie sank into a chair and Fergus sat opposite. He took a breath. 'Edie, it was you. You were trying to get into the hut.'

She clasped her hand across her mouth.

'We think you must have been sleepwalking.' He reached across and squeezed her hand. 'Has this been happening a lot lately?'

Edie shook her head vigorously when she should have been nodding — for it had started again, but she couldn't bear to admit it. At the moment her main concern was that she'd frightened poor Amelia. 'Oh, goodness me. Is Amelia okay? She will have been terrified.'

'She got a bit of a fright to begin with, but she's fine. More worried about you.'

'So that's why I had socks on when I woke up? I couldn't work it out.'

'Yes. Amelia put you to bed and was worried your feet were cold and muddy, so she thought the best thing to do was slip on some socks.'

'The poor girl. I owe her an apology.' She lowered her chin and sighed.

He waved his hand dismissively. 'Not at all. She's fine. She's more worried about you.'

'And you must have been worried about her if you felt the need to stay over?'

'She had a bit of a fright, and so she asked if I would stay until she went to sleep.'

Edie watched him as he spoke, noticing something flit across his eyes. Was it concern? Or affection? Or something else? 'Oh, Fergus, I am so sorry for giving you all a scare. I'll go and see Amelia later and try to explain.'

'I know she's been a bit worried about you, Edie. Is everything okay?'

Hot tears sprung up in her eyes and she shook her head. She was not going to cry. 'I'm afraid not,' she said. 'I've had some bad news.'

'Oh, Edie. What's the matter?'

'It's my sister. You know the one I told you about?'
Fergus nodded.
'She's dying.'
'I'm sorry.' He clasped his hand across hers.

CHAPTER TWENTY-TWO

Later that morning, there was a tap on the cabin door. Amelia opened the door and smiled at both Edie and the pink sweatshirt she wore with the words '*Happy Thoughts*' written across the front. 'Come in. How are you, Edie?'

'I'm fine, thanks, although a bit mortified. I think I owe you an apology, my dear.'

'No, you don't, Edie. Not at all. Are you okay though? That's the main thing.'

Edie nodded. 'Yes, I am. I'm so sorry, I don't know what got into me.'

'Do you normally sleepwalk?' asked Amelia.

Edie took a long, deep breath. 'Not for a very long time.' Her eyes clouded over. She was silent for a minute.

'Is there anything on your mind, Edie? You look worried.'

Edie frowned. 'Well . . . no . . .' She looked to be on the verge of saying something but shook her head. 'Which reminds me, I wondered how you feel about helping out with the Christmas fair?'

Amelia laughed. 'Of course, but you need to tell me more about it.'

'Every year we have the Christmas lights switch-on followed by our Christmas fair. There are stalls, a bar and food, and everything you can think of. And the ceilidh on Christmas Eve . . .'

'Sounds wonderful,' said Amelia.

Edie smiled. 'It is quite magical.'

'The only thing is . . .' Amelia wondered how to articulate herself. 'Will it be okay for me to still be here at Christmas?'

Edie clapped her hands together in delight. 'Of course.'

'It's just . . . Well, we've never talked about how long you want me to stay.'

'As long as it takes,' began Edie. 'There's no rush or deadline on my part.'

Amelia felt her shoulders drop in relief. She had been dreading the whole Christmas question and what she should do. She didn't fancy spending any more nights on Suna's floor, and although Jack and Ray would have welcomed her to their home in a heartbeat, she couldn't afford a flight to Boston at such a peak time of the year.

'Amelia,' said Edie, softly. 'You can stay here for as long as you want to or need to.'

Amelia nodded gratefully. 'Thank you. It's tricky . . . I don't have anywhere to go back to.' She automatically moved her fingers over to touch her wedding band, forgetting she'd removed it the day after she arrived. 'The thing is . . . my husband left me.' She sighed. 'Then I lost my job . . .' She had finally admitted it to someone other than Suna or Jack.

'Oh, Amelia, I am so sorry to hear that. You poor love.' Edie reached over and pulled her into a hug. She stroked her hair gently. 'What an awful ordeal to go through.'

Amelia wiped a tear away and shrugged. 'It wasn't exactly what I had planned for my first year of married life. I thought we would be decorating our tree and looking forward to Christmas together . . .'

'Life can be so cruel at times, dear. I am glad you are here though.'

'Thank you.' Amelia forced a smile. 'You'd better tell me what you'd like me to do at this fair.'

Edie rolled her eyes. 'Doris from the distillery wondered if you would help with the bar? She has a new gin she's trying to flog too.'

Amelia smiled. 'It's okay, Edie. Doris has beaten you to it. She has already signed me up for that.'

Edie's eyes widened. 'Really? Oh, that is wonderful news. Though she didn't tell me. Mind you, I haven't seen her for a few days. Anyway, thank you. At least that keeps her off my back. She can be a bit tenacious over the planning details.'

'I'm delighted to help.'

'Marvellous. Why don't you come up to the cottage and I can show you the plans?'

* * *

The women spent the rest of the morning together, with Edie scribbling down notes as Amelia offered ideas on how she could help with the fair. 'Christmas jumpers and reindeer antlers!'

'That's a tremendous idea. Why did I never think of that?' Edie yawned.

'Why don't we leave things there for now?' suggested Amelia. 'Maybe you could take a nap and I can walk Molly?'

Edie looked up from her notepad and let out a long, slow breath. 'If you're sure, that would be good. Thank you, Amelia.'

As Edie walked upstairs to her bedroom, she thought once again how lucky she was that Amelia had answered the advert for the job. She was a bit of an angel who sprinkled something magical around her. Since her arrival she had transformed the place and Edie loved having her around. She had a feeling Fergus was fairly taken with her too.

CHAPTER TWENTY-THREE

Amelia and Jack spoke several times a week, both on phone and FaceTime calls, and she sent lots of pictures as she explored the island. Some days she took the local bus, which wound its circular route. A couple of times she borrowed Edie's car and stopped at secluded bays and coves, taking as many pictures as she could and scribbling notes. Sometimes she would pack her rucksack with a flask of coffee, a blanket and her journal and find a quiet spot in which to contemplate and write. Being in charge of her own day was liberating, and she tried to take one day at a time, focusing on the moment.

She loved exploring all the coastal walks and this morning was walking to the King's Cave, where Robert the Bruce had sheltered and had his famed encounter with a spider. She parked at the forestry car park and followed the tree-flanked track down through the wood, pausing to admire the holly bushes. She continued down the narrow, steep path, which took her onto the pebbly beach. It was so peaceful. Picking her way over the rocks, she admired the views across the Kilbrannan Sound. Edie had told her that Paul McCartney used to live across the water back when he and Linda had lived on the Mull of Kintyre. 'He was never my favourite Beatle though,' she added. 'I always preferred John.' Amelia stifled a laugh as she stood watching the waves gently lap the shore and thought of Edie's comments. She was some woman.

When she'd spoken to Jack last night, she'd told him about Edie and the sleepwalking, omitting the details about Fergus coming to her rescue, which she hadn't been ready to share.

'Is she worried about something?'

'I don't know, and I'm not sure she would tell me anyway.'

'Is she likely to go and get herself checked out by the GP?'

'I suggested that, but she keeps telling me that she's fine. She's quite independent and it's that delicate balance between caring and interfering,' she said.

'I agree. It can be tricky. I would keep an eye on her and see how things are. Particularly if you think there's something on her mind. Her being able to talk about it will help. Does she have anyone close to her?'

Amelia thought for a moment. Edie had plenty of people around her, but Amelia had no idea who she confided in. She was friendly and warm with everyone yet nobody was particularly close, aside from Fergus, and even then she kept him slightly at arm's length. Amelia couldn't imagine her speaking privately to Thea or Doris. From what she could gather, Edie was very private and quite happy in her own company. Maybe she could enquire discreetly when she met Thea later for a drink.

Now, as she stood alone on the beach, she felt as though she was in the middle of nowhere. She lifted her face to the soft breeze, gulping in the fresh, salty air. The weather had stayed dry throughout November so far, albeit with a chill in the air, but Amelia didn't care. She revelled in having the time and space to explore. She was keen to try Goatfell next. At 874 metres, it was the highest peak on the island, but she was a bit anxious about doing the climb on her own.

The best thing about all the walking, aside from the fact it was free, which meant she wasn't spending much money at all during her stay, was the space and time it allowed her to think. Not just about Declan but what she wanted to do next with her life. She couldn't imagine herself returning to London. However, she didn't know where to go next. She knew that sorting out the hut website for Edie wouldn't sustain her forever. The Christmas fair would keep her busy for a while, but what next? It was now the third week of November and this existence wouldn't last forever. Should she be thinking about trying to make a plan or a strategy for the New Year? She didn't want to outstay her welcome as Edie had been so kind and generous, but she remained vague about the length of the 'job'.

Over the past few weeks, she'd grown fond of Edie. Although she couldn't bring herself to talk about Declan, somehow she knew Edie understood. She appeared to sense Amelia's heart had been wounded. Amelia knew she had been through her own heartache with the loss of her husband. She was still worried that something troubled Edie, especially with the sleepwalking. She said it hadn't happened again but Amelia and Fergus were both worried that she might end up hurting herself.

Later, she ventured out to the bar at the local hotel; it was extremely busy for a Wednesday night.

'Is it always like this?' she said, smiling at Thea, who sat at the bar.

'Quiz night, which I totally forgot about. But I think they're just winding up.' Pointing at a table of older people, all with grey hair, she laughed. 'They are complete demons on the quiz circuit. If you arrive and they are here, then it's game over.'

Amelia laughed. 'They take it seriously?'

'Oh, yes. That would be an understatement. What can I get you?'

'I'd love a glass of red wine, please.'

'I like your taste. That's exactly what I feel like too.' Thea turned to the barman and ordered the drinks. 'How are you settling in, then?'

'Great, thanks. Though the time is flying. I can't believe the weeks have passed so quickly.'

'Edie said you're helping her market the shepherd's hut and developing a website?'

Amelia nodded. 'Yes, I've been writing up the content and taking the pictures.'

'It's good you're helping her with it. I have to say I was quite startled when she told me she was buying the hut. I thought she was joking. Then I saw it arriving . . .'

'Yes, but she's obviously quite shrewd and knows it will make an income for her. Glamping is so in and this is such a gorgeous place.'

'Yes, I would agree with that. She and Fergus have done an amazing job with it.'

'They have. Cheers,' she said as the barman placed two glasses of wine next to them.

Amelia took a sip. 'Have they always been close?'

Thea looked thoughtful for a moment and shrugged. 'I suppose so. He's very good to her and looks out for her. He's always offering to do errands and likes to check in on her, probably because she's on her own.'

'That's very kind.'

'Indeed. Grant, my partner, loves working with him. They're so laid-back and never argue. They work well together as a team.'

'Are you into your outdoor sports? Wild swimming?'

Thea almost spat out her wine. 'Good God, no. I can't think of anything worse. I don't mind a bit of kayaking in the summer but the thought of going in the sea at this time of year . . .' She shivered.

'You don't fancy doing Goatfell?'

Thea pulled a face. 'Grant or Fergus are your men for that.'

'How long have you had the shop?'

'About five years now.'

'I must come in and have a proper look around.'

'Please do, and I can show you some of Edie's work too.'

'Has Edie always lived on her own?' Amelia asked.

'As long as I've known her. She was widowed many years ago when she lived in Edinburgh but that's about all she has told me.'

A loud cheer from the group in the corner disrupted their conversation. One of the older ladies punched the air and the other two gave each other a fist bump, which made Thea and Amelia burst out laughing.

'What did I tell you?' Thea raised an eyebrow. 'It's a competitive business.'

The two women spent an hour or so chatting over wine and enjoying the warm glow from the log fire in the middle of the pub until Grant arrived to collect Thea. He gave Amelia a friendly and welcoming handshake. 'I've heard all about you.' He laughed when he noticed her frowning. 'Don't worry, most of it is . . . good.'

'Grant! He's winding you up. Ignore him.'

Amelia couldn't stop herself from blushing. 'That's reassuring . . . I think.'

Thea laughed. 'And Doris has managed to persuade her to help with the Christmas fair.'

Grant raised an eyebrow. 'Wow, fast moving on her part. That practically makes you a local.'

Amelia smiled. 'I'm more than happy to help. Sounds like fun.'

'Yes, it will be if everything goes to plan . . .'

'A couple of years ago the lights didn't switch on after the countdown and Doris was furious,' explained Thea.

'Oh dear, what happened?'

'Someone had forgotten to plug them in,' said Grant.

'But the way Doris was marching around you would think we were switching Oxford Street's lights on.'

Eventually they said goodbye, and as Amelia turned to walk away, she overheard Grant say to Thea, 'Do you think she'll hang around for a while?'

'I hope so. She's a breath of fresh air.'

Amelia smiled. To think that when she arrived here a few weeks ago she wanted to be alone. She had been so miserable and unhappy, yet in a short space of time she could now see a ray of light at the end of the tunnel.

CHAPTER TWENTY-FOUR

Some mornings, Amelia liked to wrap up warm and take her coffee down to the end of the garden to sit on the bench and watch the sea. She enjoyed listening to the gulls and the odd bark from a dog. It was lovely seeing the village wake up and come alive, and she watched parents walk along the beach taking their children to school, and heard the sound of cars in the distance. There would always be walkers, some preoccupied with their dogs and others holding coffee cups, chatting and laughing as they walked. Life was lovely and uncomplicated in these moments when she simply focused on being.

She looked across to the Holy Isle and reminded herself that she needed to try to get over to visit sooner rather than later. She had visited the website and noticed they held yoga retreats, which she thought sounded interesting. She and Suna used to go to yoga together sometimes, early before work. She smiled as she thought about her friend and how much she missed her. They kept playing phone tag with each other, and at that very moment she wished Suna was sitting on the bench next to her.

Pulling her phone from her pocket, she pulled up Suna's name and hit the call button.

'Hello,' Suna said.

'Good morning. Oh, you've no idea how good it is to hear your voice,' said Amelia.

'I'm sorry. Things have been a bit manic,' Suna said, her voice still more distant than usual.

'Have I caught you at a bad moment?'

'No,' she said, her voice muffled. 'Give me a second.'

Amelia waited a moment until Suna came back on the line. 'Sorry about that. Too many folks bustling around in here. So, how are you? What's been happening?'

'Oh, this and that. Lots of walking and exploring. And last night I went to the local pub.'

'What, they've got a pub up there?'

Amelia tried to dismiss her comment, even though it irked her. 'Several actually . . . and I had a lovely red wine.'

'Sounds good. So, are you ever going to come back?'

Amelia glanced across the beach, wondering if she was being overly sensitive or whether there really was an undertone in Suna's voice. 'Not sure yet,' she said.

'What about Christmas?'

Amelia shrugged. 'I'm not sure, Suna. I'm just playing it all by ear.'

'Oh . . .'

'How are things with you? How is work?'

'Same old stuff, you know. I don't think you're missing much.'

Amelia wanted to ask her why she was so keen that she return but bit her tongue. 'You could come and visit?'

'In winter? Are you joking?'

Amelia frowned. 'I bet you can't guess where I am at the moment?'

'On the beach?'

'Oh . . . How did you know?'

'Because that's where you are most mornings. You tell me either on text or in the voicemails you leave.'

'Suna, I don't understand. Is something wrong?'

'Nope. Sorry, I don't mean to be short. Just because you're having a great time messing about on a freezing beach in the back of beyond doesn't mean we all need to share your enthusiasm.'

Amelia felt as though she had been slapped in the face.

'Look, I had better go. It's getting busy in here, and they'll be wondering where I am.'

'Okay. I'll catch you later. Bye.' Amelia hung up, Suna's words still ringing harshly in her ears. What on earth was wrong with her? What had Amelia done to piss her off? She knew she'd been a high-maintenance friend over the past couple of months with the wedding and all the rest of it. But wasn't that what friends were for? She hoped she would have offered support to Suna if their roles had been reversed. She'd sounded so angry with her and Amelia couldn't help racking her brain, wondering what she could have done to upset her friend so much. She walked slowly back up the garden path to the cabin.

CHAPTER TWENTY-FIVE

Later that afternoon, Amelia opened up her laptop to show Edie her work on the new website.

'Oh — hold on a minute, dear, and I'll get my glasses.'

Amelia had played about with several names for the shepherd's hut and offered a list of potentials: Coorie Cabin; the Wee Shelter; Shepherd's Hoos; the Cosy Cabin; and the Bothy.

'Oh, I love all of these.' Edie's eyes shone in excitement as she read the list over Amelia's shoulder. She stood for a moment and sat down on a chair next to her. 'Do you have a favourite?'

Amelia laughed heartily. 'I'm glad you like the shortlist! I had loads of them and needed to whittle it down. Coming up with names has been such fun. I like Coorie Cabin best because it's nestled in your garden.' She opened up another page. 'Look, this is what I've done to give you an example of how the website would look in the first instance. We can finalise the name later. See what you think.'

Edie watched the screen closely as Amelia flicked through all the different pictures of the cabin, which looked fantastic. Somehow she had captured it at its best at different times of the day. Amelia had managed to take some with the fading light and the crescent moon in the background; there were some sunset shots too, and others when she had made the most of the sunshine and caught the cabin in a warm, dappled light. Her staging was exquisitely done. A pristinely made bed with perfectly plumped cushions and neatly laid throws. Fresh flowers, a cafetière of coffee with a set of matching mugs and plate of croissants from Cèic. The log-burning stove with its warm and welcoming glow. She had set up the garden furniture, arranging the wrought-iron chairs and table with a wine cooler, fizz and glasses. Despite the time of year, the filter Amelia had used gave the pictures a middle-of-the-summer look.

'What do you think?' Amelia leaned back in her chair.

'I think it looks tremendous. You've done a fabulous job.'

Warmed by her comment, Amelia continued to scroll, and stopped when she landed on the mock home page. 'Here you go. Read the description and see what works or if you would like to add anything.'

> *Beautiful shepherd's hut in a secluded garden with spectacular sea views.*
>
> *Enjoy a magical stay on a peaceful island with this fabulous coastal retreat.*
>
> *Be surrounded by nature and the beauty of the ocean.*
>
> *Spend your days exploring the Arran Coastal Trail and wandering the stunning beaches. Spot the seals and otters and all the wildlife that make Arran their home. Or visit one of the many attractions, including the castle, distilleries and artisan shops where you can sample the finest cheeses, chocolate and breads. If you like to relax then you will love the wood-fired hot tub, especially under the starry night skies.*
>
> *The shepherd's hut is the perfect escape for two and is fully equipped with a small kitchen, en-suite shower room and log-burning stove.*
>
> *It's the most blissful place to be!*

'Wow!' exclaimed Edie. 'How fantastic. When can I go?'

Amelia beamed in delight. 'Oh, I'm so glad you like it, Edie.'

'The only problem is that we don't have a hot tub.'

'Oh, yes, I was going to talk to you about that. I was getting caught up in writing about this amazing romantic retreat and imagining what I would like if I was going there with someone I loved.' She smiled wistfully. 'I thought a hot tub would be amazing . . . But maybe something you could think about adding later.' Amelia wanted to kick herself. She'd obviously got completely carried away when writing this the other night and forgotten to take that bit out.

Yet Edie was amused by the idea and thought it a fantastic plan. 'A hot tub under the stars . . . I can imagine it now. Brilliant idea. Genius.'

'Hello,' hollered a voice, and Molly started barking.

Amelia's stomach tightened when Fergus walked into the kitchen. She hadn't seen him since they'd kind of spent the night together. 'I was just passing and thought I'd drop in and say hello.'

'Perfect timing,' said Edie. 'I was about to put the kettle on.'

Fergus pulled out a chair and sat down, clasping his hands on the table. He smiled at Amelia. 'How are you?'

She raised her eyebrows. 'Okay.' Though she did actually feel as though they had spent the night *together* because she felt shy and unable to meet his gaze. 'Edie's briefed me on the Christmas fair,' she blurted.

'Doris did ask . . .' Edie looked innocently at Fergus. 'She thought with Amelia's marketing background she would be a splendid asset.'

Fergus groaned. 'Oh dear, there's definitely no going back now.'

'I'm sure it will all be fine.' Amelia tried to keep the panic out of her voice. Surely pulling a few pints of beer couldn't be that difficult, could it? Unless she was missing something.

Fergus paused. 'Put it this way, Doris will keep you right.'

Amelia nodded, then smiled briefly. 'Super.' She hoped she didn't sound too sarcastic.

'So, will you be staying on? For Christmas?' he asked, casually.

'Looks like it.' She blushed. *Oh God*, how could she stop herself from going red? He was only asking her an innocent question.

A glimmer of a smile played on his lips, as he took the mug of tea Edie was holding out to him. He looked like he was about to say something else but Edie beat him to it.

'Wait until you see what Amelia has done with the website. It looks amazing. And she's come up with a shortlist of names. Coorie Cabin, the Bothy, the Cosy Cabin and Shepherd's Hoos.' She sat down opposite Fergus. 'What do you think?'

'Shepherd's Hoos.' He laughed. 'Brilliant. Though I like the Coorie Cabin most. What do you think, Amelia?'

'The same.'

'And you'll never guess what brilliant idea she's come up with . . . ?' said Edie.

'Let me try — alpacas in the garden?'

Edie burst out laughing. 'Well, you know I do have a soft spot for them, Fergus. They're docile and sweet, just like you.'

Now it was time for Fergus's cheeks to flush.

'Alpacas are not a bad idea . . . But not quite yet. First of all, we need to get a hot tub.'

Amelia's fingers were now tingling, and she gripped them tighter around her mug of tea. This was not good at all.

'Amelia, dear, are you okay? Your face is a bit red. Is the thought of seeing Fergus in his Speedos getting you a bit fired up?'

Fergus roared with laughter. 'Edie, you are so naughty. I much prefer a two-piece these days.' He glanced over at Amelia. 'Oh dear, are we embarrassing you?'

'Erm, no, I'm a bit hot.' She had noticed the tingles rising up her arm. This wasn't just about feeling awkward with Fergus in the room; she must be having some kind of allergic reaction to something. 'Edie, do you have any antihistamines?' She was now clawing at her hands, which were red and itchy.

Edie hurried over to the drawer by the sink and opened it, rummaging around and pushing plasters and paracetamol to the side. 'Yes.' She held the packet triumphantly to the sky.

Fergus reached over to touch her arm. 'Looks like some kind of contact rash. Do you have any allergies?' She screwed up her face and shook her head as it dawned on her.

'Latex. It's the latex.'

Edie raised an eyebrow and smirked.

'Hang on, I think I'm missing something,' said Fergus, shaking his head.

Amelia was also bemused. 'I think I'm missing something too.' She pushed a tablet from the blister pack and swallowed it with the rest of her tea.

Fergus shrugged, clearly none the wiser as to what Edie was inferring.

'At least you're being careful,' said Edie.

'Well, I mean, I've not been that careful. I was trying to do a spot of cleaning.' She tried desperately not to claw at her hands. 'I totally forgot that I normally use special gloves.'

Edie clapped a hand over her mouth, only lowering it to utter, 'Whoops.'

There was an awkward pause as the penny finally dropped as to what she had been insinuating.

'Edie McMillan,' said Fergus, shaking his head in disbelief. 'You should be ashamed of yourself. I can't believe the conclusions you jumped to there!'

Edie exhaled, her face apologetic. Meanwhile, Amelia tipped her head back and roared with laughter, tears streaming down her face.

CHAPTER TWENTY-SIX

Fergus had logs to leave at Edie's cottage and he also needed to drop off the promised wetsuit to Amelia. As he neared the door of the cabin, he hesitated when he heard Amelia sobbing. Should he go in and check on her? No doubt she would be mortified if she thought he was outside the door and privy to her heartfelt anguish, so, instead, he gently laid the suit next to the door and tiptoed back to his van. He would text her later to make a plan for their first swim together.

He of all people knew what it was like to be sad and alone. She put on a brave face, but he could tell it was a facade. She was definitely hiding something about her past and what she had run away from. He wished he could wave a wand and make everything okay for her. But his own personal experience told him that would only come with time. He walked back towards the van, climbed in and sat for a moment. The flashbacks to the day of the accident were decreasing but he still remembered it all vividly.

'This isn't a good idea,' he'd shouted after Ellen as she'd strode away from him. 'It's fine to be daring and like a challenge but you're being reckless.'

'Are you coming or not?' She glared at him. 'I'll be fine. I've been out in much worse than this. Are you scared of a bit of snow?'

Fergus bit his lip. She infuriated him when she was like this — headstrong and determined — although those qualities had also made him fall in love with her. 'I don't want anything to happen to you, Ellen. Come on. I don't have a good feeling about this,' he pleaded.

She shook her head defiantly, her eyes flashing. 'You can't tell me what to do. I'll be fine. I know these mountains like the back of my hand. Just leave me.'

Fergus shook his head. 'No. I'm coming with you.' He sighed. 'Sometimes you can be so infuriating. Do you know that?'

She tilted her head to the side and gave him a coquettish look. 'That's why you love me so much.'

He couldn't disagree. Her stubborn streak was one of her attractive qualities. She gave him a lingering kiss and walked on with a spring in her step. 'Let's go.'

On the slopes, Fergus couldn't shake the discomfort growing in the pit of his stomach. The wind had picked up and visibility was poor. As Ellen closed her helmet she gave him a dazzling smile and headed off in front of him. He called at her to be careful but his words were whipped away by the wind. Her orange jacket became a small dot ahead, and he willed himself to go faster, a rush of panic coursing through him as he lost sight of her. Then he was behind her, yelling at her to slow down. That was when things started to unravel far too quickly. It was surreal, as though they were in a film with the stunning backdrop behind them. Unease clawed at his stomach as she went faster and faster and suddenly flew into the air and landed in a heap about fifty metres ahead. He came to a stop, desperately fumbling with his gloves and collapsing over her.

At the hospital, the consultant delivered the news in a small room where he sat with Ellen's parents. 'There's no response from her brain. I'm afraid she's not going to wake up.'

Fergus couldn't grasp what he meant. 'What are you saying?'

Ellen's father put a firm hand on his shoulder, holding his distraught wife with his other arm.

'There's nothing we can do. Ellen suffered a severe head injury in the accident. She's braindead,' said the consultant.

His words hung in the air and Fergus shook his head. 'You must be able to do something.' He waited for someone to say something but all he could hear was the sound of Ellen's mother sobbing inconsolably. Her father was shocked into silence.

'I'm so sorry,' said the consultant.

'But . . .' Fergus's voice pleaded.

The consultant looked at him sympathetically. 'I'm sorry. But we can't do anything else for her.'

That was when the news sank in, and he broke down.

Fergus started the engine and drove out of the driveway at Coorie Cottage. Tears started to well in his eyes as the crushing pain of loss swept through him again. It didn't matter that it happened four years ago. Every time he thought about it, it felt like yesterday. He wished he could tell Amelia that the pain of whatever she was going through would lessen. But what would be the point? It would be a lie.

CHAPTER TWENTY-SEVEN

'Your slogan is just marvellous,' said Doris.

Amelia grinned as Thea nodded in agreement. 'It's bloody brilliant. *Mistletoe Gin: Let's Hang out This Christmas.* You're a genius. This will fly off the shelves.'

The women sat in the hotel bar with a bottle of the festive gin. After much laughter and fun, definitely fuelled by the tasting session, they were trying to come up with a rhyme.

'Well, now I wish I had gone bigger and produced more bottles rather than such a small batch,' Doris said. 'This was a last-minute experiment. I wasn't sure whether Christmas gin would be popular or not.'

Amelia picked up the red bottle, striped with white circles to make it look like a candy cane. 'How many bottles do you have?'

'Fifty,' said Doris. 'Although we're now down to forty-nine.'

'Isn't the bottle fabulous?' Thea reached to examine it.

'Yes, I have to say that I am rather pleased with the results.' Doris beamed.

Amelia couldn't help but think this was an experience she wouldn't forget in a hurry. What a fun night they'd had. It was just what she had needed after feeling so low earlier on. Fergus had messaged her to say he had left a wetsuit for her outside the cabin and suggested they meet the following morning for a swim. She smiled as she looked at Thea and Doris. It was just a shame Edie couldn't join them. She'd made an excuse about having some errands to run and insisted Amelia went along without her.

Amelia turned her attention to the gin and her head was down as she furiously scribbled notes in her pad. She asked a few questions, which provoked a flood of words. Frowning, she scored a few out, then quietly read it back under her breath, adding a word and scoring another one out. Then she put her pen down and looked up. 'Well, that was a bit easier than I thought it would be, thanks to your creative juices flowing.' She smiled. 'Okay, tell me what you think about this:

Celebrate Christmas with this festive tipple!
With its mix of cinnamon, nutmeg and lime
Spicy orange and cloves and a hint of pine
Mistletoe Gin is the perfect drink — and that's official!'

Thea and Doris clapped enthusiastically and were joined by the couple sitting at the next table, who declared their rhyme terrific and asked if they could buy a bottle to take away with them as a souvenir. They were visiting from Stirling.

'We're not even stocking it in the shops yet.' Doris's voice was hushed. 'It is a rather exclusive batch.' Amelia watched with amusement as she reached into her handbag, pulled out a bottle and gifted it to the couple. She was, literally, full of the Christmas spirit, which meant they were down to forty-eight bottles.

Thea raised her brows and stifled a giggle. She mouthed to Amelia, 'That was unexpected.'

'So, you think the rhyme works then?' Amelia paused before closing her notebook.

'It's brilliant. Right, ladies, I must be on my way.' Doris suddenly stood. 'Places to be and things to do.'

'Have you got a date tonight, Doris?' asked Thea cheekily.

'Yes, I do. With McDreamy. I'm watching reruns of *Grey's Anatomy*.'

Amelia laughed. 'My brother's a doctor, and he says it is nothing like that.'

'Well, if there's a chance your brother looks like any of the cast, I would love to meet him,' said Doris.

Thea blinked in apparent disbelief. 'I don't think I've ever seen you like this. I like this new, more liberated version.'

Amelia laughed. 'I don't think he's your type.'

'Not sure I have one. Anyway, I will see you girls, and thanks, Amelia. I can't tell you how much I appreciate what you've done. Maybe we can think about some special cocktails for the fair.'

'Sure. Great idea.'

'Come on.' Thea stood up. 'Come back to mine. My flat is around the corner and we can do some more brainstorming and try making a few cocktails.'

'That sounds like a very good idea,' said Amelia, cheerfully.

CHAPTER TWENTY-EIGHT

Wincing as she opened her eyes, Amelia reached out to the bedside table, glad to find a large glass of water. Then she flopped back against the pillows. How much gin had she drunk last night? They'd finished the bottle of Mistletoe Gin, and when they'd gone back to Thea's she'd decided that Amelia should try the whisky from the local distillery, which had seemed like a great idea at the time. From what she remembered, she'd enjoyed the honey-coloured liquid slipping down her throat and had been given a lesson on the best ways to drink whisky: neat, with ice, or with some water. She'd chosen the first option which, on reflection, given the way her head throbbed, had perhaps been the wrong choice. Had they made cocktails too? Had she eaten anything? And how on earth had she got home? She racked her brains, wondering if she'd walked back. She had a vague recollection of Thea's partner, Grant, dropping her off and opening the hut for her. Oh dear. How mortifying.

She reached for her phone and saw a missed call and text message from Fergus.

Are you still meeting me for a swim?

Oh, no. How could she have slept in and missed it? Not that she would have made it feeling like this. She quickly sent him a message of apology and as an afterthought added, *Please can we do it another time?*

His reply was immediate. *Sure;)*

Amelia groaned. What must he think of her? Especially when he had gone to the trouble of dropping off the wetsuit. She had been so looking forward to seeing him too, albeit nervous of the planned activity — and whether or not she would get the wetsuit on.

Eventually she pulled herself from bed, swallowed some paracetamol and forced down as much water as she could stomach. The thought of food made her want to vomit. Instead, she had a long, warm shower and pulled on some fresh clothes. She was never ever drinking alcohol again. She made her way across the garden to the cottage and, glancing through the kitchen window, spotted Edie sitting with her head in her hands. That didn't look good. She walked briskly round to the front door, double knocking and waiting for a moment before pushing it open.

'Morning, Edie,' she called, as brightly as she was able, given her delicate state. She caught a glimpse of her reflection in the hall mirror and shuddered at her pale face. Edie hadn't replied and so Amelia went through to the kitchen where her friend remained seated, still with her head heavy in her hands. She wore her dressing gown, which was strange for Edie as it was past ten o'clock.

'Edie,' she prompted gently.

Edie looked up, dazed and slightly confused.

'Is everything okay?' Amelia asked, walking over and putting a hand on Edie's shoulder.

The woman crumpled under the touch of Amelia's hand, dissolving into huge sobs.

'Oh, Edie. Whatever is the matter? What's happened?'

Edie was unable to speak, as her body convulsed with sobs.

Amelia wasn't sure what to do. She kept rubbing her hand around Edie's back in a circular motion, hoping it was soothing as she wasn't quite sure how to help make things better. Edie was normally so calm and collected, and it was awful to see her in so much distress.

Amelia sat down next to her, waiting for her cries to subside and her breathing to calm and become less ragged.

'How about I put the kettle on? Have you eaten any breakfast?' Amelia didn't wait for Edie to answer; instead she stood up and busied herself making a cup of tea and slipping a piece of bread into the toaster. She got the butter out of the fridge and when the toast popped up, slathered it with a generous helping. 'There you go. Have a sip of tea and a nibble of the toast.'

Edie managed to chew a square, swallowing it down with the hot, sweet liquid Amelia had made her. 'I am sorry, dear. I didn't mean you to find me like this.'

Amelia shook her head. 'I'm just glad I came over when I did.' She sat down next to Edie. 'Do you want to tell me what's wrong?'

CHAPTER TWENTY-NINE

The truth was Edie had finally decided she needed to do something about her sister. That was why she didn't go to the pub the night before. She had phoned the hospital in Glasgow. This time, though, she hadn't hung up. Christine had always been prone to exaggerating things when they were younger. Edie had thought maybe she was being over-dramatic about the prognosis and perhaps it wasn't terminal at all.

Now, as Amelia bustled around looking after her, Edie wanted to tell her everything. It hadn't been her intention to spill her story out in this way to someone she had only known for a few weeks. However, once she started talking, the floodgates opened and she couldn't stop. Somehow it seemed easier telling someone she didn't know too well.

'I'd better start at the beginning.'

Amelia sat beside her. 'Take your time.'

'I was once married. My husband was Jim and we lived together in Edinburgh. That's him there.' She pointed at the photo in the window. 'He worked for one of the banks and went up and down to London frequently on the train. I lectured at the university.' She took a fortifying sip of tea. 'We married a bit later in life, well, in our thirties, which probably doesn't seem old now but then it was more unusual to marry when you were the grand old age of thirty-six . . . anyway, I am digressing. We had a good and happy life together. We didn't have children and we were fine with that; it was very much our choice. He truly was the love of my life.'

Edie paused and Amelia gave her hands a reassuring squeeze.

'One week he had been in London for a couple of days and he phoned from the office to tell me he was heading for the train. It was a Friday afternoon, and he'd managed to leave a bit earlier, so he could take me to supper. I remember being so excited because things had been a bit tricky. He had been spending a lot more time in London than usual and I felt a bit abandoned . . . it felt a bit like I was losing him.' She shrugged. 'I managed to get a cancellation at the hairdresser's that afternoon, so I would look nice for our dinner date.'

For a moment Edie stopped talking and looked wistfully out of the window.

'Then what happened?' Amelia asked gently.

'He didn't make it home. The train derailed and the carriage he sat in was the worst affected. He and three other passengers died.'

'Oh, Edie, I am so sorry. That must have been awful.'

Edie nodded and squeezed Amelia's hand in return.

'It was horrendous.' She grimaced as she relived the moment a policeman had arrived at her door to tell her. It was a moment she would never ever forget for as long as she lived. That was when her world had crumbled.

'How did you cope?'

'As best as I could. I don't know if I coped really. I existed and drifted from one day to the next.'

'Can I ask what brought you here?'

'I wanted to start again and be somewhere there weren't constant reminders of Jim, or people looking at me with pity in their eyes or crossing the road to avoid having to make awkward conversations with me. I wanted to run away.'

Amelia noticed a crumpled letter on the table next to her. 'Is that something to do with this, Edie?'

'Actually, yes.' She sighed. 'I don't tell many people this at all. I'm sure you will have gathered I'm quite private and independent. It's just how I've become since losing Jim. After he died . . . well, my sister and I had always been close and even though she lived and worked in London, she suddenly became quite distant. Don't get me wrong, she was a rock to me when he died. I was actually quite taken aback at how emotional she was. In fact, she was devastated too.' She rubbed at her eyes. Going over this never got any easier. 'Turned out she was also grieving for Jim. You see, they'd been having an affair.'

Amelia gasped. 'How awful for you! Did you suspect anything at the time?'

She shook her head. 'No. I mean, we had a bit of a rough patch, what with his constant commuting up and down to London, but I didn't for a minute suspect he was having an affair with anyone, never mind my sister.'

'How did you find out?'

'His belongings were eventually returned to me and I found letters in his briefcase.'

'Oh, Edie. That must have been awful after being widowed in such a terrible way.'

'I confronted my sister and initially she denied it, but eventually she admitted that, yes, they were having an affair and she was sorry. I haven't spoken to her since.' She held up the letter. 'Now she's written to me telling me she's got cancer and doesn't have long to live.' She spread her hands across the table. 'I don't know what to do,' she said.

Amelia exhaled. What a difficult decision to make. She desperately tried to think what the right thing would be to say. 'Edie, do you want to see your sister?'

Edie wiped away a few tears, which had started to roll down her cheeks. 'Yes, yes, I do.'

'And where is she? Is she still in London?'

Edie shook her head. 'No, she's in hospital in Glasgow. She moved back there about ten years ago. It's where we both grew up.'

Amelia hesitated. 'Can I ask you a question? Do you know how long she's got?'

'I phoned the hospital.' She shook her head in despair. 'She's telling the truth. She hasn't got long to go. This Christmas will almost certainly be her last. If she makes it that long.'

Edie choked back another sob as Amelia enveloped her in a hug.

CHAPTER THIRTY

Amelia sat beside the log burner, curled up on the chair with her journal. Today's prompt was: *Are you courageous?* She set the timer on her phone for five minutes and began to write.

> *Am I courageous? Well... until now the thought of being alone and venturing out into the world on my own and not as part of a couple terrified me. I mean, I didn't leave my marriage or my job. They left me. I always wanted to be married. I loved my job. It wasn't as though I was bravely making radical changes in my life. I wouldn't have chosen to walk away from my husband or steady employment. Doesn't that make me weak and pathetic? Doesn't that make me the opposite of courageous?*
>
> *I didn't take a huge risk or leap in life. This was all forced upon me...*

She exhaled loudly and glanced at her watch. This was hard. Only two minutes had passed. She doodled some hearts and then tried again.

> *Am I courageous? Now I am writing for the sake of it and to fill time because I don't know what to say. I think*

I am weak. If I had been stronger, then I would have been more aware Declan wasn't happy. I would have been more tuned into my apparent domestic bliss. Today, I don't feel courageous. I feel like a fool. Edie is courageous. She has been through real loss and heartache, and I admire her for her grace and dignity. At this very moment she's my heroine. I am not courageous compared to her.

Amelia slammed the notebook shut. She wasn't quite sure of the point of doing this. Some days, writing her thoughts down did help — even the process of actively writing helped her unpick her feelings and untangle thoughts that were on her mind. But today she was irritated about the prompt. She knew that meant it was worth persevering with, but she didn't have the energy. Good and bad days were par for the course, and she thought she'd been doing quite well. She'd not called or texted Declan for almost two weeks — a record. His lack of communication actually helped as it made her realise things were definitely at an end. Even though his words and actions made that quite clear, Amelia had still been holding on to the slightest chance he might change his mind.

Of course, it probably helped that she was completely distracted with trying to build a new existence for herself here. She wondered about looking for other jobs, which she could do after Christmas. When she was in Cèic earlier that day, Cano told her his wife, Naza, hoped to go over to Glasgow in the New Year to help out with their daughter who was expecting a baby in January.

'How exciting,' Amelia said, as Naza came through from the back of the shop.

'I know, a lovely way to start the New Year. This will be our fourth grandchild,' she said, her eyes sparkling.

'Will you manage without her?' Amelia said to Cano, as Naza waved and went to greet a customer who had just come in.

'Oh, it will be tough,' he said. 'I might take someone on to help.'

'That's a good idea.' The thought swirled around in her mind all day, and she wondered if she could offer to work there. The website for the shepherd's hut was almost finished, and she knew Edie should really be starting to advertise it soon to generate an income from it. Perhaps if she picked up some shifts at the café she could offer to pay rent until bookings started to come in. Then she would look for alternative accommodation. That's if she decided to stay.

The thought of going back to live in London wasn't at all appealing. Packed Tube carriages, busy roads, overpriced artisan soup, working all hours. What a different world to the simple one she lived in now. She knew which she preferred. Yet she did miss Suna and wasn't quite sure what to do about the distance that was so obvious whenever they spoke on the phone.

At least she was being distracted from such things by Fergus, who was dropping in on Edie to keep an eye on her. He was good at coming up with a variety of excuses. He offered to fix the broken latch on her window for her, or he dropped off some more logs for her stove. Sometimes Amelia was there, and they would chat about the weather and he would try to persuade her to join him at the beach for the morning swim that had not yet happened. He had teased her relentlessly for her recent hangover, the reason she'd stood him up. He was so warm and likeable, yet guarded about his past, which she could understand as she was the same about hers too.

She wondered whether she should tell him about Edie's sister. She knew he would offer to take her to the hospital in Glasgow in a heartbeat. Perhaps she should mention it to Edie first?

* * *

Edie watched the pair of them chat and laugh together, and saw how their faces lit up and their eyes danced. Now she understood a bit more about why Amelia had come here, she knew they were both vulnerable and she hoped they would take their time to nurture this friendship they were building. She constantly reminded herself she shouldn't get involved and so said nothing to either one. Not after her faux pas with the latex comment, when she'd presumed they'd succumbed to a moment of passion. There was something about Amelia that clearly struck a chord with Fergus. Aside from being funny, smart and attractive, she intrigued him and, as far as Edie could tell, few women managed to.

CHAPTER THIRTY-ONE

Amelia decided that she had to do something about Edie's situation, so the following day she walked up to the other end of the beach where the outdoor centre was based. The sky was low and grey, and she watched as Fergus finished talking to a group of teenagers putting away their kayaks.

He smiled when he saw her. 'Hello there.' He was clearly surprised. 'Is this part of your sightseeing brief? You should've let me know you were coming and I would have got the boys to leave the kayaks out. We could have gone out for a session. Or are you desperate to make sure that open-water swimming is ticked off your list?'

Amelia glanced over at the group of teens who were scrutinising her. She heard a few sniggers and felt herself blushing as she dithered for a moment. 'No . . . Look, sorry if this isn't a good time. I just wanted to talk to you about something.'

Fergus looked over at the group. 'Right, boys, put these away and go and hose your stuff down, please.' His voice was firm and he obviously commanded their respect as they immediately followed orders.

A gusty breeze made Amelia shiver and she pulled her scarf tighter around her neck. Fergus gave her a searching look and once again she couldn't help notice the colour of his deep brown eyes.

'I'm just about finished and could do with a break. Come on into the office and I'll make you a cup of tea,' he said. 'It's too cold out here to hang about.'

'That would be great.' Why was he so annoyingly charming and warm?

Fergus grinned, and she followed him into the office, which also doubled as a shop and visitor centre. 'It's a large, upcycled shipping container, clad in larch,' he explained.

'It's actually surprisingly warm in here,' she admitted.

'Yes, people tend to expect it to be freezing. We've even got underfloor heating and running hot water!'

'I think it's great.'

'Take a seat,' he pointed at the chairs in the corner, 'and I'll put the kettle on.'

'Hey there,' said Grant. 'How are you doing?'

'Good, thanks. Much better than the other night. Thanks for taking me home.'

He laughed. 'No worries. You and Thea certainly put a lot of booze away.'

'Never again. That's me off it forever.'

'Famous last words.' He laughed.

'What a great place this is.'

'It is now but it hasn't always been like this. We used to work out of our cars.'

'Well, you've done amazing things and it's brilliant seeing the local kids getting so much out of it.'

'Yes.' He nodded. 'Normally we're mobbed with visitors during the holidays. So it's nice to be able to spend some time with them. Makes a huge difference to their self-confidence.'

Fergus had previously explained to Amelia that they did a lot of project work with teenagers at risk of social isolation and those who didn't seem to fit in at school.

'Tea or coffee?' Fergus held up a tin with *TEA* on the front in one hand and a jar of coffee in the other.

'Tea would be great, thanks. And I take it black.'

'Good, because we're out of milk,' said Grant. 'I'm popping to the shop to get some. I'll catch you later.'

She smiled at Grant as he left. She glanced idly over at Fergus, averting her gaze as he turned to bring their drinks over.

'Thank you.' She gratefully clasped her cold hands around the cup.

'The cold weather takes a bit of getting used to. The trick is to make sure you're dressed for it. Gloves?'

'Good point. That's something I don't have.'

'I've got loads of spares. Remind me to give you a pair before you leave.'

She sipped some tea and cleared her throat. 'I hope you don't mind me coming by to chat to you like this . . .'

'Not at all.' He leaned forward, fixing his gaze entirely on her. 'What did you want to talk to me about?'

'Edie. I'm a bit worried about her.'

He frowned. 'More sleepwalking?'

She shook her head. 'No, but she has told me what's been bothering her.'

Picking his mug up, he waited for her to continue.

'She's had a letter from her sister, who is ill in hospital. She's got cancer, and she's dying, and she wants Edie to go and visit her.'

'Ah. I did wonder when she would tell you.'

'You know?'

He nodded. 'Yes, she told me the other day but swore me to secrecy. Not that I would ever discuss other folk's personal business. But I did wonder if she would tell you.'

'Edie called the hospital in Glasgow and it would seem her sister doesn't have too much longer. They suggested that if Edie was going to visit, she may like to do so sooner rather than later.'

Fergus exhaled. 'And does Edie want to go and visit her?'

'Yes, I think she does. But she's a bit overwhelmed. That's what I wanted to talk to you about. Do you think you could go with her? Could you take her to see her sister?'

'Of course I will, no problem at all . . . Do you want me to go and talk to her? I can offer?'

'I think that would be better. You know how independent she is. I don't think she'll ask.'

'Of course. No bother.'

They finished their tea in quiet, companionable silence and Amelia stood up. 'I'd better leave you to it. And . . . thanks, Fergus. I'm so glad you're going to take her. It will mean the world to her.'

He shrugged. 'I'll do anything for her. She's a special person.'

Amelia nodded in agreement. 'She is.' Just then, Grant arrived back with his pint of milk.

'You should come to the pub with us later,' he said earnestly.

'Oh, okay, that would be great. Remember, though, I've sworn to stay off the alcohol after the other night.' Amelia tried to sound nonchalant. She was conscious of how close Fergus was standing next to her and his arm brushed against hers.

'Especially when it made you miss your first Arran dip,' said Fergus, laughing. 'Tell you what, why don't I come and collect you? I'll pop in and chat to Edie first and come and pick you up. Around eight?'

'If you're sure?'

'Of course. I'll see you later.'

'Thanks.' Amelia turned to walk away with a definite spring in her step.

CHAPTER THIRTY-TWO

Edie watched Fergus as he left, pulling the door closed behind him. He was such a good soul, and she was lucky to have him as a friend. Indeed, she looked upon him as the son she'd never had, and she always hoped that he would settle down and have his own family. But she knew why he kept himself at a distance. He too had lost the love of his life in an accident. Earlier in the year, he'd opened up to her, quite unexpectedly, and had told her about his late fiancée, Ellen, and her death in a ski accident. Fergus blamed himself for what happened because they'd gone out in tricky conditions despite his misgivings. Edie had tried to reassure him that her death was not his fault. That was when she'd shared her story of losing Jim. In a way the pair of them were kindred spirits. Yet she hoped that Fergus would come to realise his life still stretched out ahead of him.

His offer to take her to Glasgow to see Christine would certainly help settle the sense of dread that had been hanging over her these last few weeks. It was a journey she really didn't want to make alone.

* * *

Amelia rummaged through her limited wardrobe options, unsure as to what she was even looking for. Jeans, sweaters, leggings, trainers and boots were all she had. She put on a fresh pair of jeans and a bright red jumper and pulled a brush through her hair. Just as she was about to apply some make-up, her phone rang. It was Jack.

'Hi, Jack, how are you?'

'Good, thanks. How are you?'

'Well, can I phone you back? I'm in the middle of something.'

Jack paused. 'Um, okay.'

She put down the tube of tinted moisturiser. 'Look, don't worry. Is everything okay with you?'

'Well, sis, your husband called earlier . . .'

The mere mention of Declan made her wobble.

'He's been on the phone to me and, well, it sounds like he's a bit contrite.'

'A bit *contrite*?' She couldn't believe what he was saying.

'I know, don't worry, I gave him a piece of my mind.'

'If he's *contrite*, then why hasn't he been in touch?' She remembered his voicemail from several weeks ago. He'd said he needed some space, which were hardly the words of someone who felt like apologising. She clenched her free hand as she tried to contain her rage. It wasn't as though he had been calling her every two minutes to tell her how sorry he was.

'Good question, and I did put it to him. He said he's worried about your reaction.'

Amelia bit back a surge of frustration. 'But he's not bothered to reply to any of my gazillion messages or texts, Jack. He has totally blanked me . . . aside from one message, which basically gave me short shrift.'

'Look, you don't need to tell me this. I understand. I get the sense he's too ashamed to call you, but if you got in touch with him again, he would know that you did want to talk to him.'

She felt a tug in her stomach. 'Whose side are you on?'

'Hey,' he said, gently. 'I am always on your side. You should never need to question that.'

There was a knock at the door. Brilliant, she thought. 'I need to go. I'm heading out.'

'Where you off to?'

'Just to the pub with some locals.'

'Oh,' he said wryly.

'I'll call you soon.'

'Have a think about what I said.'

'Yip, I will.'

'Have a great night, sis. Love you.'

'Love you too. Bye.'

Her head was spinning as she opened the door to Fergus. 'Come in out of the cold. I'm almost ready.' Except she wasn't really, as Jack's call had interrupted her. Fergus wore dark jeans, trainers and a black quilted jacket. Still casual yet smarter than his usual work gear. 'I need to get something from the bathroom.'

'Take your time.'

She disappeared for a moment and caught her reflection in the mirror. At least the fresh air had given her some colour in her cheeks. Either that or the fury she currently felt about Declan calling her brother rather than her. She quickly smeared on some pink lip balm. This wasn't a date, she reminded herself. It was merely a casual get-together with friends. Who cared what she looked like?

'Ready?' He smiled.

'Yes, I am.' She grabbed her coat and hat from the hook by the door.

'Oh, I almost forgot,' he said, pulling a pair of gloves from his pocket. 'Here you are. I meant to give them to you earlier.'

She felt the prick of tears at his kindness and the fact he'd remembered.

'Thank you, Fergus.'

'Well, it's cold out there.'

'You can tell me about Edie on the way.'

'Sure. The moon's high tonight, so shall we walk along the beach?'

'Yes, that sounds like a plan.'

CHAPTER THIRTY-THREE

As Amelia walked along the shoreline with Fergus, she realised she didn't feel at all guilty that she was with another man. After speaking to her brother, she actually felt really pissed off with Declan for being such a coward. Tension swirled around her stomach as she momentarily wondered if she should offload to Fergus.

'Are you okay?'

'Erm, yes, sorry, bit distracted. My brother in Boston called a few minutes before you arrived.'

'I could have waited if you'd wanted to talk more to him?'

She shook her head. 'Tell me about Edie. What did she say?'

'Watch your step there,' said Fergus, holding her arm and steering her over the pebbles.

'Thanks . . . good I've got my sensible footwear on,' she joked.

Fergus laughed. 'I just said you were a bit worried about her, that we both were, especially since the night of the sleepwalking . . . and offered to take her to see Christine. That's when she told me about the latest news from the hospital.'

Amelia exhaled, blowing her cheeks out. 'Oh, good. I'd hate her to think I'd betrayed her confidence or was gossiping about her — particularly when she's been so good to me.'

'Don't worry, she volunteered all the information and told me time is pressing. She did look relieved when I said I would take her.'

'When are you going to go?'

'The day after next. She's keen to get it over with, I think, and she doesn't want to miss the Christmas fair.' The lights switch-on was only a few days away.

'I can understand why she wants to go now. She must be thinking about it all the time.'

He nodded. 'Yes, she is. She needs to work out the timings and the ferry crossings. I know she would rather just go and come back home as soon as she can.'

'Will it take long to drive up to the hospital when you're on the mainland?'

'No, about an hour if the traffic is quiet,' he said, kicking a stone in front of him.

'It will be a long day for her. I just hope there's no hassle with the ferries otherwise you may have to stay over if the last one is cancelled.'

'Yes, keep your fingers crossed. And don't worry, she'll be in good hands. I'll keep an eye on her. I'll take her to the door and be there waiting for her when she comes out. And I've reassured her you will walk Molly and look after her should we get stuck. I hope that's okay?'

'Of course,' said Amelia. 'I'll do anything to help. I'm glad she's definitely decided to go.'

He gestured inland. 'Let's cut up this way to the bar.'

Amelia followed his lead and caught a whiff of his lemony scented cologne. As she looked up at the inky black sky, scattered with stars, she couldn't help but think that continuing a walk along the beach and chatting with Fergus seemed the more pleasing option than heading into a busy pub.

CHAPTER THIRTY-FOUR

In the bar, Grant ordered drinks for everyone and brought them over to the table Thea had commandeered in the corner of the pub.

'I hope wine does the job?' he said, passing Amelia a glass.

'Perfect. Thanks. So much for me staying off the booze. That resolution didn't last long,' she said.

'You doing good?' asked Thea.

'Yes, thanks. Really enjoying my new job, though a bit guilty that it doesn't seem much like work.'

Thea laughed. 'The best kind of work. If you love what you do you will never work another day in your life.'

'Very true. You feel that way about the shop?'

'You know, I think I do. I lived in Glasgow but there was no way I could have afforded my own shop there. Rents are too expensive. Then I met Grant and moved over and it all kind of happened.' She glanced over at him and smiled. 'And I love that I can showcase local produce and talent. That's the most exciting bit.'

'That's such a brave thing to do. And I love the way you've designed the shop window — it's so stylish.'

'Thank you. This time of year is great. I love all the festive themes, and there's always a competition for the best-dressed shop window . . .' She lowered her voice. 'I've won the past three years so I feel a bit of pressure to maintain a certain standard.'

Amelia laughed. 'I'm sure you'll be fine. I'm looking forward to the festivities. I've heard so much about it all. I can't wait!'

'Well, you don't have much longer to go. Only a few days until the lights go on, and the fair. And then there's the big ceilidh on Christmas Eve.'

Amelia spotted Fergus looking over from the bar and flushed under his intense gaze. Fortunately, Thea's phone beeped and she was distracted with that rather than noticing Amelia's red cheeks.

'It's great having you here, Amelia,' said Thea. 'It's nice to have someone a bit more my own age.'

Amelia was touched. 'That's so nice of you to say. Thanks for being so welcoming. Everyone has been so nice. It feels like a great place to be.'

'It is,' she said, before raising an eyebrow as Fergus appeared at the table with another round of drinks.

Beeps were sounding from somewhere on Fergus. He groaned and reached inside his pocket, pulling out a pager. Grant did exactly the same and they grabbed their jackets.

'Am I missing something?' Amelia was confused.

'They're both on the lifeboat crew,' said Thea. 'That's their pagers, which means they're about to disappear.'

'Right,' said Amelia. She watched Fergus as he hurried out the door. Was there anything he *couldn't* do? 'When will they be back?'

Thea shrugged. 'Who knows? Could be five hours or five minutes. Depends what is going on.'

'What kind of things are they called out for?' She was fascinated about this other side of Fergus that she didn't know anything about.

'Anything from a broken-down fishing boat . . . or a kayaker . . . to someone who has got into difficulty on a cliff trail.'

'And do you worry when Grant's out?'

'I try not to but it can be hard,' admitted Thea. 'Especially when the weather's bad and I don't know where he is or what has happened. But I guess I've got used to it.' She jerked her head over to the door. 'Looks like this was a false alarm.'

Amelia felt a jolt of excitement when she saw Fergus and Grant making their way back through the bar towards them.

Grant flung himself into a seat with a huge sigh of relief. 'False alarm.'

'It's even colder out now and the wind has picked up. Can't say I'm disappointed.' Fergus slipped off his jacket and sat next to Amelia. 'And I was so looking forward to drinking this pint.' He picked up the glass and took a gulp. 'We'd better turn our pagers off now, Grant, as we're not meant to be on the rota anyway. And it means we can enjoy our beer.'

'Cheers,' said Grant, raising his glass.

* * *

Later, Fergus insisted on walking Amelia home from the pub, despite her assurance that she would be fine.

'You might trip over a seal or a rock,' he said, his voice husky and gentle.

'I've only drunk two glasses of wine, Fergus. I'm capable of making my way home.'

He sighed. 'Humour me, please? Plus, I promised Edie I would see you home safely. I'm more scared of her. You don't know what she's like when she's cross.' His voice was light and Amelia didn't mind when he then gently touched her back and steered her down to the shore. It was dark but the full moon lit the way and cast a soft glow over the shoreline.

Amelia stared up at the stars scattered across the sky. 'It's beautiful,' she said softly, standing for a moment to admire the view. 'This is definitely a first.'

'What's that?'

'A moonlight stroll along the beach after a night at the local when half the party do a brief runner.' She shivered and pulled her collar up. 'I had no idea that you were also on the lifeboat crew.'

He shrugged. 'You're cold.' He moved closer to her.

'That will be thanks to my city wardrobe. I need to invest in some thermals.'

She gratefully leaned into him and they continued walking. Amelia was now a little breathless though. Maybe that was the winter air. The temperature had definitely taken a drop these last few weeks. Too soon, they arrived at the narrow gate to Coorie Cottage and moved through in single file.

'You can leave me here,' she said, smiling.

'Edie will never let me hear the end of it. I need to walk you to the door.' He was laughing, which made Amelia giggle too, and soon they were cackling away.

'Sssh,' she said. 'You'll wake her up.' They reached the door of the cabin. 'Well, thank you for a lovely evening, Fergus. I really enjoyed it and I appreciate you coming to collect me and also bringing me home.'

Fergus looked down at her, his eyes crinkling, and she had a sense he wanted to kiss her by the way he was looking at her. Her breath quickened and she hoped he couldn't hear her heart pounding. She felt his warm breath as he held her close. The prospect of kissing another man, who wasn't Declan, was weird but also exciting.

Her arms tightened against him as he held her closer. He rested his cheek against her hair and inhaled its scent. A tear rolled down her cheek, then another. Shit. His body tensed.

'Amelia. What's wrong?'

She couldn't move and stayed rooted to the spot, eyes closed, with her head against his chest. Eventually she pulled away. 'You'd better come in.'

CHAPTER THIRTY-FIVE

Fergus felt a flutter of nerves in his stomach as Amelia beckoned him into the cabin.

'Did I do something wrong?' he said, raking a hand through his hair.

'No. The opposite. You actually helped,' she said, sniffing.

Fergus wondered if she'd felt the same warmth and comfort that he had. It had reminded him that he *really* missed being touched and held.

'Here, sit down,' she said, pointing at the bed.

'No, first let me make you a warm drink,' he said, noticing her shivering.

'This is becoming a bit of a habit, isn't it?'

He shrugged. 'I'm used to making warm drinks. It's my speciality.'

'And saving damsels in distress?' she said jokingly, 'I've got some whisky in the cupboard, if you want something stronger?'

'Nah, you're okay. Tea's fine.' He bustled around the kitchen.

Amelia kicked off her boots and curled up on the bed. Fergus brought their mugs of tea over and pulled up a stool.

A few minutes passed before she started to tell him about her husband, Declan, and what had happened.

Fergus didn't say anything. He just listened as she let her doubtless pent-up emotions from the past few months come tumbling out in a mixture of words and sobs. He longed to reach for her and stroke her back or hold her. Instead, he focused his gaze on her and listened.

'My brother called me tonight to say Declan had been in touch with him. This is despite me calling and texting him begging for an explanation. He's completely blanked me.'

'And what did he say to your brother?'

She shrugged. 'He's sorry and wants to talk to me but is too scared to call.'

'Scared or cowardly?' He shook his head and smiled at her. 'Sorry, it's none of my business. I shouldn't have said that. I'm sorry about everything that's happened.' He stood up and placed the blanket at the end of the bed over Amelia. 'Another cuppa?'

Amelia nodded gratefully and he could tell she was watching him as he walked to the kitchenette and bustled about.

'Peppermint?' he asked when he realised it was the only option. 'Looks like you're out of builder's.'

'Perfect. Thank you. What about you? Have you ever been married?' she asked.

He didn't respond immediately and instead focused on straining the teabags. 'Almost,' he said. 'I was once engaged.'

'What happened?' she asked gently.

He exhaled loudly. 'It didn't work out . . .' He looked at her intensely.

'Sorry, have I said something wrong?'

'No. I find it hard to talk about,' he said, his voice flat. 'I don't share much about my personal life with anyone.'

'Please don't feel you have to tell me,' she said, sitting up on the bed. She held his gaze for a few moments.

He rubbed a hand over his jaw and pursed his lips. 'You've been so open with me, it's only fair I tell you what happened . . .'

Amelia hugged her knees to her chest and waited for him to continue.

'I was engaged. Her name was Ellen . . . She was the love of my life,' he said tenderly. 'We were working in a ski resort in Canada. I was there working as a ski instructor and writing a travel piece. That's what I used to do . . . before. After Whistler, we went to New Zealand, where she was from, and where we planned to settle.'

'What happened?'

'We were out skiing . . . on a horrible day. It was blustery and conditions weren't great. I didn't want to go but she insisted. She was very headstrong,' he said. 'She would have gone regardless and there was no way I could let her go alone. I thought I could look after her . . .' Amelia moved to sit beside him, reaching over to clasp his hand. She squeezed it as he continued to talk.

'She fell and hit her head. Even though she wore a helmet, the impact was too much . . . she died two days later.' Now Fergus wiped away his tears. Amelia handed him a tissue.

'I'm so sorry, Fergus. I had no idea.'

'It was awful. And I blamed myself. Nobody else did. Just me. I kept thinking if we hadn't gone out it wouldn't have happened.' His voice broke with the emotion.

'Oh, Fergus, you mustn't think that. Ellen sounded like she was independent. As you said, she would have gone regardless. You couldn't have known what was going to happen. It was a tragic accident.' She gripped his hand. 'I'm so sorry,' she said again. 'There are no words for what you've been through.'

Fergus appreciated the way she was holding his hand and *really* listening to him. 'Her parents were great and told me not to blame myself, that she had always been stubborn. They said she died doing something she loved and she was happy. I tried to stay on for a while afterwards because I felt close to her there, you know? But I saw pity in people's eyes. That's why I left and came back.' He looked gratefully at her and cleared his throat. 'Sorry, Amelia. I bet this wasn't what you were expecting?'

'I'm glad you are comfortable enough to tell me. And I'm grateful for your friendship, Fergus. At a time when life has been a bit crap, you have helped coax me out of my shell.'

He smiled. 'Well, you're a fairly easy friend. You're not too high maintenance.'

'Hey,' she said. 'I'm not high maintenance at all!'

Looking at his watch, he stood up. 'I'd better go. I've got an early class in the morning.'

'You're welcome to stay here if you want some company?' said Amelia. She blushed. 'I didn't mean it like that!'

He raised an eyebrow. 'Edie would kill me. And accuse me again of a dirty stopover . . . when she means stop out.'

His joke lightened the mood and they both laughed.

'Well, thanks, Fergus, I appreciate you.'

He pulled her towards him and nestled his chin on the top of her head. They both stood for a moment, then he softly kissed her on the hair. She felt so comfortable and warm in his arms.

'I'll catch you soon,' he said, gradually drawing away.

'Goodnight,' said Amelia.

As Fergus walked home, he realised he had managed to share his story with someone else and survive, and he was actually okay. Though a small voice in his head told him that was because Amelia was kind and warm. He smiled.

CHAPTER THIRTY-SIX

The following day, Amelia couldn't stop thinking about Fergus and the story of Ellen's death. Poor man. What a horrendous thing to go through. Her impending divorce paled into insignificance. It made her realise that things could have been so much worse. At least Declan hadn't died and they had started married life on a high.

She thought of their honeymoon in Italy, when they'd spent a glorious fortnight on a romantic adventure. They'd spent a weekend in Rome exploring the Vatican and the Coliseum, and eating in small restaurants tucked off the tourist trail. Then they'd flown to Sardinia, with its breathtakingly beautiful beaches and turquoise waters, where they swam and snorkelled. Declan had seemed tense in Rome and she'd wondered if his mood had been post-wedding exhaustion. The crowds exacerbated his mood, and it was only when they'd got to the island beach resort that he'd started to unwind. Those days were when they'd been at their best. They'd spent lazy days on the beach with siestas in the afternoon when the sun became too hot to bear. On their last evening, they'd enjoyed a candlelit dinner on the terrace and afterwards he'd reached out and put his arms around her. She'd melted into his embrace and it had been the perfect moment. She'd wished they could stay forever. He'd even told her he didn't want to go back to London. She'd dismissed his comments at the time. That was normal, wasn't it? Everyone felt like that when they'd had a great holiday and the prospect of the drudgery of real life loomed. Looking back, she realised it was when they'd returned that the cracks had started to appear. Even thinking about those happier days made her feel the familiar prickle of tears behind her eyes.

He'd started working later and later, as though he was avoiding her, and she couldn't work out what she had done wrong. Things had been so good on their honeymoon. Admittedly, things weren't great between them those last few weeks because of his avoidance tactics, but his departure note had still knocked the wind out of her sails.

She gave herself a shake. There was no point feeling sorry for herself. She decided she would take Edie's car and head over to the other side of the island today.

CHAPTER THIRTY-SEVEN

Edie woke up with a knot of anticipation and dread in her stomach and she couldn't immediately work out why. She gave a huge sigh when she remembered what was happening today. Fergus was taking her over to Glasgow to visit Christine. It was time to make peace and say their goodbyes. As she lay there staring at the ceiling, she sent up a silent prayer for support to help her through the day. Taking a few slow, meditative breaths in and out, she reminded herself that she would work through this. After everything she had been through in her life she had learned she was stronger than she ever thought she could be. And she had to stay strong today for Christine. This was about her sister and doing what was right for her at this moment.

Edie realised that when she'd learned of her sister's illness, all the anger she'd harboured towards her had disappeared. What was the point? Instead, sadness had replaced the rage. Molly seemed to sense something as she moved close and licked her hand.

'What would I do without you, old girl?' she said, stroking the velvety fur behind her ears. 'Come on, let's go downstairs and you can have your breakfast.' Molly's ears perked up and she stood up, did a quick downward dog stretch, then leaped onto the floor. Wagging her tail, she led the way down the stairs and waited to be let out.

Edie opened the door, breathing in the sea-salt-tinged air, and Molly shot outside. Edie stood for a moment, waiting for her to return, and just took a few slow, deep breaths. She went into the kitchen and filled the kettle, absent-mindedly looking at the photo of Jim.

What would you say, Jim? If you were here with me right now, what would you advise? If only I understood why, Jim? Why my sister? And what would you do now?

She made a pot of tea and took it over to the window seat where she gazed out at the dawn sky. She warmed her cold hands on the cup. This time she was drinking from a seashell-themed mug, which she'd varnished in shades of blue. Although just after eight, the sky was unseasonably bright.

Sipping the tea, she closed her eyes. She would never totally lose the grief she felt over Jim's death, which came in waves. Sometimes they were gentle and constant, always there, lapping around and about her. Other times they would crash down on her out of nowhere, engulfing her and leaving her completely breathless and bereft. With time, things had got a bit easier and the waves had settled down, only to be triggered again on a special date like their wedding anniversary or his birthday.

Then, when she'd found out about the affair, she'd pushed away friends who had been supportive. She'd just wanted to retreat and stay in her own safe bubble. She'd been too emotionally exhausted and embarrassed to explain to people why her grief was so complex. The suddenness of his death had been bad enough, without the added layer of duplicity, which had just served to heighten the grief. She knew people couldn't understand why she wasn't yet 'over' Jim's death and she just hoped that they would never have to go through anything similar. Perhaps the largest lesson in all of it was learning to reserve judgement on any situation until she had walked in another person's shoes. It was all too easy to comment, assume and judge from the outside. She just told people that she had to do what worked for her; a coping strategy that meant taking things slowly and at her own pace.

Opening her eyes, she gazed at the sky and could hear Jim in her mind saying, 'Follow your instinct, Edie. You have always known the right thing to do. Sometimes it's best to forgive and move on.'

She could almost imagine him sitting next to her, his hand resting in hers. There was nothing else for it — she just had to accept the situation and try to make amends. She sat for a moment longer and enjoyed the view, the only noise the tick of the clock in the background. Then she stood up and stretched, knowing she must hurry if she was going to be ready for Fergus in just under an hour.

* * *

'Hi Edie, are you all set?' asked Fergus as she came out of the cottage towards him.

Amelia reassured Edie that she would look after Molly. 'Don't give that a second thought. She will be fine with me. And I will organise something for your dinner. You've a long day ahead of you.'

She nodded at Fergus, who smiled. There hadn't been much of a chance to chat since their heart to heart a couple of days back.

'I will take very good care of her,' he said. 'Don't worry about that.'

'Stop fussing. Come on, let's be off, otherwise we will miss the boat.'

Edie checked one final time that the letter she had written to her sister was safely tucked in her bag. Amelia reached out to give her a hug before Edie climbed into the van. After closing her door and getting himself sorted, Fergus drove slowly out of the driveway, tyres crunching over the gravel.

The journey seemed to drag on, and whenever Edie looked out the window of the ferry, the scenery didn't seem to change. She wondered if they were moving at all. Fergus queued for the café and bought her an overly stewed cup of tea, which just didn't taste the same from a cardboard cup. Then she idly started to wonder if she should try to sell some of her work on the ferry route.

When Edie arrived at the hospital, the heavens opened and it started to pour. Fergus drove as close to the reception area as he could to drop her off before going to park. When he came back to find her, she was standing ashen-faced by the lifts.

'What's happened?'

'I'm just scared,' she said quietly. 'I haven't seen her for years. And now I feel bad about it because she's dying. If she weren't dying, would I care about seeing her?'

'Only you know the answer to that, Edie. But this is the situation and she has reached out and apologised again. I think if you can do this, you should be very proud of yourself. Otherwise, if you walk away now without seeing her then maybe you'll come to regret it. Being able to say goodbye properly to someone is a privilege.'

Edie squeezed his shoulder. 'You're right, Fergus. How come you got so wise?'

He shrugged. 'Just life and teachers like you. Now, shall I come up to the ward with you?'

She nodded. 'If you don't mind. Even just to the door of the ward?'

Neither of them spoke as they went into the lift and she pressed the button.

As the doors opened, Edie moved slowly towards the entrance to the ward.

'Remember,' said Fergus. 'Just be yourself. Just be your kind and lovely self.'

She allowed him to walk her a little further and then shooed him away. 'I'll be fine. I promise.'

CHAPTER THIRTY-EIGHT

Cano's eyes lit up when he spotted Amelia walking towards the café with Molly.

'Hello! Where have you been?' he asked. 'We missed you this morning. Ed was asking after you, too.'

'Ah, slight change of routine today,' she said, waving at Naza through the window. 'But I am fine, thanks, though desperately in need of a coffee.' She was pleased and rather touched that he regarded her as a regular.

'No problem, Amelia. You take a wee seat here and I will bring it right out. Just the usual?'

She nodded, thanked him and then sat down, closing her eyes for a moment to feel the warmth from the early afternoon sunshine. She could hear the gentle slosh of the water against the pebbly shore and the odd squeal from a seagull. The sea breeze felt icy on her skin but she was well wrapped up with her thick coat, a hat and the gloves Fergus had given her. She couldn't help but wonder how things were with Edie, and hoped Fergus would text her soon. Cano brought her coffee outside and placed it on the table, and she pulled the mug towards her gratefully.

'Where is Edie today?' asked Cano, bending to pat Molly between the ears.

'She's just got some business to attend to over on the mainland,' she said. 'I'm on dog-sitting duty.'

'And how are you doing?' His voice was kind and he paused before asking, 'Any more man trouble?'

She laughed. 'I'm good, thanks, and fortunately no, not at the moment.'

'That is good.'

'And how's your daughter?' she asked.

'Oh, she is well, getting very ready to have the baby though.'

She pondered for a moment, gazing out at a bobbing boat in the bay. 'Cano, I thought . . . well, would it help you . . . if I helped in the café when Naza has to go to the mainland?' There, she had managed to say it. When he didn't respond immediately, she started to shuffle uncomfortably in her seat. Had she offended him? Or said something she shouldn't?

Cano looked down at her. 'Oh, Amelia. I don't know what to say . . . that is so very kind of you. I am quite overwhelmed. I had been wondering what to do. It can be a struggle to recruit staff, especially at this time of year when we're out of season.'

'I would be delighted to help you,' she said. 'You've been so kind to me since I got here and, well, I would like to repay the favour.'

'Amelia, wait until I tell Naza, she will be thrilled. I know she's been worried about leaving me. Though I can't think why. She must think that things will collapse without her.' He raised an eyebrow and smiled. 'Though that is quite a possibility.'

Her dilemma as to whether or not she should offer now became irrelevant — she was so glad that she had been bold and taken a leap of faith.

'Are you sure, though? We do pay the National Living Wage and there will be tips too.'

She nodded. 'Absolutely, Cano. It would be my pleasure.' She didn't want to admit to him that she would have worked for free for him as he had done so much to welcome her when she'd needed it most.

He placed a hand on her shoulder. 'Thank you. Now let me make you another coffee,' he said, noticing she had drained her cup already. 'On the house.'

Amelia laughed. 'See how much I needed your coffee this morning! I drank it in seconds.'

Cano went back inside and Amelia quickly looked at her phone to check for news from Fergus. She sent a brief message.

Thinking of you and hope all is okay? X

Her phone beeped seconds later.

Yes, here safely and at the hospital. I've just taken her to the ward where her sister is. Fingers crossed . . .

Amelia really hoped Edie would manage to work things out with Christine. She couldn't even begin to imagine how she was feeling or the millions of thoughts that must be racing through her head.

CHAPTER THIRTY-NINE

Edie gave Fergus a wave and turned to speak to the nurse who had come to greet her. She told them she was Christine's sister and the nurse ushered her through. 'She's been waiting for you . . . you're the only person she talks about.'

Edie felt another twinge of guilt. Christine didn't have anyone else. Just Edie.

The nurse gently touched her arm. 'She's just through here.' She pointed to a room at the end of the corridor. 'And just to let you know, she's quite frail. I'm not sure when you saw her last?'

Edie didn't reply. She nodded and walked towards the door, bracing herself as she walked into the bright and warm room. She was surprised to see Christine sitting up in the bed against the pillows, her head turned to look out the window.

'Christine?'

She slowly moved her head round and a small smile spread across her face when she realised it was Edie.

Edie moved towards the bed and sat down on the chair next to it, trying to disguise her shock at how fragile Christine looked.

'You came,' she whispered.

Edie reached for her hand, feeling her sister weakly try to squeeze it.

A strangled sob escaped and Edie muttered under her breath, 'Sorry, this isn't helping, Christine . . .' She tried to make light of her own upset by saying, 'Trust me to make a song and dance of this.'

'It's okay, Edie,' her sister said quietly. 'Thanks for coming. I am so glad you are here.' She pointed at the cup of water and Edie stood up to help her sip through the straw. Christine let her head melt back into the pillows. 'Losing you is my biggest regret in life, and now you are here . . .'

The sisters sat in a companionable silence for a while, just holding hands. Christine drifted in and out of sleep and Edie observed her chest slowly rise and fall.

'Tell me about Arran,' Christine whispered. 'Is it as magical as it was when we were kids?'

'Yes, yes. It is. I have been very lucky. I live in a beautiful cottage overlooking the Holy Isle.'

'Tell me about it.'

'Well, it's a whitewashed house called Coorie Cottage with a huge garden and a hedge all the way around it, which is brown just now but in the summer is a patchwork of shades of green. There's an apple tree, laden with fruit in September, and I make chutneys and crumbles and whatever else I can.'

'Just like Mum,' said Christine.

Edie squeezed her hand. 'Yes.'

'Are you happy?'

'I am. I've got a spaniel called Molly and lots of friends. A young woman, Amelia, is staying with me just now. She's come from London and she's staying in the garden.'

'In the garden?' Her eyes widened in surprise.

Edie laughed. 'I bought a shepherd's hut for the glampers to stay in during the summer.'

'Glampers?'

'Yes, those folks who quite like the idea of camping but don't like tents. But they also don't want to stay in a hotel.'

Shaking her head, Christine giggled, which made her wheeze. Edie helplessly watched her sister, who was clearly in a lot of pain.

'You always were a bit of an entrepreneur, Edie . . . Has it got a name, this shepherd's hut?'

'Coorie Cabin.'

Another wheezy laugh. 'Lovely,' she whispered and smiled, closing her eyes again.

Just then the nurse came over and put a hand on Edie's shoulder. 'I think she's getting tired,' she said quietly in her ear.

Edie looked desperately at the clock, knowing that their time together was drawing to a close. Christine needed her rest, and she should go. But there was one more thing she needed to do before she left. 'Just five minutes?' she asked the nurse.

'Yes, but no more.'

'Thank you,' she said, gratefully. 'Christine, I need to go soon.'

Christine's eyes closed and she nodded her head slowly.

'But I wrote you a letter . . . would you like me to read it to you?'

Christine's eyes fluttered open and she whispered, 'Yes.'

Edie got it out of her bag, unfurled the paper and took a big breath before she started to read.

Dear Christine,

I am sitting looking out over the sea. The winter sun is setting on the horizon and casts an orange glow into the living room of my house. I love all the seasons here for different reasons. In winter, the days are cold and bright but the cottage is cosy and I love sitting beside the log burner with a cup of tea and a good book. You always loved reading too and more often than not I would finish a novel and wonder if you would like it or if you had read it. Sorry, I digress.

Spring is all about new life and starting over. The sight of snowdrops and crocuses gives me hope, and the bursts of yellow daffodils remind me that warmer days are coming. They seem to appear in every nook and cranny. They even appear at the beach where the grass meets the sand.

Summer is beautiful and I have enjoyed many days of dipping my toes in the sea, eating ice cream at the pier and laughing. There has been a lot of laughter and joy in my life and I am grateful for that.

Autumn, when the leaves are reds and oranges and vivid and bright, is stunning as long as it's not too wet. After years of life being so grey and drab after Jim died, it has been colourful too. I just wanted to paint the scene for you to let you know that I was able to move on with life. I have been okay.

Since I got your letter I've not been able to sleep because I realise how much we have missed out on. For that I am sorry. You are and always will be my adored sister . . .

Edie paused for a moment to compose herself. She had to finish this for her sake and for Christine's. She closed her eyes and took another steadying breath.

Today I may have to say goodbye to you and I'm not sure how to do that. Especially when we have only said hello after such a long time. But I keep reminding myself that at least we do have the chance to say hello and I thank you for that. Our relationship hasn't always been the best through these years and I am so sorry for that. Maybe I should have made more effort to be more forgiving but I was lost in my own grief.

Should I say goodbye, Christine? Because I truly believe that we will be together again. Like Jim, you will always be in my heart. You may find it hard to believe but I have so many wonderful memories of you and of us as kids.

Of the summers we spent together on Arran, playing on the beach, crabbing and going to the sweetshop to buy our sweeties. Do you remember the time we came home completely soaked and Mum and Dad just laughed and laughed? We thought they would be cross with us but the opposite. Perhaps that is why I was drawn back . . . because I knew it had a special place in your heart too.

When I walked along the beach the other day at Brodick, I was comforted knowing that the place was a constant presence and was there when we were kids and will still be there when we have both passed. Life goes on . . .

Edie shook as she tried to keep going.

I haven't said everything I planned to. I tried to write this letter from a place of love. And I hope you know that at the end of the day that's what matters, Christine. You are my sister and I love you and I always had forgiven you.

Be at peace, my darling sister, because you are so very loved. This is just a hello until we meet again.
Edie x

Edie wiped away the tears that now rolled down her cheeks and placed the letter on the bed next to her sister. Standing up, she walked round to the other side of the bed, leaned down and gently hugged her. 'I love you, Christine, and always will, no matter what. Sleep well, my darling sister.'

Christine gently opened her eyes and mumbled something to Edie, who had to stoop closer to hear what she said. 'Thank you . . .' she said, in a croaky whisper. 'Beautiful . . . love you.' She closed her eyes and was soon dozing again.

Edie looked down at her sister one last time, kissed her own fingers and touched them to Christine's forehead. Then she quietly gathered her coat and bag and tiptoed out of the room. When she reached the door, she looked round once more at her sister, who now clutched the letter in her hand. Edie managed to choke back her emotions until she was well out of the room and halfway down the corridor. Then her sobs engulfed her. The kind nurse spotted her and gently ushered her into a nearby visitor's room where she handed her a box of tissues and sat beside her while she broke down.

CHAPTER FORTY

The return journey was mainly spent in companionable silence, and Edie dozed while Fergus turned the radio down low, making it just a distracting noise in the background. The day had been long and emotional, and she was glad of Fergus's company. She couldn't have made the journey alone. When her tears had subsided, the nurse had made her a cup of tea and sat with her until she'd been ready to leave.

Fergus had waited outside the ward and seemed to instinctively know what to do and say. She would never forget his kindness and was grateful that she didn't have to worry about making small talk with him as they drove home. He knew what losing someone you loved was like. He had experienced the raw, visceral grief that consumed you, and Edie knew he too had learned that talking about what had happened helped to heal the constant and awful heartache.

After Jim died, Edie had eventually had counselling, and she'd urged Fergus to speak to someone when he'd opened up and told her about losing Ellen. However, he'd said that even just talking to her had helped him, and that the hurt had started to fade to a dull ache. She just hoped he would be able to open himself up to love again one day.

Edie thought about the different stages of her grief and the way in which she'd decided to make a fresh start away from Edinburgh and reminders of Jim. Investing in a new life had helped her and she still cherished their marriage and the memories they'd shared. Somehow she clung onto them and made sure they weren't tarnished, despite the affair. Edie's way of coping was to continue to talk to Jim in her head and ask for his advice.

Edie opened her eyes and felt relief as she heard the metallic rattle of the van driving onto the ferry and spotted the CalMac staff in their hard hats and fluorescent vests waving them towards the back of the hull. Glancing over she noticed Fergus stifle a yawn. He drove forward slowly into place, following instructions, and turned off the engine.

'We're on the boat now and we need to go up to the deck,' he said gently.

She rubbed her eyes. 'Thank you, dear. I'm just glad we made it and the ferry is running. I am so looking forward to getting home.' She unclipped her seat belt and slowly opened the door, making sure not to touch the vehicle that was parked very closely next to the van. 'I'm sure you must be tired too. It's been a long day for you with all the hanging around. Come on. Let me buy you a cup of tea.'

They followed the other passengers up the flights of stairs onto the deck with the bar and café. The crossing wasn't busy, due to the time of year, and outside was in complete darkness. Edie could only see her own sad reflection in the windows.

Once they were settled with their drinks in a corner of the café, she thanked him again for what he'd done.

Fergus shrugged. 'It's absolutely fine, Edie. I'd do anything to help you.' He took a sip of tea and broke a finger off the KitKat she'd bought him. 'I am just so glad for your sake that you've made your peace.'

Edie nodded. 'Yes. I'm glad I made it in time. I don't think she has much longer . . .' she said sadly. 'She is so frail and her face white. I almost didn't recognise her. The cancer has ravaged her.' She attempted to smile but it was futile. 'Cancer is such an awful disease.'

Fergus reached over and held her hand. 'She's in the best place, Edie.'

'I know, but I found it hard, seeing her so ill.'

'You'll be okay, Edie. You're the strongest person I know.'

She smiled gratefully and put her other hand on top of his. 'I'm not sure about that. But thank you. I guess we just need to deal with what life throws at us.'

He nodded and offered her a piece of his chocolate biscuit.

'Oh, okay then,' she said, realising she hadn't eaten much at all today. 'I'm looking forward to getting home.'

'Me too,' he said. 'It's a bit of a culture shock being in the city again. Feels a bit grimy and busy.'

'Have you never regretted coming back to the island then?'

'Nope. It's the best thing I have done since . . . well, since Ellen died. Even though I don't have any family here anymore, this is home for me and I'm not leaving.'

'Yes, there is something very grounding and healing about Arran. It's been my haven over the years. Living by the sea is certainly very restorative.' Her thoughts drifted to Amelia and how much more rejuvenated she was compared to her pale, sad demeanour when she'd arrived four weeks ago.

Fergus told her that Amelia had been in touch just to check how everything was and that she had some dinner ready for their arrival.

'She's a good girl, isn't she? I'm lucky she answered that advert.'

Fergus nodded. 'That reminds me, is everything set for the weekend and the fair?'

She laughed. 'Oh, yes, Doris is in charge and everything is ready to launch. Mind you, I took a quick look at my phone earlier and clocked the messages from her. She obviously thinks I've done a runner. She's holding a final meeting tomorrow and wants to check I can make it.'

'Did you tell anyone else you were coming over to Glasgow?'

She shook her head. 'Well, I mentioned I had some business in Glasgow but that was all. Only you and Amelia are aware of the real reason.'

'I thought that would be the case. You keep your own business off the radar. Like me . . .'

'I understand that, Fergus . . .' Edie paused and drew in a calming, steadying breath. 'Can I offer you some advice from an old bird? Don't keep everything to yourself. Remember to let yourself trust. You're still young. You won't feel like this for ever.'

He pursed his lips together and nodded.

'You've got a lot of folks around you who really care about you. Don't forget that.' She sipped her tea. 'Okay, lecture over, I promise.' Just then the announcement was made that they were approaching the pier. 'You'll be glad this is such a short crossing as it limits my time to dispense advice.'

He grimaced good-naturedly. 'You're right. And thank you . . . looks like we'd better start making our way to the van.'

As they drove back to Coorie Cottage, the sharpness of loss pierced her heart again. But when she saw Amelia waiting at the door for her, she managed to smile. She wasn't quite so alone.

CHAPTER FORTY-ONE

Amelia's phone pinged the next morning as she lay in bed, enjoying the cosy warmth of her duvet.

I'm heading for a swim if you fancy joining me?

She yawned and considered it for five seconds. She could just about make out a tiny chink of light in the curtains, so at least it wasn't completely dark. Though that maybe wasn't a good thing given what she was about to do.

You're on. See you at your usual spot?

If she didn't bite the bullet now, she never would, and, well, why not? She pulled the wetsuit on over her swimming costume, scraped her hair back in a ponytail, threw on her coat and trainers and ran down the garden path before she changed her mind.

He was standing waiting and watching for her coming along the shore. 'I didn't know if you would actually come.'

She grinned. 'Thought I should be brave.' Pulling off her jacket, she threw it beside Fergus's things and shook her head. 'I forgot a towel.'

'I've got that covered.' He pointed to his bag of kit. 'Here, you'll need these.' He handed her a pair of neoprene gloves and boots.

She pulled the boots on, zipping them so they fitted snugly to her feet. Then eased her hands into the gloves. 'Is that me?'

'Not quite. Take this, too.' It was a woolly hat. 'It'll help keep you warm.'

'Just as well you're around, otherwise I'd be completely unprepared.'

He laughed. 'That's what I'm here for.'

'Do I just go in fast and hope for the best?'

He shook his head. 'Follow my lead. We need to start by getting you acclimatised to the water. So come and stand with me.' He reached for her hand and she followed him into the water, where they stood. 'Splash your face like this.'

She gasped as the icy cold water shocked her system.

'Just give it a bit longer and you'll get used to the temperature. Come on, a bit further in.'

Amelia focused on her breathing as she waded out and the water covered her up to her chest.

'Are you good?' His voice was encouraging, which definitely helped and stopped her from doing a U-turn and running screaming back to the cabin. Then, with a surge of confidence, she allowed her shoulders to go under the water.

'Look at that. There you go.'

Amelia smiled, feeling a rush of adrenaline surge through her as she started to swim. 'I'm okay now. This isn't too bad.'

'Don't go too far away though. Or out of your depth. You also need to be able to get back.'

Amelia gave him a thumbs-up sign as she trod water for a moment, looking around her. She tipped her head back, looking at the sky, and had a sense of complete exhilaration. Who would have thought she would be swimming in the sea in Scotland in December? Fergus stayed close, keeping an eye on her until she shrieked as a wave hit her in the face.

'You okay?'

She laughed. 'Amazing. This has to be the best thing I've ever done.'

He nodded appreciatively. 'Gives you a buzz, doesn't it? I kind of needed to ground myself after yesterday.'

'Hospitals do that to you, don't they?'

'Yes . . .'

Amelia could have kicked herself. She'd totally forgotten to consider how Fergus had felt being back in a hospital again. What an idiot she was. 'Was it hard being there?'

'No,' he said a bit dismissively and quickly changed the subject. 'I'm so glad this is on our doorstep. It's like a reset for my mind. I just hope Edie will cope.'

Amelia nodded. 'I'll look in later and check how she's doing.'

'Are you shivering?' he said teasingly.

She grinned, splashing him. 'Not really . . .'

'That's probably enough for your first day though. You don't want to catch a chill. If you can still feel your fingers and toes, that's a good sign. If they're numb you know you've stayed in too long.'

Amelia didn't argue. She had thoroughly enjoyed the swim but was ready to get out of the water. 'Look at that.' She pointed to a seal bobbing quite near to them.

'That's Sammy. As long as you're not too close to him he doesn't bother.'

'Sammy the seal. I wish I'd brought my phone. Nobody will believe me.' They walked towards their bags.

'Here.' He pulled out his phone and zoomed in on Sammy then took a photo of Amelia. 'Smile.'

She couldn't stop grinning. 'I am so proud of myself. I honestly can't tell you how amazing that was. Thank you, Fergus. How about a selfie?'

'Sure,' he said, chuckling.

Amelia leaned back against him, enjoying the feel of his solid frame behind her. She wished he hadn't snapped the picture so quickly, because she then had to move away.

Reaching down to his bag, he pulled out a towel poncho. 'Okay, what I want you to do now is put this on and walk briskly back to the cabin. That will let your temperature start to adjust.'

Amelia was completely transfixed as he expertly talked her through the instructions.

'Give me your gloves and boots and I'll sort them out. Just put your trainers back on.'

'Thank you, again. I obviously completely forgot that I might need a towel or a change of clothes. What about your wetsuit?'

'Just hold on to it . . . that's if you want to try swimming again?'

'Definitely.'

'In that case, just hose it down and hang it on the washing line to dry.'

'I can't thank you enough,' she said.

'So you enjoyed yourself, then?'

'Oh my God, Fergus, I can't believe how much I loved it. My skin is completely tingling.'

'When you get back, jump in the shower but make sure it's not too hot, and then fix yourself a warm drink.'

Amelia's teeth had begun to chatter.

'Off you go.'

Reluctantly, she turned away and started to walk along the pebbles to the gate at the cottage. When she looked back, Fergus had already changed. He raised his hand and waved. Amelia licked her lips and tasted the salt. She felt as though she had just had a really life-affirming and healing experience. Who would have thought that a brief dip in the sea could work such magic?

After her shower, she pulled on her jogging bottoms and sweatshirt and a pair of fleecy socks. Thank goodness she had packed them. She lit the log burner and looked out at the bay. What a magical way to start the day. She opened her journal and saw the prompt for the day was: *How do you feel today?* Smiling, she grabbed her pen, knowing this would be easy.

Zingy, alive, loving life, proud, brave, awake . . .

CHAPTER FORTY-TWO

Over in the cottage, Edie poured herself a cup of tea and was immersed in her thoughts when the phone rang. Even though she had been expecting the call, the news was still a shock. Christine had died in her sleep during the night. She had been at peace and was comfortable, the nurse told her. Edie thanked her for the call and said goodbye. She sat down at the kitchen table and stared out of the window. She looked at the smoke curling up from the chimney of the cabin. It drifted lazily in the early breeze, barely visible in the smir that had started to fall. There was something reassuring about knowing Amelia was only a few hundred metres away. But she had a tremendous sense of longing for Jim and wished he would just appear behind her and wrap his arms tightly around her. 'I really loved her,' she said out loud. *And I forgive you, Christine. And you, Jim. What I would give to have just one more day with you. How I wish you could give me a sign that everything will be okay.*

Just then the rain started to fall harder and she shivered as it began to bounce off the windows. She brushed a lock of hair from her face as she continued to watch the pelting water. Then it stopped as quickly as it started and the sun appeared, flooding the kitchen with bright light. She stood and edged nearer to the window. Peering out, she smiled when she saw the perfect arc of a rainbow with its colours dazzling against the dark sky. *Is that a sign, Jim?* She smiled, knowing that must have been, surely? She loved rainbows and their symbol of hope and faith. A sense of calm descended on her and she knew that everything was as it should be. She would get through this, and Jim was never far from her side.

Later that afternoon, Amelia called in as planned so they could walk to the high street together to attend the final meeting of the Christmas fair committee.

'I'm so glad it's stopped raining,' said Amelia, as she walked into the kitchen.

'Yes. And I think that will be it for a few days,' said Edie, who checked the weather forecast religiously. 'Fingers crossed, the coming days are set to be fine, albeit cold.'

'You'll never guess what I did this morning, Edie.'

'I won't. Just tell me.'

'I went for my first sea swim.'

'Oh, you are crazy. But well done . . . dare I ask what it was like?'

'Amazing.'

'Well, you're a braver soul than me.'

'I don't know about that. Anyway, how are you feeling today?'

Just as Edie was about to tell Amelia about her sister, she heard a car pull up outside, its wheels crunching over the gravel.

'Oh, that will be Fergus,' Amelia said. 'He mentioned coming to collect us.'

Edie raised an eyebrow. 'Mmm . . . so much for walking then?'

Amelia shook her head and stifled a laugh. 'Now, Edie, just behave . . . He sent me a text earlier when the heavens opened.'

'It's fine. I'm glad he's here.'

'Who, me?' said Fergus as he walked into the kitchen.

'Just the very man. I'm glad you're both here actually. It means I can tell you together.'

'Tell us what?' he said, confused.

'Now,' she said, clapping her hands together. 'Please don't make a fuss. I'm fine. But . . . well, the hospital called this morning to let me know Christine . . . passed away.'

Amelia gasped. 'Oh, Edie. I'm so sorry to hear that.' She ran over to Edie and put her arms around her.

Edie allowed herself to be held for a moment then pushed Amelia away. 'Thanks, dear. But really, I am okay. I was expecting the news. And . . . I'm lucky that I managed to visit her in time . . . and that we made our peace.'

'Sorry,' said Fergus gruffly. He hovered awkwardly, unsure as to whether he should also give her a cuddle.

Edie waved him over and hugged him. 'Thank you, Fergus. If it hadn't been for you I wouldn't have gone to see her.' She stepped away. 'Thank you both for being there for me when I needed you.'

'What about a funeral?' asked Amelia.

Edie shook her head. 'She didn't want one.'

'Oh,' said Fergus.

Edie shrugged. 'She just wanted a private cremation and asked that I scatter her ashes here, in Arran.'

Fergus and Amelia looked at each other, then back towards Edie.

'Now, come on. There's no point in sitting around being maudlin. Let's get to the meeting.'

'But, Edie . . .' began Amelia.

Putting a smile on her face, she dismissed their concerned looks. 'Come on, we just need to get on with things. The best thing to do is keep busy. And if we don't get up there soon, Doris may end up taking over.' She clocked Amelia and Fergus looking at each other in surprise.

'I think she perhaps already has,' said Fergus, with a grin.

She looked at them both and nodded. 'Let's go. I'll be fine.'

CHAPTER FORTY-THREE

When they arrived at Cèic, where the final meeting was being held, Doris already held the attention of the table. Clearly she had entered into the Christmas spirit of things, as she wore a jumper with a flashing Christmas tree on its front. Thea and Grant looked up as Edie, Fergus and Amelia walked in, and they rolled their eyes.

'There you are. Nice you could make it,' said Doris.

Amelia felt herself bristling at the tone of her voice.

'Ladies, you sit down and I'll get you a coffee.' Fergus casually walked over to Cano.

'I'll give him a hand.' Grant couldn't get away fast enough.

'I just said that everything seems to be in hand. But you just never know, do you?' Doris's lips were pursed as she looked outside at the few clouds in the sky. 'I mean, after that downpour earlier, who knows what will happen. What if it rains? Or snows?' She tapped her hands briskly on the table. 'This is the last year I do this. I mean, does anyone have any idea how much work is involved?' Her phone rang and she sighed dramatically, excusing herself.

'It's the same speech every year,' said Thea, stifling a smile. 'She thinks she does all of the work and is the chief executive officer of the world. She loves the stress of it all. Positively thrives on it.'

'Something smells good,' said Edie, looking over at the counter.

'It's Naza's festive brownies. She's been trying out some new recipes.'

'It's hard to believe Christmas is just a few weeks away,' said Edie. 'Where has the time gone?'

Amelia smiled sympathetically at her.

Edie gasped. 'I don't even have my Christmas tree up yet. Normally I like to have it up before the fair.' She seemed to be blinking back tears.

'I can help you with that, Edie. In fact, I would love to if that's okay?'

'Thank you, dear.' She patted Amelia on the hand.

'Do you think she'll notice if I go?' Thea gestured to Doris, who was pacing around an area at the side of the café. 'There's obviously an issue. I think she'll be a while.'

'Poor Ed.' Amelia could see the elderly man was a bit perturbed by the way Doris kept circling his table.

'Go. Make a run for it,' said Edie. 'Escape while you can.'

Thea laughed, her pale skin flushed at the warmth inside the café. Waving over at Grant, she quickly darted between tables and chairs, avoiding Doris's gaze.

'How did she manage to get out of this?' Fergus placed a mug in front of Edie and Amelia. He sat down opposite.

'Because she's a smart cookie. That's why.' Edie laughed and lifted the cup. 'Thanks, dear.'

'You've got yours to go?' Amelia gave him a meaningful look. He winked at her and she couldn't help but feel a pang of *something*. Why was he so annoyingly charming and warm? What was the matter with her? She was acting like a lovestruck teenager.

'The quicker we can get this done, the quicker we can escape,' said Edie.

Amelia's mind drifted to the previous Christmas when she and Declan had decorated their tree. He'd brought a huge, real tree home with him, which he'd picked up on his way back from the pub. Snow had started falling and he and the tree had both been covered in a light dusting of it. He'd struggled to get it up the stairs and into the flat, and it had dominated their small living room. But how they'd laughed as they'd tried to straighten it, using books and magazines to balance the fact it had been extremely lopsided. He'd tipsily asked Alexa to play Christmas tunes and they'd draped it with tinsel and baubles. The fairy lights had been broken.

Usually Amelia loved Christmas and was super organised with the presents and wrapping because of her busy work schedule. Otherwise, Christmas tended to be a bit of a scramble. She had a spreadsheet, which detailed who she needed to buy for and what. Because her family weren't exactly local, she'd spent the last couple of years with Declan's family in Brighton. It was strange to think she didn't need to worry about any of that this year, other than perhaps some small gifts for Edie, Thea and Fergus. She idly wondered if Suna would appreciate a bottle of the festive gin. She made a mental note to send it soon. She didn't even know what Suna's plans were and for that she felt bad. Suna normally visited her parents in Essex, but she still felt a twinge of sorrow about the way in which their friendship was drifting.

She hoped Edie was still happy to have her for Christmas lunch. She would check with her later and offer to help. That was the least she could do. Although who was to say Edie did a turkey meal? Everyone had their own traditions. She blinked back the tears as she was reminded that life was very different for her this year. Everything had changed in the blink of an eye. She took a deep breath and told herself to focus on enjoying this time. She looked around the café and saw many familiar faces she was very fond of, including Ed, who raised his hand and waved at her. She realised there were far worse places to be.

CHAPTER FORTY-FOUR

On the morning of the fair, Amelia and Fergus had arranged to meet for another swim. This time she had suggested it. She had been awake all night worrying about another message from Declan. She'd felt a mix of panic and uncertainty when she'd listened to his voicemail.

'Thinking of you. Can you call me?'

What did he want? Hearing his voice unsettled her hugely. Jack had again mentioned that he was holding out an olive branch to her. But she just wasn't ready to go there yet. Not when she was starting to find herself again. They didn't even live in the same city anymore. Yet she had a sense of dread that needled in her stomach. It was like those early days when he'd walked out, when everything had felt out of her control. She felt her eyes fill with tears, and when she looked out at the sea she knew that a dip would be the perfect tonic. She needed to do something to keep hold of the positive feelings she'd rediscovered. She wanted to stay in control and didn't want to have that horrible sense of life spiralling downwards again.

She walked briskly down the path, noticing the dark green moss caking the pale slabs. She would do something about that when the weather got a bit warmer. As she sauntered along the shore, deep in thought, she smiled on noticing the light dusting of frost on the pebbles and seaweed. As she waited at the usual spot, she became transfixed by the low morning sun, which glowed faintly on the horizon. An icy breeze created gentle ripples in the water, yet she couldn't wait to get in.

'Sorry I'm late.' He was panting as he ran over the grass and crunched over the layers of shingle.

'That's okay. It was my idea. I'm just glad you're here, otherwise I may have bottled out of it.' She gulped.

He looked at her with his head tilted to one side. 'Hey . . . are you okay?'

'Yes. Well, no, not really, but I'm hoping this will sort me out. I'm thinking of it as self-care.' She sounded a bit dubious.

He looked concerned. 'Do you want to talk about it?'

She shook her head. 'No. I just want to get in the water.'

'Let's go then.'

She reached for his hand and they walked through the dark green waves together. The water was icy and she braced herself, knowing that this was the hardest part but that it would pass. *Things are always changing, Amelia,* she reminded herself. In a minute or so she would be fine and swimming along marvelling at the sky and the view of the beach from the sea. Being in the water gave the world around her a whole different perspective. Fergus wore his neoprene hood today, and she watched as he powerfully sliced his arms through the water. Remembering his advice, she stayed in her depth and floated on her back, splashing her legs to keep warm. Her spirits lifted as she saw Sammy the seal watching from a distance.

'Better?' he said, swimming over.

She nodded. 'It can only get warmer, right?'

'Actually, no . . . it drops to its coldest temperature in March.'

'You're kidding?'

He laughed. 'No. This is still quite balmy for December.'

'What is it about this that is so magical?'

'When you're exposed to the elements it reminds you what's important.' He dipped his shoulders under the water. 'And being in the sea with Mother Nature, well, it's quite humbling. You have to respect the tides and nature.'

She nodded. 'You're right. It just strips everything away, doesn't it? All the crap in life.'

'Come on,' he said, when he realised she was shivering. 'Time to get out.'

They waded out of the surf side by side, 'I can't tell you how much better that makes me feel. It's amazing.'

He nodded. 'It really recalibrates you, doesn't it?'

'When did you get into it?'

He unzipped his wetsuit and she tried not to stare at his broad chest and ripped abs. 'When I moved back. I mean, I swam as a kid. But I hadn't really bothered that much as an adult.' He pulled a T-shirt on, followed by a fleece. 'It saved me from . . . the hole I was sinking into after Ellen's death.'

Amelia had managed to shimmy halfway out of her wetsuit to pull on a couple of dry layers. 'It sounds like it has been really healing for you and I get that.'

'Being in the water at first light, or last thing when the sun is setting, is therapeutic. Especially when it's just me and Sammy.'

Amelia smiled. 'Well, thanks for introducing me to it and being so encouraging.' She felt calmer and now a cheery sense of anticipation washed over her rather than her earlier sense of dread.

'Right, you had better go and get warmed up. I'll see you later at the fair?' He grinned lazily at her and she wondered if he was flirting.

'Of course.' She raised an eyebrow. 'And remember your Christmas jumper.'

'I will, if you remember your reindeer ears.'

'I'll go and put them on now so I don't forget.' With a laugh and a last lingering look, she turned and headed back along the bay.

CHAPTER FORTY-FIVE

As the late afternoon light faded away, the fair took on a magical glow with the twinkling fairy lights strung between lampposts. Each of the shops had their own Christmas display and a myriad of coloured lights flashed from each window. As families with younger children started to drift off home, the feel was slightly more relaxed. The mulled wine stall had done a roaring trade, as had the bar. Amelia had been rushed off her feet selling wine and fizz and shots of the festive gin, which had sold like hot cakes.

'I told you this was a great idea, Amelia,' shouted Doris, who had clearly enjoyed a few tipples herself. 'I should have produced more bottles. Next year for sure.' Her face was flushed and her eyes bright. 'Or maybe we could produce a special Easter blend or a summer edition.'

'Great idea.' Amelia was actually desperate to go and use the ladies.

'And these jumpers have been a tremendous idea.' Doris was wearing her sweater with the flashing Christmas tree. Amelia's had a giant Christmas pudding on the front.

'Can you cover me for a bit, please? I need to go to the loo.'

'Of course,' said Doris. 'Away and have some fun.'

'What, at the toilet?' Amelia said, bemused.

Doris winked. 'I think Santa's been looking for you. *You'd better watch out . . .*' she sang.

Amelia looked at her quizzically. How much gin had she drunk? That was just wrong on so many levels and she tried not to shudder. Davey, the lollipop man, who was about eighty, was Santa, and it was just totally inappropriate to think she'd caught his attention in that way. As she made her way through the crowds, she giggled. Wasn't it ironic that she could attract the attention of pensioners but not guys her own age?

She cast her eyes around looking for Edie and waved when she realised she was chatting to Cano. Edie's eyes lit up and she smiled back. Amelia hadn't seen Fergus at all, and she wondered if he was even here. Then she realised she was disappointed she hadn't seen him. She actually missed him. There was a lovely scent of cinnamon and ginger in the air and Amelia paused to look at Grant, who was juggling Christmas baubles and had attracted quite a gathering.

She stopped at Thea's shop and stuck her head inside. 'Is it okay if I use your loo, please?'

'Of course.' She waved her in. 'Off you go through the back.' Thea, who wore flashing robin earrings, turned to talk to her customer.

Amelia caught sight of her reflection in the mirror and was pleasantly surprised. Her cheeks were smudged with colour and her eyes were bright, which was perhaps a result of the festive gin she'd been sampling. Her hair was piled into a ponytail and she had dusted some glitter powder across her eyelids and cheeks.

'Thanks for that,' she said to Thea. 'I was desperate.'

'No problem at all.' Thea's eyes were twinkling. 'Are you having fun?'

'It's been amazing. What a brilliant atmosphere,' she said. 'It really has been great.'

'Wait until Doris starts the dancing . . . that is a sight worth seeing.' Thea laughed.

Amelia tilted her head and raised an eyebrow. 'Should I be worried?'

'A bit . . .'

'Well, I'd better head back to bar duties and let her get on with it.'

'Oh, don't worry too much. Things tend to look after themselves.'

'See you later,' she said.

'Yes, I'll pop down to the bar soon. I could do with a drink.'

'Great, I'll look out for you.'

'Oh, and Amelia . . .' Thea said mischievously, 'Santa has been looking for you.'

'Super,' said Amelia, starting to feel slightly worried.

'You've definitely got an admirer there.'

CHAPTER FORTY-SIX

Amelia made her way back down the High Street to the bar, smiling at all the proud and happy faces of people in the community who had made the day such a success.

But her grin soon turned into a grimace when she realised Santa, clearly on a mission, was making his way towards her quite determinedly. Oh dear. She frowned as she tried to hotfoot it in another direction. But Santa was gaining speed. Who knew pensioners moved so fast? As she began to weave her way through the crowds, her mind raced. How on earth did she handle this? How did you politely but firmly turn down an octogenarian? She appreciated Thea and Doris giving her a heads-up. But *seriously?* Wait until she told Jack, who would find it all completely hilarious. She quickened her pace and was about to make a beeline into a shop when a hand rested on her shoulder.

'Ho-ho-ho.'

Her stomach sank and she plastered on a smile as she turned to face the man himself. Santa Davey.

'There you are. I've been looking for you for ages. Didn't anyone tell you?'

'Um, yes.' Her voice started rising in indignation. 'They said Santa was looking for me.'

Fergus grinned.

'*Really?*' She managed to stifle a giggle.

'Oh, you think this is funny, do you?' He gestured at his outfit. 'Ho-ho-ho.'

'You look a lot older than you do usually. And my oh my, look at that beard. I didn't realise they grew so quickly.'

He gave her a sexy wink, which should have been wrong but somehow worked.

'What happened to Davey?'

'Bad back. He pulled out at the last minute and they were desperate.' He shrugged. 'I couldn't let the children down, could I?'

He moved closer. Amelia felt the warmth of his breath on her neck and became conscious of others around them.

'I'd better get back to the bar. Doris will be waiting.' She was *not* going to let herself become enchanted by him. She felt her cheeks flushing.

'Oh, I think she's just fine. Make the most of your getaway while you can before she sends out the search party. Are you having a good time?'

'Yes,' she said truthfully, dropping her eyes from his penetrating gaze. 'I am.' She was happy and free and, *Oh God*, he was now holding her hand. How did that happen? Not that she was complaining but . . . 'I never thought Santa was such a catch.' Did she actually say those words out loud? She cringed.

'Thanks. I should take you to my special chair and get you to sit on my knee and ask you what you want for Christmas.'

'That would be very wrong.' She tried to keep a straight face.

'Yes.' He nodded, trying to look serious. 'You're right.'

Once again she sensed he wanted to kiss her and she wished they weren't standing in the middle of the street with him dressed as Santa.

Amelia waited with bated breath. How typical that they were at this potentially crucial moment, possibly on the verge of locking lips, and he had a wig and beard on. She never thought she'd be lusting after Father Christmas. Then he touched her nose. Her *nose*!

'There's some glitter.' He blew it away.

'Just my eyeshadow. I should have offered you some to go with your get-up.'

'Santa in make-up. That would have got the locals talking . . .'

Tears of laughter started to stream down her face.

'Are you laughing at me?' he asked innocently.

'I am, Fergus. And this ridiculous situation.'

'Is this any better?' He unhooked the beard.

'Well, you still look like Santa but a much younger version. You'd better make sure none of the kids spot you or you'll ruin their Christmas.'

'It's okay. Nobody can see us in this dark corner.'

'Next you'll be inviting me into your grotto,' she said.

'Don't tempt me.'

She pulled her padded jacket around her, zipping it up.

'I can't see your Christmas pudding anymore.' He flashed her a wicked grin.

'You're full of good chat today, Fergus.' He was *definitely* flirting with her and she couldn't meet his eyes.

'You're right. That sounded naff.'

Amelia, distracted by a crowd of folk who had gathered, said, 'Oh look, here she comes. I don't know whether to laugh or cry.'

They watched as Doris led the Gay Gordons down the street.

'She's like the Pied Piper . . .'

'I think people are too frightened to refuse her. They'll be toeing the line or else . . .'

'Quick, hide, or you'll soon be twirling your way behind her.'

They ran back to the drinks stall, which people had abandoned in favour of the dancing throng.

Fergus laughed as he suddenly stopped. 'Wait a second. Look where we are.'

'Will you look at that.' She pointed up at the mistletoe. 'We'd better move or folks will talk.' She began to edge away from him but he pulled her close.

'Let them talk,' he said quietly, looking at her intently. He smiled again and touched her cheek. Then he leaned down, cupped her face in his hands and kissed her gently on the lips.

Amelia gripped his shoulders and kissed him back.

CHAPTER FORTY-SEVEN

When the crowd started trickling back into the bar, exhausted and thirsty from their dancing, Amelia reluctantly let go of Fergus's hand. His smile was playful. 'This is definitely to be continued.'

Amelia couldn't wipe the grin from her face. She had forgotten how good kissing could be, and Fergus was excellent at it. 'I should head back behind the bar . . .'

'Give me two minutes and I'll come and help you. I'll lose the outfit first though.'

Amelia couldn't stop grinning, and when his hand gently touched her waist, her stomach flipped. They worked side by side, pulling beers and dispensing drinks to the rowdy crowd. She sensed he was watching her and it was exciting to share a secret together.

'That's the gin finished,' Amelia called to Doris.

'The bottled beer is almost finished too,' shouted Fergus. 'I'm going to go out the back to fetch some more.'

'Does everything normally run dry so quickly?'

'It must be a particularly thirsty crowd tonight.' Grant had arrived with Thea. 'I've never seen it this busy.'

'Wow, what a day,' said Thea. 'I'm exhausted. I can't ever remember having so many visitors here before.'

'Yes, there were a lot of unfamiliar faces,' said Grant. 'The ferry from Ardrossan will have been busy today.'

'Rob did say the hotel was full. But it's great. Business has been booming. I've done a roaring trade at the shop, so I'm not complaining.'

Edie appeared wearing her red sequinned sweater and reindeer ears. She yawned. 'I'm calling it a night. It is way past my bedtime.'

Amelia looked at her watch. It was approaching eight o'clock.

'Thought I should let you know in case you were looking for me.'

'Are you okay, Edie?'

'Yes, it's been a long day and my wee feet are tired.' She smiled. 'I'll leave you youngsters to it.'

Fergus glanced over. 'Do you want me to walk you back, Edie?'

'Thank you but I will be quite fine. I'm only two minutes along the road. You all enjoy yourself.'

'Bye, Edie,' they chorused, and she did a little curtsy before making her exit.

'Someone looks happy tonight.' Thea jerked her head towards Fergus. She winked at Amelia. 'Santa found you then?'

Amelia laughed, her face red, when she realised Thea knew a lot more than she was letting on. 'He certainly did. Why didn't you tell me? I spent a while dodging him completely.'

'Well, there is nothing wrong with being elusive. You never want to be too keen.'

Amelia blushed as she remembered the passionate kiss they'd shared. It was a bit late for that.

'I hope he gives you the Christmas that you truly deserve.'

Amelia burst out laughing. 'You're quite naughty, Thea. I'm saying nothing.'

'You don't have to. It's written all over your face.'

'That obvious?'

'Just to me. Don't worry . . . Look, when we're finished here, a few folk are coming to ours for some drinks. It would be great if you joined us. Santa too.'

'Sure. I'll find out what he's up to. He may have other plans . . .' She didn't want to assume anything at all. 'But that sounds nice. Thank you.' Amelia's heart raced at the thought of continuing what they'd started earlier. She truly had not thought she was able to experience feelings like this for someone other than Declan. But Fergus had kissed her passionately enough for her to know that she wanted more. 'I better go and check whether he needs a hand with that beer.'

'Sure.' Thea winked.

Amelia went through the curtain at the back of the bar and round the corner to the makeshift store area, which had piles of boxed beers. Fergus was crouched down on the ground trying to read the label. She shivered. 'Perfect for chilling?'

He stood when he saw her. 'Come to join me?'

'I wondered if you needed any help with the beer?'

'Oh, yes, please.' His smile widened.

She felt as though she was walking on air as she went over to him and reached up to give him a brief kiss. He responded hungrily and this told her it *definitely* was not a one-off.

'Wow,' he said, leaning down to kiss her again.

She broke away, reminding herself they were in a public place. Anyone could appear at any minute. 'Thea and Grant are having a few friends back later . . .'

'I'd rather we had our own private party.' Raking a hand through his hair and grinning, he reached to gently touch her face.

'We'll see . . .' She smiled and turned to walk back inside the bar. She was desperate to drag him to the cabin right then, slightly surprised at how easy this all was. But she had to show some restraint, didn't she?

He caught her hand and twirled her round. 'Not so fast.' He kissed her again, holding her tightly to him.

Amelia couldn't stop smiling when she returned to the bar, and when Thea caught her eye she sniggered. When had she last felt so happy and carefree? Life had somehow magically turned around for her, and this thing with Fergus was completely unexpected. She smiled at the sing-song

Grant had started in the corner. He'd managed to persuade everyone to do an interesting version of Mariah Carey's 'All I Want for Christmas'.

'I know what I want for Christmas.' His breath was warm on the back of her neck. Her skin tingled at his proximity and she knew if she turned to look at him, she wouldn't be able to keep her hands off him.

A pretty woman with dark hair and eyes pushed her way forwards at the bar. Thea frowned as the woman knocked her elbow, causing her to spill her drink.

'Oops, there you go.' Amelia passed her a pile of napkins and looked over curiously. She didn't recognise the newcomer.

'Is Fergus here?'

Amelia smiled brightly at her but the woman glared back.

'Yes,' Amelia said, looking around. 'He must be out back. Can I tell him who's asking for him?'

The woman flicked her hair over her shoulders rather aggressively. 'Kelly.' She paused for deliberate effect. 'His *girlfriend*.'

Thea had been watching and listening with interest and her eyes widened in surprise, especially at the woman's rather surly tone.

'Girlfriend?' said Amelia as casually as she was able to through gritted teeth. How could she have been stupid enough to think that he hadn't already been snapped up?

'Yes. That's right.'

Amelia turned away so the woman couldn't see her face fall. She felt as though she had been punched in the gut, and just like that all the happy and carefree feelings evaporated in an instant.

CHAPTER FORTY-EIGHT

Fergus froze when he saw Kelly waiting for him at the bar. He looked as bewildered and surprised as everyone else.

'What are you doing here?' He couldn't disguise his shock at seeing her standing there.

'Well, that is hardly a nice way to greet me, is it?' She reached across the bar, planted her hands on his shoulders and covered his mouth with hers. A few bystanders started whistling at the steamy display.

Amelia's heart pounded and her mouth turned dry as she watched the scene unfold. Fergus didn't exactly seem to be in a rush to push her off. *What on earth was going on?* She tried her best to plaster on a smile and busy herself with drink orders, but it was a struggle. The bar area wasn't huge and so it was difficult not to hear snatches of the conversation between them, especially when everyone else was trying their best to eavesdrop too.

'You don't look all that happy to see me.' Kelly now stood with her hands on her hips and swayed slightly.

'I didn't expect you to come here,' said Fergus, his voice terse.

'Clearly,' she said, glaring. 'But you never answer my calls or messages so I thought I would see you in person.'

God, that sounds like my life, thought Amelia. *A man who doesn't return calls.* She wished she had stuck to her initial gut feeling about him being too good to be true.

Grant made a face into his pint and shook his head in pity at Fergus. Then he gestured to Thea that they should think about leaving.

'Oh God.' Thea went round the other side of the bar, helping Amelia and Doris to clear up. 'This is not ideal at all.'

'Did you know he had a girlfriend?' whispered Amelia.

'No! I have never seen her before in my life and he's never mentioned her.'

'It would seem like he's keeping a lot of secrets then, doesn't it?' Amelia tried to remain calm but she could feel anger rising from the knots in her stomach. She knew she should walk away but she remained rooted to the spot as she observed Fergus and Kelly's heated exchange. How could he have kissed her like that when he had a secret girlfriend on the side? How dare he do that to her? Did he get some kind of kick from leading her on?

'I've been worrying about you,' said Kelly coyly, fluttering her eyelashes.

'Oh, for God's sake. Will you look at that?' Thea shook her head in disgust. 'She's going to take someone out with them. They're like bloody branches.'

Amelia appreciated Thea's attempt to make light of the situation but she wanted to be sick.

'Grant, come and help us, will you?' Thea's voice was sharp. 'The bar is now shut.'

Grant hastily finished his pint and went round the tables collecting the glasses.

'Doris, will you be okay from here?' Thea clearly sensed she had to do something to move Amelia away from the situation.

'I can help too.' Cano magically appeared just at that moment. 'What needs to be done?'

'Oh, just the tables need putting away and the floors mopped,' said Doris gratefully.

'We can't leave Cano and Grant to do that all by themselves.' Amelia looked over at them. 'That's not fair.'

'We'll be fine,' insisted Cano. 'Come on, you ladies head off. It's been a long day.' He put a hand on Amelia's arm. 'Honestly. Leave us and we will organise it. I am glad you're wearing your trainers. It is not your shoes that are making you look sad.'

She smiled gratefully at him and shook her head. 'Thank you.'

He nodded at her and gave her a knowing smile. 'It will all be okay, Amelia.'

Fergus seemed to be trying to catch her eye but she completely ignored him. Inside, she shook with rage.

She pulled on her coat and Doris hugged her. 'Thank you so much for everything you did today. You're a superstar and we need to think about more work for you.'

Amelia kept a smile plastered on her face as she hugged Doris back.

'Amelia,' said Fergus gently. He touched her hand and she recoiled.

'Goodnight, Fergus.' Her voice was brisk and she couldn't meet his eyes.

'This is not what you think,' he said urgently. 'Look, I'll come over later and explain.'

Kelly wandered to his side, snaking an arm around his waist. He appeared to flinch. He looked at Amelia pleadingly.

'I'd rather you didn't, actually,' she said crisply. 'I'll catch you later.'

'Who's she?' Amelia heard Kelly ask as she walked away. 'Is there anything you need to tell me?'

Fergus didn't answer.

Amelia was shivering by the time she finally got back to Coorie Cabin. She glanced up at the cottage and, seeing Edie's bedroom light on, was glad to see her friend was home safely. She locked the cabin door behind her, wiped off her glittery make-up and pulled off her clothes, leaving them in a heap on the floor.

Then she stepped into the shower, letting the warm water slide over her. She angrily lathered her hair with shampoo, trying to forget how amazing Fergus's lips had felt on hers. How could she have been so stupid? She was an utter fool.

CHAPTER FORTY-NINE

Fergus couldn't quite believe what had happened and his heart ached when he remembered the look in Amelia's eyes. He hoped she would give him a chance to explain.

In the meantime, he needed to sort out this mess with Kelly, who waited for him in the bar at the hotel where she was staying for the night with her friends. When he arrived, he spotted her in the corner, nursing a glass of wine.

'Hi,' he said, taking a seat.

'I thought you would have been happier to see me.'

'You surprised me, that's all. I wished you'd called . . .'

'I did. Several times.'

He winced. He deserved that. 'I never meant to give you the wrong impression . . .' How could he tell her kindly that he'd *never* thought of her as his girlfriend? Never! 'I thought our understanding was casual?' Oh dear, he thought, wincing at his clumsy wording.

Kelly threw him a look. 'I thought it was more than that. I missed you, and when my friends suggested a trip, I thought I would surprise you. Which clearly I did.'

He shook his head. 'Sorry, Kelly. The last thing I would ever do is deliberately hurt you.'

'Is there someone else?'

He couldn't lie.

'Who is she?'

'Look, there hasn't been anyone else until recently.' He took a breath.

She shook her head in disgust. 'Well, good luck to her. That's all I can say.'

She glugged back the rest of her wine and stood up.

'I'm sorry.' What more could he say? He now felt completely awful as Kelly wiped away a tear.

'Nothing. I'm sorry I came.'

Fergus stood and reached towards her to give her a hug. But she recoiled, turned away and stomped off.

Fergus slipped back into his seat and shook his head. *Seriously?* What a mess of a night this had turned out to be. How could he explain to Amelia? Should he go and try and talk to her now? Or leave it until the morning? He nodded to Rob behind the hotel bar and left to make his way down to the beach. The waning moon cast a soft glow across the shore and he watched its reflection in the water. Standing at the edge, he bent down to pick up a pebble, which he skimmed across the flat surface. He watched it dance across the water, leaving circles rippling behind it. Then he picked up another, effortlessly throwing it and making it hop and skip.

He thought about earlier in the night when he and Amelia had kissed for the first time. It had been just as amazing as he'd thought it would be. There'd been such an easy, relaxed atmosphere between them. He'd been wanting to kiss her for a long time. Probably from the first moment he'd set eyes on her that night at the ferry terminal when she'd arrived. He felt a tug of impatience at how events had unfolded tonight. Surely he could do something to make it right again?

He skimmed a final pebble and listened to it plop into the water, and decided he would go to her and try to explain. Surely she'd understand once he'd told her the whole story? When he reached the gate, he pushed it open and walked quietly towards the cabin. But his heart sank when he saw it in darkness. Letting out a heavy sigh, he turned and walked back home.

CHAPTER FIFTY

Amelia didn't sleep well at all and spent most of the night tossing and turning. She stretched out her arms and lay thinking about Fergus, wondering if and when he might be in touch to offer an explanation. But her imagination started to run wild as she pictured him with Kelly, kissing her the way he had Amelia a few hours ago. She traced her fingers across her lips, remembering how good it felt.

Eventually she got up and cleaned the entire cabin. She wiped down the bathroom, sorted out the kitchen drawers and scrubbed the sinks, and organised her few items of clothing. After that she couldn't help pace restlessly. She remained furious, despite her attempts to keep busy. A girlfriend? Fergus and a girlfriend? Why had he lied to her? He'd had every opportunity to tell her the truth, yet managed to miss out that tiny but explosive detail. Honestly, what an eejit. Though perhaps it said more about her? She obviously attracted all the tossers.

A sharp knock at the door made her jump. Who on earth could that be? Her heart started to race in anticipation. Fergus? Could it be Fergus? *Oh, for God's sake, Amelia. Pull yourself together.* Maybe he wanted to explain. Might there be a logical explanation? There had to be. Why would he kiss her like that if he hadn't meant it? Even the thought of it sent tingles down her spine. Those kisses felt *special*. They definitely shared a connection; she hadn't imagined it. Yes, she told herself, Fergus was at the door to smooth things over and explain. She rushed over to open it, but as the door swung back, she gasped.

'What . . . wh-what are you doing here?'

'Well, that's not quite the reaction I expected,' he said, looking Amelia up and down. 'I thought you might be a bit happy to see me.'

'But . . . why? What are you doing here?' Amelia frowned in disbelief at Declan, who stood in the doorway of the cabin.

Declan had a nervous and worried expression on his face. 'I came to see you.'

'But how . . . how did you know where to find me?'

'Let's say that I have my sources.' He grimaced.

Amelia couldn't quite get her head round the fact Declan was stood here at her door in Arran. Oh God. Why was this happening? He was the last person she'd expected to turn up.

'Well, you might have called first to tell me you were coming, rather than turning up like this, Declan. I don't think this is fair at all.' Amelia knew she wasn't being particularly welcoming but what did he expect? He shivered and she noted, with disapproval, that he wore a thin jacket, hardly appropriate for the island's climate.

'Can I come in? Please?'

She stepped aside to let him in.

'Thanks. It's bloody freezing here.' He ducked under the doorframe as he came into the cabin. She'd forgotten how he filled a space with his height, and he seemed out of place here in her sanctuary, with his designer jeans and boots. He looked like he should be heading to a city wine bar. Yet it was Declan. Familiar Declan. And . . . what should she do? Was she supposed to hug him or kiss him?

'It's good to see you.' He smiled, leaning down to kiss her on the cheek. 'I've missed you. A lot.' His eyes flickered around the cabin as he took in her new surroundings.

They stood in awkward silence. Amelia's head began spinning. She couldn't work out why he had appeared so suddenly, after everything, and how he'd got here and what he wanted. Suddenly overwhelmed, what with last night's events and now this, her temper flared. 'What makes you think you can swan in here like this?' Her hands were firmly on her hips. 'After everything you've done.'

'You are right, and I can't even begin to apologise.' The corners of his mouth turned down, but his eyes were warmer.

As she looked at him, she remembered their wedding day and the way she'd gazed into those eyes. This was the man she'd promised to spend the rest of her life with. 'You broke my heart, Declan. You walked out on me and ignored all my calls. I hadn't even finished writing the thank-you notes for our wedding presents.'

'I know,' he said, clutching at her. 'I monumentally cocked everything up and I'm sorry. I'm so sorry.' He clammed up and wiped a tear away from the corner of his eye.

Declan had never cried in front of her before and his tears unsettled her. Being emotional was so unlike him. She let herself be drawn into his arms.

'Oh God, I am so sorry, Amelia. I love you.' His voice shook with nerves and he stroked her hair as he choked back another sob.

Then tears began to slide down her cheeks. After thinking that she had cried every last drop for this man, she surprised herself. Perhaps it was the mixture of pent-up hurt and sadness from these past few months and the emotion of last night. But standing there in his arms, she realised to her horror that she still had feelings for him.

He tightened his arms around her for a moment before he pulled away. Without another word, he reached down and kissed her gently on the lips. 'I've booked into the hotel at the bay.' He stood back from her. 'I appreciate this is a shock and I took a risk turning up like this. But I wanted to come and hold you and say sorry . . . and to ask if you would give us another chance.'

Amelia's mind whirred. 'But you owe me an explanation, Declan. You upped and left.'

'What I did was wrong. I panicked. I am a complete tool, Amelia. I realise that now. I just needed some space and some time to think.'

'But you should have done that with me. You should have been able to speak to me. I'm your wife. No, sorry, correct that. I used to be your wife . . .'

He looked at her intently. 'I didn't want to hurt you. I had to figure things out for myself.'

'But . . .'

'Look, Amelia, I'm at the hotel in the bay. I am booked in for the night. I'm on the ferry back tomorrow afternoon. I would love it if you came with me.'

Amelia had no idea what to think. Was his apology supposed to make the last few months disappear and make everything okay? Just like that?

'I didn't know what else to do. I'm sorry I turned up like this and shocked you. But I figured if I told you I was coming you'd have put me off. That's why I thought I would turn up and surprise you. I thought we might talk and try and sort this mess out.'

'Your mess, Declan. You caused all of this.' Amelia's heart thudded as anxiety and panic pooled in her stomach. Did she want this?

He held his hands up apologetically. 'You're right. I did. I take the blame for all of it.'

He drew her to him again. His familiar smell of cologne reassured her and she fleetingly wondered if she might make things work again with him?

CHAPTER FIFTY-ONE

Edie sensed something was afoot. Amelia had been keeping an extremely low profile since the Christmas fair. She'd expected her to pop in for a cup of tea or a chat but there had been no sign of her at all. After receiving a phone call from Doris, she soon realised why.

'Well, you certainly missed all the drama after you left, Edie,' she said breathlessly.

'What's that?' Edie didn't care much for gossip, but she knew to let Doris get whatever news she wanted to share off her chest.

Doris took a sharp breath. 'To be honest, you couldn't write the script. I felt as though I was watching an episode of *River City* or something like that.'

Edie rolled her eyes. Doris always did love a bit of drama.

'Santa only had eyes for your Amelia, which may possibly have been controversial if it had been Davey.'

'Any news on how Davey is?' enquired Edie.

'Yes, he's fine. Right as rain. Apparently he is a bit put out by his younger replacement. Did you know there was such a thing as Santa envy? Anyway,' she said, dismissively, 'the new Santa and Amelia looked rather friendly together . . . they were also spotted under the mistletoe.'

'Oh, for God's sake, Doris. It's hardly groundbreaking stuff.' Honestly, she did like to make a drama out of nothing. 'There was mistletoe everywhere due to the time of year.'

'Edie,' Doris said with a knowing tone. 'The mistletoe was merely the beginning.'

'Mmm, go on.' Edie moved to look out from her usual spot at the window. The sun was trying its hardest to break through those clouds.

'Someone claiming to be Fergus's girlfriend turned up. A woman called Kelly.'

'Oh,' Edie said, surprised. That wasn't a name she recognised.

'What do you think of that?' Doris said triumphantly. 'Do you know her? In fact, did you even know he had a girlfriend, because apparently it was breaking news to everyone else.'

Edie took a deep breath. 'And so?'

'Well, he didn't look happy at all to see her. The girlfriend. Well, not to begin with. Though soon enough they were certainly smooching for all and sundry to see.'

That didn't sound at all like Fergus, Edie thought, but let Doris continue.

'Kelly started to act very possessive. If looks could kill, Amelia, and in fact any other female within one hundred metres of Fergus, would be dead.'

'Okay . . . and then what happened?'

'The atmosphere was a tad frosty, to say the least. Young Amelia wouldn't meet Fergus's eye, although you could tell he desperately wanted to talk to her. Meanwhile, Kelly didn't leave his side. And Amelia made a sharp exit. She wasn't having any of his nonsense. I think she might even have been . . . *crying.*' She added the last word with dramatic effect.

Edie frowned. Poor Amelia. No wonder she'd not been seen today. Edie had noticed the pair of them last night at the fair looking amorous, though she wasn't letting on to Doris about any of that. It would only fuel her speculation. A mystery girlfriend turning up would have been a shock. Surely Fergus would be able to offer some kind of explanation?

Edie listened vaguely to Doris going off on a tangent about the ceilidh, while looking out at the garden. She smiled at the robin, hopping on top of the bench outside. Then her interest was piqued when she spotted a man she didn't recognise heading down the path.

'Meanwhile, I've popped off some of our other gin to Rob at the hotel. He needed some for the bar, and I overheard a handsome young man ask where to find Coorie Cottage. Well, actually, it was the shepherd's hut he specified.'

'Oh,' Edie said as she watched the man look around and make his way towards the cabin.

'And you're not going to believe this, Edie. Do you know who it is?'

Edie shook her head in irritation. In fact she had a good idea who the man was. This did not sound good at all. Sighing, she said, 'No, but I'm sure you're about to tell me.'

'It's Amelia's husband. I mean, did you even know she was married?'

Oh dear, thought Edie, the poor girl's head must be all over the place. 'Well, that's really none of our business, Doris, is it?'

'Well,' Doris spluttered. 'I thought you might be interested to hear a bit more about the woman living in your garden.'

Edie shook her head. 'Well, I'm not, Doris. I've never been interested in gossip. I thought you realised that. Whether Amelia is married or not is neither here nor there.'

'But this is all happening right under your nose. Aren't you intrigued to know what is going on?'

'No. And you shouldn't be either. Amelia worked wonders last night for you. If it hadn't been for her, you would still be trying to shift all those bottles of festive gin. She helped you because she is kind and has more integrity in her little finger than you do in your entire body. Please remember all of that.' Edie slammed down the phone angrily. No doubt that would be something else for Doris to gossip about, but honestly, sometimes she just went too far.

Edie looked out into the garden again. She couldn't help wonder what was going on in the cabin. Had Amelia's husband come to beg forgiveness and declare his undying love for her? And would she give him another chance? Perhaps their relationship was worth another go? Although what about the bond between Amelia and Fergus? Their gentle flirtation had surely done wonders to help heal their broken hearts? Edie didn't want Amelia to leave, for her own selfish reasons, but she was old enough and wise enough to know it was none of her business. Amelia needed to make the choices that were right for her.

In her reflective moments, she asked herself what she would have done if she had known about Jim's affair with Christine before he died. Would she have turned a blind eye? Or would she have left him? She would never know the answers and had decided that those questions were better left alone. There was no right or wrong, and she couldn't change the past. Instead, she had managed to forgive him and let it go for her own sake, otherwise she wouldn't have been able to move forward with her life. Being bitter would have destroyed her. She had coped with her sister's betrayal by pretending she didn't exist. That had been a good coping strategy until Christine got in touch.

Life, she'd learned, wasn't straightforward, and she couldn't throw away all those happy years of marriage they had shared together. They didn't simply disappear because of his betrayal. Jim had died but it didn't mean their marriage had to be erased, and the fact she could still feel his presence so strongly had to mean something, didn't it?

'Oh, Molly, I hope Amelia does the right thing for herself. I hope she puts her happiness before any sense of expectation or duty.' Molly wagged her tail and pressed her nose against the window. She started barking when she saw who was walking down the path.

'Oh dear.' Edie's eyes widened. 'It never rains but it pours.' Fergus was heading straight to the cabin. 'Time we busied ourselves elsewhere, I think. Come on, Molly, I need to go and do some sorting out upstairs.'

CHAPTER FIFTY-TWO

'You don't need to tell me your decision right now. Take some time to think,' said Declan.

'But what about my life here?'

'You've only been here for five minutes, Amelia. We've got a past and a history. We have a future to build. Remember our plans? To buy a house and settle down? We can start a family and even buy the puppy we always talked about.'

Amelia smiled sadly, but Declan took that as a sign to kiss her again. She flinched when she realised someone else now stood in the open doorway. Pulling away, her face flushed crimson when she saw Fergus watching.

He looked from her to Declan and back again. 'Sorry. I'm obviously interrupting something. I'll come back later.' His brow furrowed and he scowled. 'You're clearly busy.'

Amelia remained frozen to the spot. *How could this actually be happening?*

Declan watched him for a moment, assessing and thinking. He held out his hand. 'Hello, I'm Declan. Amelia's husband. And you are?'

'Fergus.' His voice was tense.

'Nice to meet you. Well, we're in the middle of something, mate.'

'I can see that.' He glared at Declan. 'I'll leave you to it.' His voice was sharp.

'I'll catch up with you later.' Amelia kept her voice even, reminding herself that Fergus was the one with the girlfriend. She hadn't done anything wrong.

'Don't worry — it's not important. Enjoy your time together.' His voice was flat and he wouldn't look at Amelia. He banged the door shut behind him.

A surge of anger rippled through her. How dare he act as though she had done something wrong. What about him? She may have a husband but he also had a girlfriend. At least she had been honest about Declan. Unlike him.

Declan raised an eyebrow. 'Something you want to tell me?'

The way he looked at her accusingly . . .

'He's a friend.'

'Looked like he was disappointed to find me here.'

'It's not any of your business, Declan.'

'I'm sorry.' He held up his hands. 'You're right.'

* * *

Amelia and Declan spent the rest of the afternoon talking, yet she still wasn't convinced that leaving with him to go back to London was the right decision. This was all too rushed and sudden. She needed more time. He was overly bright with her, and when she offered to cook some dinner, his comment over the lack of television irritated her.

'It's nice here,' he said softly. 'I can see why you came. Though I don't know how you've coped. I mean, it is pretty basic and you like your luxuries.'

'Maybe I've realised that simple is better.'

He yawned. 'How long were you going to hide out here?'

She turned from the sink and frowned. 'I wasn't aware I was hiding. I was just trying to pick up the pieces of my life, Declan. The one you trampled on.'

He had the grace to look embarrassed. 'You're right. I'm sorry, and it took guts to come over here on your own. Especially in the middle of winter. What are the locals like?'

'Great.' She smiled. 'Edie who lives in the cottage has been wonderful. Then Cano at the café has been a good friend. They've all been very kind.'

'That Fergus guy . . . is he just a friend?' He tried to keep his voice light, but there was a definite undertone to his question.

'Yes, he is.' She sighed and placed a bowl of pasta in front of him. 'I've already told you.'

'Thanks,' he said. 'Although I could have taken you for dinner at the hotel.'

That was the last thing Amelia wanted. She wasn't ready to be seen in public with Declan after last night. She wanted to keep her private life private. Declan looped his foot around hers as he twirled the fettuccine on his fork. It was comfortable and familiar and, after a glass of wine, she relaxed a bit and realised it was actually okay-ish.

'I think we can make this work.' His voice was earnest. 'I've got a new flat, which you'll love until we can buy our own place and . . .'

'I don't have a job though.'

'Yes, but you'll get one. I'm sure you will.'

Amelia's heart sank. Did she really want to go back to that existence? A marketing job in the city? That was real life, wasn't it? Doing things you didn't want to? Maybe she should just face up to reality. Sitting for a moment, she glanced around the cabin. Had she been deluded to think that a new life and fresh start was possible?

'Was there someone else?' she asked suddenly.

'No,' he said, shocked. 'Why would you think that?'

'Just one of the many thoughts I had, Declan, when I had time on my hands to pore over what I had done wrong. Did I push you away?'

He put down his fork and gripped her hands. 'No, please don't ever think that. You didn't do anything wrong. It was all me.'

Amelia yawned, emotionally exhausted with all the chatting they had done.

'I should go. You're tired.'

Amelia didn't challenge him. She wanted to collapse into bed and have another night here, especially as it might be her last one. She wanted to be alone.

'It's fine,' he said wearily. 'I don't have any expectations, Amelia. I want you to know how sorry I am. And I love you and you would make me the happiest man on earth if you would come back with me tomorrow.'

Amelia didn't answer.

'Sleep well.' He leaned in to kiss her and Amelia found herself kissing him back. But she couldn't get the image of Fergus out of her head.

CHAPTER FIFTY-THREE

After another restless night of tossing and turning, Amelia lay for a moment and watched the dark early morning sky gradually fade until it turned a pale grey. She sat up and reached for her journal and started to write.

What if I go with Declan? What if it works out and we make a go of our marriage . . . it could turn out to be the best thing I've done. It might be the most courageous decision I've made. Perhaps we'll look back and have something to tell our children and our grandchildren. Our marriage may have had a rocky start but surely that makes our story more interesting, doesn't it? But what if I'm acting from a place of fear? What if I'm doing this because I'm too scared to be on my own?

But you have been on your own, Amelia. You came to Arran and made a life for yourself. You're not weak, you're strong and proud. You must do what is right for you.

But what if things all go wrong? What if I make a mistake? What if, what if, what if . . . it all goes wrong? I can come back, can't I? Or go somewhere else? Surely the biggest lesson I have learned in all of this is that I am stronger than I think. I will always be okay. The question is, what if I go back with Declan? Will it be different?

What if I'm not happy? I can leave. What if I don't like being back in London? We can leave. I can leave. What if I don't go?

She looked out of the window thoughtfully and chewed her pen for a moment.

If I don't go, I will always be left wondering what if? I might regret not trying out what if?

A tight coil of emotion lodged in her throat as she realised she had made her decision.

She closed her journal and got out of bed, pulling on some clothes. She wanted to have one last walk along the beach.

The air was cold and she inhaled the tangy, salty scent as she made her way down the garden path. Her hand rested on the wrought-iron gate and she closed her eyes, willing herself to remember this moment forever. Opening them, she gazed over at the Holy Isle, saddened that she hadn't managed to make the trip. Perhaps she would return one day. But in her heart of hearts, Amelia knew that if she left with Declan there would be no returning. Was she really able to give all of this up? Just like that?

She walked along the shore, studying the lacy trail the tide left over the pebbles as the water gently pulled in and out, and hoping she could commit these pictures to memory for ever. The water was still and she half wondered if she might see Fergus having an early swim. But the beach and the sea were deserted. She walked briskly, crunching over the shells and listening to the sounds, which she'd started to take for granted. The lapping water, the shrieking and swooping gulls overhead, the sound of cars up on the road. She knew she should really go to the café and say goodbye to Cano and Thea at the very least. But she couldn't face them, which made her a coward. They would find out soon enough from Edie, though it wasn't fair to leave her to tell them. Oh, Edie, how on earth was she going to break the news to her? That was going to be the hardest part of all of this.

She drank in the view once more, taking a few last photos with her phone. There were several messages from Jack, checking she was okay. She'd answered briefly and said she was busy but she would be in touch. She couldn't face getting into it all right now and explaining what had happened. She felt utterly drained. She was about to walk back to the cottage when she heard someone call her name. She waited and looked back. For a moment, when she saw his face, she remembered the man she loved, or used to love. That was what confused her. She didn't know anymore.

He jogged along the shore to join her. 'Hi,' he said. 'I couldn't wait any longer.'

Amelia squirmed. She had just wanted to enjoy this last walk here on her own.

'Have you made your decision?' he said earnestly.

She looked at him, smiled and nodded.

CHAPTER FIFTY-FOUR

The late morning sunshine cast a warm glow on Edie's kitchen and Amelia paused to look through the window and watch for a moment. The scene comforted her, and Edie had been such a huge support to her. Could she really just walk away?

Knocking on the door, she opened it and walked in, kicking her shoes off and leaving them by the mat. She couldn't help but think back to that wet night when she'd arrived and how welcome Edie had immediately made her. If only she could rewind to that night and relive every second of her time here. She hovered in the doorway, feeling the warm tiles underfoot, smelling the shortbread scent of the kitchen and the burning logs in the stove.

'Hi, dear, come on in. Nice to see you.'

Amelia smiled awkwardly.

'How are you?' Edie cocked her head, trying to read Amelia's conflicted expression.

She shrugged. 'Ah, Edie. I'm not quite sure . . .'

'What about?'

'Declan, my husband — or ex-husband, I'm not sure what he is — turned up yesterday. He was the last person I expected to turn up at my door.'

'Oh . . . and how did that make you feel?'

'Angry, hurt . . . all those feelings came flooding back again. Yet also happy. I was happy to see him, Edie, and relieved.' She held herself still and steadied her breathing. 'He wants us to give our marriage another go,' she said flatly. 'That's why he's here. He's rented a flat in London and wants me to go back with him and try again.'

Edie looked taken aback for a moment, though quickly regained her composure. 'Okay, dear.' She looked intently at her. 'And what do *you* want, Amelia?'

'I think I still love him, Edie. Don't I owe it to him and myself to give us another go?'

* * *

There were lots of things Edie wanted to say but didn't. She couldn't bear to see Amelia get hurt again by her so-called husband. What sort of man walked away from his marriage and ignored calls from his heartbroken wife? Then just arrived and snapped his fingers for her to go running.

Amelia sighed. 'Look, I know what you're probably thinking, but he's had a hard time of things lately. He said there was stuff he had to deal with at work, which wasn't helping his frame of mind, and he couldn't think straight. I have to believe the nice man that I married is still in there, and he's shown me a glimpse of that . . . I don't want to look back and think that I didn't try hard enough. I don't want to look back and think what if . . .'

'Only you can decide, Amelia. I just know that we will all be sorry to say goodbye. Me especially, but Fergus too . . .'

'I know.' She wiped away a tear. 'He's been a good friend to me and I thought there was something more between us. But I think I got that wrong too. I seem to be making a mess of everything at the moment, Edie.'

'Oh, love.' Edie drew her into a gentle embrace.

'I'll miss everyone. Cano and Naza and Thea and Grant. Edie, I can't bear the thought of saying goodbye to them. I feel awful and cowardly, but will you explain for me?'

Edie nodded, against her better judgement. 'They will be gutted not to see you before you go but I'm sure they'll understand. You've made good friends here. Doris, on the other hand . . .' Edie shook her head.

Amelia laughed and then shrugged reluctantly. 'I will write to them all properly.' Her hand flew to her mouth. 'Cano! I said I would help him out when Naza goes to the mainland next month . . .'

'Don't worry, he will understand.'

Amelia shook her head in despair. 'It's a lot more complicated than that, Edie. The night of the fair . . . Fergus and I kissed and I thought we had a connection. Then his girlfriend arrived.'

'Don't worry about any of that. Fergus is a big boy. This is about you and what you want.'

'Edie, I promise to keep in touch with you. I will never forget your kindness and support.'

'When are you leaving?'

'Any minute. Declan is picking me up.'

Edie gulped. 'So soon?'

'I'm sorry. He's booked on the ferry. He's booked flights to London.'

Edie raised an eyebrow. 'Did he presume he would win you back?'

Amelia grimaced. 'I have tidied the cabin . . . and left it ready for your first guests. Now the website is up and running, all you need to do is decide when you want to make dates available and I can still help with that remotely.'

'Okay,' said Edie. The thought of anyone living in the garden other than Amelia was not appealing. She cleared her throat. 'Are you absolutely sure about this?'

Amelia didn't answer, then was distracted by her phone beeping. 'It's him. He's just leaving the hotel.'

'What about Fergus?'

'What do you mean?'

'Aren't you going to say goodbye?'

'I'm sure he won't notice I'm gone.'

* * *

The truth was, she couldn't face seeing him, it would be too hard. She'd been kidding herself that she and Fergus could have a future together. They both had too many issues and too much baggage — and she had a husband.

Edie put a supportive hand on Amelia's arm. 'You are sure about this?' she asked again.

Amelia went quiet and couldn't quite meet Edie's eyes as she shrugged. 'I think so.'

The doorbell rang. 'That will be Declan.'

Reluctantly she trailed her way down the hallway behind Edie. Molly must have sensed the sombre mood as her tail was down and firmly tucked between her legs.

'Is this all you've got?' Declan said, lifting up her rucksack which was sitting by the door.

'Yes, that's it. Declan, this is Edie. Edie, meet Declan.'

'Nice to meet you,' he said, extending his hand.

Amelia watched as Edie took his hand without her usual warmth. Molly sniffed around his feet and Amelia could tell Declan was antsy about her putting a muddy paw on his designer jeans.

'Well, we'd better get going. We don't want to miss the ferry and be stuck here.'

Amelia flinched at his words and smiled apologetically at Edie, but she just looked back warmly at her.

Amelia fought back the tears. This was much harder than she'd expected it to be.

'I'll give you a minute,' said Declan. 'Bye, Edie.'

Amelia lifted her gaze sadly to Edie and then gave her a warm hug. The women clutched each other tightly, neither wanting to let go.

'Now you remember you will always be welcome here, Amelia,' Edie said fiercely. 'You will always have a place to stay here when you need it. I will never forget what you did for me and how much you helped me with my sister. I am always here if you need me. Remember that.'

'Thank you, and I will. I promise.'

As they walked outside, Amelia took one last look around at Edie's garden, patted Molly and took a dramatic breath of the salty air. 'How I will miss that smell. And how I'm going to miss you, Edie.' She looked at the car and then back at the cottage, and was about to say something about passing on a message to Fergus, but stopped. There seemed little point.

'Take care, my love. Safe travels . . . and . . . Amelia?'

'Yes?'

'Be happy, my dear.'

'Thanks for everything.' Amelia nodded, the tears now stinging her eyes.

She climbed into the hire car, and as Declan turned out of the driveway and waited to turn right onto the main road, she spotted an orange van driving past. It was Fergus. But he didn't look her way and she was glad.

CHAPTER FIFTY-FIVE

Edie stood in the doorway watching until they had driven away; she couldn't help but feel sad. Saying goodbye to people was becoming a recurring theme in her life these days. She walked over to the holly bush by the gate, pleased to notice it was now bearing red berries. Yet it didn't feel like Christmas. Not now Amelia had gone. She had been looking forward to putting the tree up and decorating it with her. Maybe she would just give it a miss altogether this year. She didn't feel like celebrating.

She went back inside, calling Molly to come with her, and closed the door. Leaning against it for a moment, she wiped the tears from her eyes. Sighing, she wandered back through to the kitchen, and the silence that greeted her was broken only by Molly's intermittent whines. Edie curled up in her seat by the window and the dog lay her head on Edie's lap, sensing her sadness. Scratching Molly's ears, Edie looked down at her beloved pet. 'It's just you and me, Molly.' She glanced out of the window. 'I just hope Amelia is doing the right thing.'

Something about Declan's sudden arrival and his subsequent haste to leave and get back to London unsettled her. What was the rush? Why wasn't he giving Amelia any time to get her head around it all? And what had made her suddenly change her mind and leave so quickly? Edie knew Declan's type. The way he'd touched her on the arm when he spoke to her, as though he was trying to reel her in with his charm. Edie was far too long in the tooth for that nonsense. But she didn't want to show her disapproval to Amelia. That wouldn't be fair.

She thought Amelia had been happy here; the young woman had started to blossom and flourish compared to the uncertain and pale girl who had arrived just a couple of months ago. When Edie thought back to how nervous and reticent she'd seemed, it was obvious that her stay at Coorie Cabin had rejuvenated her and done what it said it would on the tin. She had become serene and calm and joyful. Edie was puzzled as to why things would so rapidly change. Unless of course Amelia truly was still in love with her husband, despite everything. Of all people, Edie knew how love could indeed be blind.

She looked out across the bay with a sense of foreboding as the dark clouds gathered overhead. Amelia's arrival and her company had been wonderful, their subsequent friendship unexpected but so welcome at a time when Edie had really needed her. She couldn't help but feel bereft. But that was life. At least Amelia had done an amazing job with Coorie Cabin, and in the New Year she would launch the website for her. It was just such a shame that she would miss the Christmas Eve ceilidh.

Maybe I'll give it a miss too. What was the point? She had seen everyone she wanted to at the fair and to be honest she was tired. The fair had taken more out of her than she'd thought. She had to remind herself that she was only just processing Christine's death and that it was no wonder she was exhausted. Grief could overwhelm you, and all the complicated emotions around their reunion and her sister's death were all so very fresh. She knew it would take a long time for her to process the feelings.

As she sat watching clouds darken and the afternoon light fade, she began to doze, but smiled when she felt the warmth of the sun on her eyelids. She briefly fluttered them open and noticed another rainbow.

CHAPTER FIFTY-SIX

Amelia clambered heavily up the stairs from the car deck behind Declan, feeling like a petulant child. Oblivious to her sorrowful mood, Declan muttered that he would go and get some coffees.

'Okay. I just want to go outside and get some fresh air,' she said. Her tone had turned snippy and she pulled away as he reached to kiss her.

'I'll meet you outside,' he said, and grimaced.

Amelia knew he hated the thought of being outside in the cold temperatures for any longer than absolutely necessary. But she didn't care. She wanted to make the most of the salty air while she could. Outside, the sky was low and grey, and the diminishing view of Arran made her want to weep as she watched it slowly move further away from her. Her heart contracted. Surely she shouldn't feel so bereft about this decision, should she? Leaving to return with Declan was her choice. In a bid to distract herself she sent a quick text to Suna.

Guess who's on the way to the airport to catch a flight to London?

She put her phone back into her bag when she spotted Declan walking towards her with two coffees.

'I'll be glad to get a decent cup of coffee when we're back in London,' he said, shivering and looking at the sky in disgust. 'Looks like there's going to be a downpour any minute.'

'There was nothing wrong with the coffee at the café. In fact it was one of the best cups I've tasted.' His comments had once again irritated her.

'At least you'll be able to appreciate some decent shops again,' he said, clearly trying to lighten the mood. 'Did you miss them? I know how much you love shopping.'

She shook her head. 'I haven't missed them a bit.' Amelia stared at the choppy, dark waters, which unsettled her stomach. When the raindrops started to fall, she conceded defeat and went inside. Once again she followed behind Declan, dragging her heels, and they found a seat in the café. They made the rest of the journey in an awkward silence, and when they got into the taxi at the ferry terminal, she pretended to be asleep. But instead of a restful slumber, her mind whirred with a mix of complicated thoughts. All she'd ever wanted was to settle down with Declan and start a family, and she'd never questioned that life may have different plans in store for her.

She bit her lip as she remembered walking down the aisle towards the man she was going to spend the rest of her life with. When she'd told him later that night that she couldn't wait to start a family with him, he hadn't been quite as overjoyed as she'd thought, given that she thought they were on the same page about having a baby. The amazing scenario she'd envisaged in her head, where he would gather her in his arms lovingly, hadn't quite transpired. His face had paled and he'd gone quiet, eventually coming round after a while and smiling and kissing her tenderly on the lips. But when her mind dwelled on that scene, she realised that it had been a precursor of what was to come. Perhaps if she was really being honest, then the news that he was leaving her shouldn't have come as such a big surprise . . .

Why oh why did she now feel as if she was making a huge mistake? Why had she let herself be talked into this? *Because, Amelia,* she told herself, *you have been over this, and if you didn't come back with Declan you would always have wondered what if?* She reached over to clasp his hand, reminding herself that she needed to try a bit harder. He had come to her and begged forgiveness and repeatedly apologised. If they were going to get through this, they needed to move forward and that meant she had to forgive and forget.

At the airport she went to buy a magazine for the journey while Declan hung around the departure lounge. She'd always been an anxious flyer and so wanted to distract herself with some of the glossy mags. Just as she put her purse away, she frowned when she saw her phone flashing. It had been on silent and when she pulled it from her bag, she realised there were several missed calls and text notifications from Suna. She opened the messages.

Call me now. Urgent!!!
Please call now xx
Amelia I really need to spk with u x

She dialled her number and it rang once before Suna answered.

'Suna!'

'Oh, thank God, Amelia. Where are you?'

'At Glasgow Airport . . .'

'What?' she screeched. 'What in God's name are you doing there?'

'I'm . . . I'm coming back. That's what I said in my text.'

'But why?'

'What do you mean?' she said, confused. 'Do you mean you don't know? I thought you told him where to find me?'

'What are you talking about?'

'Declan turned up on Arran yesterday. I have no idea how he knew where I was. I assumed you told him.'

'No.' She sounded shocked. 'I wouldn't have told him. No way. Absolutely not.'

Amelia detected a trace of venom in her voice, which was unlike her.

'Please tell me you are not abandoning your idyllic island life to return with that shitbag.'

'Suna, what's wrong? This isn't like you. I thought you liked Declan?'

'I did until he left you, and then . . .'

Amelia's heart had started racing. 'And then what . . . Suna, what is it?'

'Look, I have been trying to work out what to do about this. This is why I've been avoiding your calls and texts these past few weeks. I'm so sorry. I was just glad that you sounded like you were happy and settled. It sounded like the perfect place to go to try to heal your broken heart . . .'

'But . . .' said Amelia, sharply.

'But . . . Look, I just wish you weren't coming back.' Her words were harsh.

'Oh.'

'Not because I don't want to see you. Of course I do. God, I miss you, Amelia.'

'Then what?' She looked across at Declan. He watched her, a concerned expression on his face.

'Look, you may never want to speak to me again after I tell you this. But if I were you, I would rather know. Especially as you're giving everything up again for him . . . and coming back. I mean, after everything . . . Amelia, you obviously love your new life. I haven't heard you so happy for months and I won't let him ruin it for you.'

Declan was now hopping anxiously from one foot to the other. He looked at her and tapped his watch. He always liked to be near the front when they announced the flight was ready to board.

'Suna, if you've got something to tell me, please do it quickly. They're about to announce the flight is boarding . . .'

CHAPTER FIFTY-SEVEN

Declan tapped his fingers on his watch, gesturing at her to hurry up even though their flight still hadn't been called.

Amelia's face drained of colour as she listened to what Suna had to say. After a few minutes she thanked her and slid her phone into her bag. She remained serene as she slowly walked towards Declan.

'When did you plan to tell me?' she said quietly.

'Tell you what?' He sounded confused.

'Well, the truth would be a good place to start.' She became aware of a few passengers murmuring from the seats opposite but didn't care. She glowered pointedly at Declan.

'What do you mean? I don't know what you're talking about . . .'

At that point, an announcement was made that the flight would soon be ready for boarding. People started bustling around them. 'We should go,' he said, his voice tight with impatience, and he placed a hand on her arm.

Amelia shook it off. 'I'm not going anywhere until you tell me the truth.'

'Come on, Amelia. Don't make a scene,' he urged. Declan always hated fuss and attention, but Amelia didn't care.

'When were you going to tell me?'

'I have no idea what you are talking about.' Yet his confidence started to wane, and he no longer looked so sure of himself.

'When. Were. You. Going to tell me the truth? The truth about you and Cara?'

His face crumpled and he looked utterly stricken.

She shook her head in pity. 'Did you *really* think I wouldn't find out?'

'Would passengers in rows twenty-five to forty-five now come forward, please?'

'Come on. Let's get on the plane and we can chat about this when we're home.'

'No way. I'm not going anywhere with you.'

'You tell him, love,' said a woman standing within earshot.

'Move out the way of everyone,' Amelia said, pulling him to the side and away from the small queue that now snaked around them. 'I am not getting on the plane with you unless you tell me now.'

He rolled his eyes and finally spoke. 'Okay. I admit it's not something I'm proud of. I panicked . . .'

'Panicked?'

'Look, I'd rather not talk about this here. It's not the time or place.'

Amelia laughed bitterly. 'When is the time and place, Declan? You had plenty of opportunity to tell me this before. Like yesterday when you came begging, or this morning when I wasn't sure about leaving. Or the day you walked out . . . or the weeks after when you ignored all my calls. You had ample time to tell me.'

An older lady tutted and shook her head at Declan as she made her way towards the flight attendant.

'I thought we'd rushed into things with trying for a family . . . It all came so soon after the wedding. I panicked. You were so focused on the wedding and the bloody flowers and then having a baby . . .'

'But we talked about wanting a family. It was what we both wanted.'

'Well, maybe I just went along with it,' said Declan quietly.

'So this is all my fault? Is that what you're saying?'

'Eejit,' said another passenger, giving him a withering look.

'No, that's not what I'm saying. The thing with Cara was a mistake. But it was hardly my fault.'

Did he actually just say that? Amelia shook herself. *He slept with Cara, and now he's trying to say none of it was his fault.*

'Okay . . . are you telling me I am to blame?'

'No, not at all . . .'

'But you are completely contradicting yourself with every word that comes out of your mouth.'

'I made a mistake,' he yelled.

'How many mistakes did you make, Declan? Just the one or were there several mistakes?'

He looked towards the dwindling queue of passengers, clearly in a panic. The departure lounge had almost emptied.

'And to walk out with no explanation. How do you think that made me feel?'

He hung his head in shame.

'This was a mistake,' Amelia said. 'I should never have come back with you. When will I learn to follow my instincts?'

'I'm sorry . . .'

'So you keep saying, Declan, but are you?' Amelia paused before speaking again, this time in a hushed voice. 'Did you sleep with her in our bed?'

He didn't reply.

'And you think you can snap your fingers and expect me to come running back? You walked out on me three months after our marriage with no explanation. You didn't return any of my calls or messages. You left me wondering what I had done wrong. And you betrayed me with one of our friends. A guest at our bloody wedding, Declan. You made those vows in front of her knowing you'd cheated. Did you have a right good laugh about it all?' Her eyes blazed in anger. 'Did you know I was going to lose my job before I did? Did you include that as part of the pillow talk?' He wouldn't meet her eyes. 'Wow. Then you walked out as soon as your guilt got the better of you and knowing I had lost my job. You are weak and pathetic.'

'This is a final announcement for any passengers joining the flight to Heathrow. This is your final call.' The airline steward was looking pointedly in their direction.

'Please go, Declan. It's over.'

Declan looked utterly dejected. He gazed pleadingly at her one last time. 'I am sorry, Amelia. I really am.'

'Goodbye, Declan.' This time she turned and walked away and didn't look back.

CHAPTER FIFTY-EIGHT

Amelia made her way back out of Departures. She went straight to the ladies and, once inside a cubicle, burst into tears. She wiped her face, laughing when she realised they were tears of relief rather than sadness. *I knew I didn't want to go with him. When will I learn to trust my intuition?* Thank goodness she had taken her rucksack on as hand luggage, otherwise she would have nothing. But Amelia realised she didn't need anything. Who cared about stuff? What did it matter?

Sitting there in the cramped toilet at Glasgow Airport, she began to laugh.

Amelia tried not to make eye contact with her reflection as she washed her hands vigorously under the taps. However, when she glanced at herself she was pleasantly surprised that she looked better than expected. She splashed some cold water on her face and smiled. She would work through this. She was strong, and she didn't need a bloody man to mess up her life again. Particularly that man. Thank God for Suna. She quickly sent her a text to tell her all was okay, to thank her and let her know she would be in touch. Now she understood why Suna had been a bit off with her these past weeks. Her poor friend just hadn't known what to do for the best. What a stressful situation to have been in.

What should she do now? It was late and dark in December, and she was stuck at an airport in a city she hardly knew. She thought for a moment, then walked back through to the main building, smiling at the man polishing the concourse next to the check-in desks. The Christmas trees and flashing lights seemed out of place in her current state of mind. What a crazy couple of days.

She found a chair to sit on and took a breath. Pulling out her mobile, she pressed call.

'Edie. It's me. Amelia.'

'Oh, hello, my lovely. How are you?'

'I'm okay,' she said, laughing. 'In fact, I'm great.'

'Oh,' said Edie, sounding bemused. 'That's nice, dear.'

'The thing is. Well, Edie, I'm still at Glasgow Airport.'

'Oh, is your flight delayed?'

'I didn't get on the plane.'

'Did you miss it? Was the ferry late? Honestly, you just never can tell. And sometimes the traffic . . .'

'No, Edie. We got to the airport on time and I will tell you the whole story later . . . but I couldn't go back with him.'

'Oh. What happened?'

'It's a long story and one I will tell you when I see you, Edie. But I don't want to leave you and my friends and Arran,' said Amelia, smiling. 'I love it. I can't remember when I was last this happy.'

'I don't know what to say . . .'

'Can I come back, Edie? Can I come back and stay in the cabin? Just until I sort myself out?'

'Oh, Amelia, you don't even have to ask,' she said. 'You're always welcome here and there will always be a place for you to stay as long as you want. You can tell me all about it when you're back, that's if you want to. But I am so pleased you're coming home.'

Amelia choked back a sob as she realised that was what had changed. It did feel like home. Arran was a place she felt like she truly belonged.

Edie coughed. 'Erm, there's one slight problem though, dear.'

Amelia didn't care, she felt invincible, and she so appreciated Edie's lack of probing about what had happened. 'Go on, tell me about it. What's the problem?'

'Well, dear, you have missed the last ferry for the night.'

Try as she might, Amelia couldn't stop the huge roar of laughter that escaped. 'In that case I will see you tomorrow. I'll be back as soon as I can.'

CHAPTER FIFTY-NINE

Edie hung up the phone, thrilled that Amelia was returning, though not happy at the thought of what had happened to make her come back. She made Amelia promise to go and check in at an airport hotel and text her when she was safely in her room. She knew Amelia was desperate to get back as soon as possible, but it would have to wait until the morning. As her mother always used to say to her, good things came to those who waited.

She hoped Amelia would come back stronger than ever. It did sound as though the brief trip to the airport with Declan had clarified things for her. 'Who knows what happened to trigger such a quick return,' she said to Jim's photo. *But I'm glad. I already miss her.*

Since Christine's letter and subsequent passing, she realised there was no point in carrying around resentment or anger, and she hoped Amelia would accept what had happened with Declan and move on. She had learned that being angry only added to your burden. Acknowledging the hurt and taking care of it in the best way for you was the least damaging way forward. She hoped she could perhaps guide Amelia to forgive and move on.

'Well, Molly, this is exciting news. She's coming back.' Molly thumped her tail on the floor and jumped up and ran to the door. Edie turned and jumped when she saw Fergus standing there.

'Sorry, Edie, I didn't mean to give you a fright. I knocked and called out.'

'Oh, don't worry. I was miles away. Is everything okay, dear?'

'Yes. Though I wondered if you'd seen Amelia? The cabin's in darkness.'

Oh-oh, thought Edie. *What on earth do I tell him?* 'Cup of tea?' she said, turning to fill the kettle.

'Erm, okay, though I wasn't planning to stop. I'm just keen to see Amelia. We didn't leave things on great terms . . .'

Edie ignored him. 'Fergus, dear, while you're here, would you mind awfully checking the smoke alarm for me at the top of the stairs, please? It's been beeping away and I'm worried the batteries need replacing. It's a wee bit too high up for me to reach.'

'Of course, I'll do that now.' He scratched his head.

Edie mentally made a list of other tasks she could give him to do to wave him off Amelia's scent. It wasn't her place to tell him, yet she also felt awkward about lying.

He walked into the kitchen. 'I've checked it over and the batteries seem okay. I wonder why it's been beeping.'

'Perhaps I dreamt it or imagined the noise? Thanks anyway . . . So how are you, dear? I heard you had an unexpected visitor at the fair.'

He cocked his head to the side.

'News travels fast,' she said, her voice warm and amused.

His face darkened. 'That's what I want to talk to Amelia about. I called in earlier and her husband was visiting. I'm desperate to apologise. When will she be back?'

'Um, I'm not quite sure.'

'Are you sure you don't know where she is? I mean, it's dark and getting late.'

'What kind of tea do you want? Your usual? Builder's?' Crikey, this was getting awkward.

'That's fine.'

'Biscuits?' Molly looked up. 'Not for you, silly, for Fergus.'

'Tea is fine, thanks. Edie, is something wrong?'

'No, no, what makes you say that?'

'You're acting strangely.'

'Nothing new then.' She forced a laugh. 'Sit down.' She placed a mug of tea beside Fergus. 'Are you going to tell me about the mystery lady? Seems Doris is in a right fankle wondering who she is.'

He rubbed his hand over his jaw. 'A friend I hadn't seen for a while from the mainland.'

'A *friend?* The rumour is that the mystery lady is your girlfriend.'

'Well, she isn't. At least not anymore. We broke up ages ago. Look, it's all a complete misunderstanding.' He sighed. 'Edie, what's going on? Where's Amelia?'

She paused while she took a sip of tea, then bit into a square of shortbread. She chewed slowly.

'Edie . . . look, forget it. I'll phone her later on. That's probably easier.'

'No, don't do that,' she said. That was the last thing Amelia needed. The girl could do with a night's rest. 'Sit down and I'll tell you . . .'

He looked at her quizzically.

'She had to go to Glasgow today on some business. She hoped to catch the last ferry home but missed it. She'll be back in the morning.'

'Some business? With her husband?'

'Yes. That's all I know.' Edie blinked furiously. She was rubbish at lying.

'Right.'

'Mmm. She can tell you.'

He looked at her thoughtfully. 'The thing is, Edie, I don't like to put two and two together and make mistakes but . . .'

'Then don't, Fergus,' she snapped, more in frustration at her inability to throw him off the scent. 'This is none of our business and Amelia will tell you what she wants to in her own time.' She stretched her arms up and yawned, looking at her watch. 'Now, if you'll excuse me, I had better go to bed. I will tell her you called in when I see her tomorrow and I'm sure she'll be in touch.'

'Okay, I hear you,' he said, draining his mug. 'Thanks for the tea. Just tell her . . .'

She gave him a knowing smile. 'I will.'

CHAPTER SIXTY

The next morning, after a night at a hotel next to the airport where she'd slept surprisingly well, Amelia made her way back to Arran.

Once again she stood on the deck of the ferry, gripping the handrail, thinking about the surreal turn of events. Was it really only yesterday she had made this journey in reverse with Declan? What *had* she been thinking? It seemed like a bad dream. Now, as she tasted the salt air on her lips and watched the cormorants dive into the water, she was certain she had made the right choice. Her thoughts no longer swirled, and a sense of calm had descended when she boarded the boat.

She'd pulled her journal out on the train to the port and scribbled down some of her thoughts, which she reflected on as the boat sluiced through the water.

> *That was a gift. If he hadn't come for me I would always wonder what more I could have done. Now I know I did everything I could. And with that knowledge I can truly and freely move on with my life. Today is the day that I start to love myself completely and unconditionally. I deserve great things to happen and this has been a gift.*

She opened a magazine on a page with a feature on infidelity, and laughed as she read an article that may as well have been written for her.

WHY I CHEATED ON MY NEW WIFE
Suzie and Thomas were newly married when he found himself in bed with another woman.

We were only married for a few weeks when once again I found myself in bed with one of my wife's friends. There had been plenty of flirting before the wedding, and we had a one-night stand. Then after our wedding I bumped into her at the local pub near my office and I realised I still wanted her. It was never meant to be anything serious, just a little fun. I still loved my wife and had never cheated on her before we were engaged. Some of my friends had been with their partners for ages and had never felt the urge to cheat. And I had never been tempted before. Perhaps it was just the pressure of the wedding or having to settle down. I guess I felt a bit trapped. We carried on our affair after the wedding. Even though we had an amazing honeymoon and I swore to myself it would never happen again, it did. My wife was never suspicious. She trusted me completely. I don't think she ever thought I would cheat on her, never mind with a mutual friend. For that I felt awful and had to do something. Except I didn't want to end our marriage. I loved her. But I couldn't sleep for worry. I hated myself.

So I left and said I wasn't happy. I didn't tell her that I'd been having an affair as I didn't want to hurt her. Her friends and family were furious at the way I had ended things. But how could I stay with her when I had acted so badly. It was only when I left that I realised what a huge mistake I had made. I wanted her back. But she found out from someone else that I had been unfaithful and wouldn't speak to me. Our marriage never got off to a happy start because of the affair and though I finished things, it also meant the end of my marriage.

The words resonated with Amelia, and she knew she wasn't entirely blameless for the demise of her marriage.

Maybe she should have noticed that Declan was acting weirdly. He hadn't been sleeping well and she'd put it down to his stressful job. That's when she realised her head had been in the sand. She'd been so focused on having a perfect wedding and happy ever after that she didn't notice what was right in front of her. It was better she'd found all of this out sooner rather than later. What would have happened if she'd found out after they'd had kids?

She smiled as the ferry sailed into Brodick. She looked up at Goatfell, which was still on her to-do list. There was so much she wanted to do, and she choked back a sob as happiness surged through her. The announcement of their imminent arrival at the pier drew her from her thoughts. She couldn't wait to hug Edie.

As soon as she stepped off the gangplank and saw Edie waiting for her, she was absolutely certain she had done the right thing.

Edie flung her arms around her. 'It's wonderful to see you.' When they got into the car, Edie reached over and patted her arm. 'You should be proud of yourself. Look at what you've done. You uprooted from your life and came here to this wee place in the middle of winter. This is about you now and settling where *you* want to and where *you're* happy.'

Amelia smiled, feeling hugely reassured by her words. As they joined the procession of cars waiting to exit the car park, she looked at Edie in the driver's seat and gave her a quizzical look. 'Did you say anything to anyone else?'

The older woman shook her head. 'Fortunately not . . . so your secret is safe with me. Although . . .'

Amelia looked over at Edie with a wary expression. 'Yes?'

'Fergus realised you'd gone to the mainland.'

'But how?'

'Mmm. He came to see you but you weren't there. I said you'd gone to Glasgow on business but would be back. I didn't tell him any of the details and nobody else knows you left.'

'Did he think I went away with Declan?' Her voice was slightly wobbly.

'It's none of his business. He can think what he likes,' Evie said dismissively.

'That's true.' Amelia reminded herself that she didn't owe anyone an explanation, least of all Fergus with his secret girlfriend.

'Don't worry about him. I'm sure you'll think of something.'

'Did you meet his girlfriend?'

'He doesn't have a girlfriend.'

'But the girl at the fair. She told everyone that she was his girlfriend.'

Edie's lips pursed. 'Well, she isn't. Wishful thinking on her part.'

'Though Fergus must have given her that impression?'

She shrugged. 'None of our business. Anyway, you don't need to worry about her. She's away back to the mainland.'

Amelia thought it best not to push things, and she clasped her hands in her lap and focused on the scenery as they drove along the tree-canopied road. When they came round the corner and reached the top of the hill, Amelia gazed contentedly at the view of the Holy Isle. 'That's also on my to-do list.'

Edie chuckled. 'I'm glad to hear it, though I would leave it now until the spring when the crossing will be a bit calmer.' She indicated to turn into the drive of Coorie Cottage. 'Home sweet home. And I know someone else who will be delighted to see you.'

'Molly?' Amelia smiled.

CHAPTER SIXTY-ONE

Amelia took her time to unpack her bag and arrange her things in the cabin. All she needed was right here. A wave of excitement rippled through her. This place was home. She stared out the window at the view she would never tire of and wondered how she could ever have left. The last couple of days seemed so surreal.

She still couldn't get Fergus out of her head and wondered if they would go back to being friends. She felt a flutter of excitement at the thought of seeing him. Yes, she was annoyed he hadn't exactly fought off Kelly when she'd turned up. She hadn't thought it would be so hard seeing him with someone else. Perhaps that was why she had been quick to leave with Declan. Anyway, what right did she have to be jealous? His love life was none of her business, and she would much rather have him as a friend than not in her life at all. She could still be happy without a man to complicate things; this was all about her now and her future. She had to do what was right for her.

She'd left the door of the cabin ajar as she bustled around arranging her belongings, and it was a moment or two before she realised someone stood watching.

'Oh,' she gasped, when she glanced up. 'You gave me a fright.'

'Are you going somewhere?' Fergus pointed at her rucksack.

'Um, no, just sorting a few things out.'

'You decided to come back?'

'What do you mean?' She was surprised at the tone in his voice.

Fergus smiled, but it wasn't his usual relaxed grin. They regarded each other for a moment, both unsure what they should say next.

'I heard you were on the mainland . . .'

Thank goodness Edie had given her the heads-up, otherwise she might have been rendered speechless. 'Yes. I had something to deal with . . .'

'I thought you'd left,' he said abruptly, 'without saying goodbye.'

Now Amelia did feel a bit mortified, as he was correct. 'Of course not. I wouldn't have done that,' she lied.

'Did you forget something?'

'What are you talking about?' She desperately hoped he hadn't put two and two together.

'Well, you left.' He leaned against the doorframe with his arms folded, confusion and sorrow in his eyes.

'I did. And now I'm back.'

'You're not going to London then, with your "husband"?'

Amelia paused as she weighed up how to respond. She wasn't sure she appreciated his quizzical approach. 'What do you mean?'

'Well, he was obviously here to try to win you back and it seemed to be working.'

She stood with her hands on her hips. She wouldn't feel happy until she'd cleared the air with him. However, she could have done with a bit of preparation time. 'Yes, he was here. He arrived out of the blue. You happened to walk in at the wrong moment and read into it. But there's nothing left of our marriage and that's not what I want anymore . . .'

'Oh. So—'

Amelia cut him off angrily. 'I don't want to pick up the pieces of what I left behind. Quite frankly, it's not worth putting back together again.'

He scratched his chin. 'What made you change your mind?'

Amelia turned away to pour a glass of water and compose herself. 'I didn't want to leave . . .'

'Okay.'

As their eyes met and he took a step towards her, Amelia didn't trust herself not to throw herself into his arms. *Why was he so good-looking?* Instead she kept talking. 'That's not to say he's a bad guy or anything. He has lots of redeeming qualities, but he's also a cheat.'

Fergus's eyes widened. 'Oh God. I'm sorry.'

'Why?'

'I'm sorry, Amelia. You don't deserve any of this.' He shook his head and dropped down on one of the stools. 'You don't owe me an explanation.'

'It's okay.' She sat opposite him. The frisson of excitement from earlier had totally evaporated. 'You've been a friend to me and I should have told you I was leaving for the mainland . . . It was all unexpected and I wasn't thinking straight.'

'It's nice to have you back,' he said stiffly.

'Anyway,' she said, not letting his words register. 'You seemed to have your hands full.' She didn't want to tell him that the arrival of his girlfriend had *completely* unsettled her.

'She's not my girlfriend.'

Crikey, he could read her mind. 'Who?'

'Kelly.'

'I see, well, she seems to think that she is. And you weren't exactly pushing her away. Not that it's any of my business.'

'I know, but I felt I owed you an explanation, and then . . . Well, I wasn't expecting to see you with him. Your *husband*.'

She sighed. 'Fergus, you don't owe me anything.'

A confused look flitted across his face. 'Okay then . . .'

As she looked at him, more memories of what happened at the Christmas fair came back to her. His twinkling eyes — and not because he'd been Santa — the scent of his aftershave, his smile and the way his lips had twitched when they'd stood underneath the mistletoe . . . 'Anyway,' she said awkwardly. 'Thanks for coming over.'

'Okay,' he said flatly. 'I'll see you around.'

Amelia gave him a tight smile. 'See you.' She wondered if they would ever get back to the way they'd been before all of this had happened. Somehow she doubted it. But she put that to the side. She needed to focus on herself for a while and she was relieved to be back.

CHAPTER SIXTY-TWO

Edie swept the driveway of imaginary leaves as Fergus thundered back up the path towards the van. 'Everything okay, dear?'

'Great.'

She took a breath. 'Just give her some time.'

He forced a smile but his eyes were sad.

She knew he was feeling vulnerable. 'Do you want to chat?'

He hesitated. 'Kelly and I saw each other for a while but we had broken up. She is not my girlfriend and I've made that clear to her and Amelia.'

Edie's frown softened a little. But Fergus appeared to be on the verge of tears.

'Do you want a cup of tea?' She walked over to him and linked her arm in his.

'I'd better get off,' he said gruffly. 'Grant will be expecting me.'

'You sure? Just ten minutes?'

He hesitated and managed a tight smile. 'Okay.'

'Give her some time,' Edie repeated as they went into the house. 'And if it's meant to be, dear, it will be. Just trust things will work out the way they are supposed to.'

There was no point lecturing him about life and love. She could say they both needed to let bygones be bygones and move on. Yet that would be completely hypocritical given what had happened with her and Christine. Yet her sister's death also made her realise life was too short. Fergus already knew that after losing Ellen. She was aware that he was scared about his feelings for Amelia. It was something she had also been through with Jim. The very idea of falling in love again after losing her soulmate was awful.

She thought momentarily about the one brief affair with George, the artist who'd spent a summer on Arran a few years ago. At the time she'd enjoyed his company, but afterwards, as she'd reflected, it had felt like a betrayal of her marriage to Jim.

She and Fergus sat by the fire with their tea, but he shook his head when she offered him some shortbread. 'Oh-oh. That's a sure sign things are bad, Molly.'

Fergus smiled weakly, but she could tell from the crumpled look on his face that he was far from happy.

'I wish I could talk to her one last time . . .'

'I know, dear.' Edie sighed. 'Fergus, it sounds like you're feeling guilty about having feelings for Amelia?'

He looked at her in surprise and nodded.

'That's okay. It's normal to feel like that . . . I remember it with Jim. It felt like I was letting him down.'

'I want to ask Ellen if it's okay, and if she minds that I have feelings for someone else.'

Edie reached to pat his hand. 'She would want you to be happy, Fergus.'

He frowned.

'What if you had died instead of Ellen? Wouldn't you want her to move forward with life and find love again?'

'Of course.'

'There you go. Why should it be any different for you? And it's not about moving on from Ellen. It's about moving forward.'

'I mean, I saw Kelly for a bit, but that was all very relaxed . . . My feelings for Amelia are completely different.'

'Well, it's about making connections with the person who is right for you, and timing can play a big part.'

He nodded gratefully at her. 'You're right. Thanks, Edie. You always know what to say to make me feel better.'

'It's one of the advantages of age,' she said graciously.

Fergus took her hand and gently squeezed it.

'The answers are inside us, Fergus. Just trust you will work out what they are.'

CHAPTER SIXTY-THREE

'No.' Jack gasped as Amelia filled him in on the events of the past couple of days. 'Oh my God, Amelia, I am so sorry. I thought I was doing the right thing telling him where you were. He sounded so contrite . . .'

They were on a FaceTime call and Amelia pursed her lips but reminded herself there was no point in being cross with Jack. 'It's not your fault. You weren't to know what he would do, and I know it was well intentioned.'

'Thanks for being so kind,' he said sheepishly.

'I guess it has made me wonder if you ever really know someone and what they're capable of.'

'Hey, sis, come on . . . don't go all melancholy and start thinking that all men are bastards.'

'I'm not at all. In fact, quite the opposite. I've decided that there's no point in holding on to resentment. I need to move forward with my life. I'm fed up with being sad, Jack.'

'You look far from sad,' he said, smiling. 'All this drama must suit you. You've got a lovely glow on your cheeks.'

'That's the fresh air. I've been battered by the breeze.' Amelia did feel windswept and rejuvenated from the fresh air and sea. It was like a tonic that was helping her every day.

'And what about Fergus?'

'What about him? We're just friends. Far easier that way.' She couldn't stop the disappointment from flitting across her face.

'You sure you're happy with that?'

'It's a bit complicated,' she said.

'Does he know you left with Declan?'

'Well, yes and no. He knows Declan was here and that I went to the mainland with him, but I don't think he realises how close I was to going back to London. But the night before I left, we had a *moment* . . .'

'Right . . .' Jack's eyes widened. 'Tell me more.'

'Then his girlfriend arrived, except she wasn't his girlfriend.'

'Amelia. My God! This is better than daytime soaps.'

'Anyway, the bottom line is that it's all a bit messy, but we hope to be friends . . .'

'Come on! Really?'

'Yes,' she said, although she was sounding less sure.

'I guess you need to work out what you want?'

Amelia nodded. 'Yes, exactly. I'm heading up to see Cano soon at the café about a rota. I've offered to help him when his wife goes to Glasgow soon to help with their grandchild.'

'And what about the distillery?'

'No rush there — I'm not interested in being the focus of Doris's speculation and gossip at the moment. I'll wait for a while. Anyway, enough of me, how are you?'

'Super! We've been ice skating and decorated the tree over the weekend. It's lovely. Very festive.' He walked through to the front room to show a tastefully decorated tree in gold and red.

'I'm going to help Edie with hers later.' She realised she was looking forward to it. 'And what are your plans for the big day?'

'Ray's going to cook and I'm going to eat. That's about it! How about you?'

'Well, there's a ceilidh at the village hall on Christmas Eve, which everyone goes to. I could do with keeping a low profile, but Edie insists that I go with her and I think it will be good for her. She's been so brave since her sister died but you know how sometimes people become morose around this time of year. She's promised to show me all her best country dancing moves.'

'Sounds great.'

'Look, I'd better go just now, Jack. But I will call soon. Love you loads.'

'Bye-e-e,' he said, and kissed the camera. 'Take care, sis.'

She giggled, despite herself. At least she had one man in her life who hadn't let her down.

CHAPTER SIXTY-FOUR

Edie had pulled all the boxes of Christmas decorations from the hall cupboard and was now standing contemplating them in excitement.

Despite the plans to decorate the cottage around the time of the fair, Edie had kept putting it off. Floating around with tinsel and baubles, just after Christine's death, had felt wrong. Then when Amelia had left, there hadn't seemed much point at all. However, now she was back, Edie felt that was reason to celebrate and she had invited her over so they could put them up together. 'Well, Molly, looks like it will be the star on the tree this year rather than the angel.'

Molly had buried her head into one of the boxes, pulled out the angel and was now shaking it vigorously between her teeth.

Edie went into the kitchen to check on the mulled wine, which simmered nicely on the stove. The scent of cinnamon and cloves filled the air and Christmas hymns played on the radio.

'Hello,' said Amelia, walking into the kitchen.

Edie beamed. 'Wonderful timing, dear. Can I offer you some of my very special mulled wine?'

Amelia inhaled deeply. 'Oh, yes, please. It smells amazing.'

Edie ladled the rich, dark liquid into a sturdy tumbler and handed it to her. Then she filled another cup for herself. 'Well, cheers, my dears, and here's hoping for a Merry Christmas.'

'Thanks, Edie.' Amelia sipped the hot spiced wine and closed her eyes as she enjoyed the different flavours. 'It's delicious. What's in it?'

Edie tapped her nose. 'That's my prized recipe. But don't worry, I will let you in on the secret. But first have a guess.' She enjoyed a sip of the warm liquid as she watched Amelia think.

'Okay, let me see. Definitely cinnamon and cloves?'

Edie nodded. 'What else?'

Amelia licked her lips as she thought. 'Oranges?'

'Yes,' said Edie.

Amelia nodded. 'Anything else?'

'Sugar,' said Edie. 'And a slug of maple syrup.'

'Oh, that's unusual. I don't think I would have guessed that. Well, it is delicious.' She took another sip. 'I'm impressed that you made it from scratch. We just used to buy the ready-made stuff and heat it in a pot. This is far better.'

Edie noticed that Amelia didn't flinch when she referred to 'we' anymore. That was good. It was a sign that she was ready to forgive and move on, which she hoped she would do. Edie knew how resentment and anger could really suck away all your energy, and she just wanted Amelia to move on and enjoy her life. 'There is one more ingredient but I won't tell you just now. I will let you keep guessing.'

'Okay,' said Amelia, accepting a refill. 'Is this a good idea? It tastes quite potent.'

'It's fine,' said Edie, waving her hand dismissively. 'It's part of the decorating the tree tradition.'

The two women chatted excitedly as they dressed the tree that Fergus had brought over from the garden centre the previous day. Edie had let it settle overnight in preparation.

'When was that?' said Amelia casually.

'Oh, must have been about three o'clock.' She could tell from Amelia's expression that she was disappointed he hadn't called in. 'Have you seen much of him recently?'

'Not really,' admitted Amelia. 'Our paths don't seem to have crossed much at all these past few days. I guess he's busy with work and, well, it's that time of year when there's lots happening. Everything is always so frantic. I'm sure we'll catch up eventually.'

'Indeed,' said Edie, threading a thick rope of tinsel around the branches of the tree.

'To be honest, I wonder if he is busy or if he's just avoiding me.'

'You mustn't think that, dear. I'm sure he's been preoccupied with work. You know how the opposite sex can sometimes struggle to multitask at times. You'll see him soon enough.'

'Yes, that's true. I'm sure you're right.' Amelia reached for another ornament and continued spacing them around the tree. 'I have to say your baubles are lovely.' She traced her fingers across a golden glass ball.

'Thank you. I actually made them.'

'Did you? That's incredible, Edie. You are so talented.'

Edie shrugged. 'Aw, thank you, but they were very easy.'

'Well, they look most impressive. Well done. Which reminds me, what can I do to help for Christmas Day? Please let me bring something. It's the very least I can do.'

'Thanks,' said Edie, touched by the offer. 'To be honest, I haven't given it much thought other than to ask the butcher if he could help me out with a turkey, seeing as I had missed the order deadline.' She laughed. 'They only had large ones left and it seemed ridiculous to have such a large bird for the two of us . . .'

'I don't mind if we have something else. That's fine. I could make something non-traditional, like lasagne or roast beef,' suggested Amelia.

'Just a sec,' said Edie, taking their cups into the kitchen and refilling them. 'There you go. Isn't it looking lovely and festive in here?'

'What do you think? Would you like me to do something like that? It would save you cooking?'

'Ah, well, the thing is that I ended up ordering the turkey anyway and . . . inviting a few others to help us eat it.' She paused and watched Amelia glance over from the other side of the tree. 'I hope you don't mind?'

'No, not at all,' said Amelia, shaking her head, though Edie didn't think she looked all that convinced. 'That will be lovely. Who is coming?'

'Just Grant and Thea, Cano and Naza . . . and Fergus.' She kept a half-eye on Amelia's face as she continued to drape the tinsel round the lower branches.

'That sounds . . . nice.'

'I am sure it will be.' Edie sensed that she should change the direction of the conversation quickly as Amelia looked worried. 'Well, have you guessed it then?' She pointed at her cup and took another drink.

'Guessed the secret ingredient?'

'Yes. What do you think it is?'

'I'm not quite sure but it's making me feel quite tipsy and warm,' she said, patting her flushed cheeks.

Molly ran into the room, dropped the angel at Edie's feet and barked.

'Oh dear, Molly. She doesn't look healthy at all.'

'She looks a bit how I feel just now,' said Amelia, giggling.

Edie picked up the angel, whose wings still hung from her back, but only just. Her crown had been completely chewed off. 'Oh, Molly, you are very naughty.' Molly wagged her tail excitedly.

'Tell me then,' said Amelia. 'What is it?'

'Brandy. That's what gives it that punch.'

'Oh, I hope this won't give me a hangover, Edie. It's a good job that I haven't already started working at the café because I'm not sure how I'd manage getting up at the crack of dawn, hungover.' She burst out laughing and Edie sighed in relief.

She was glad she hadn't ruined the mood by telling Amelia the change of plan for Christmas Day. 'I am sure you will be absolutely fine for tomorrow. It's only a wee dash of brandy. Hardly anything at all.' She didn't want to admit that she had poured half the bottle into the pot. 'But I will go and get you some water anyway. Just in case.'

'Thank you. I feel a bit giddy. But I think I'm just happy, Edie. I'm excited about the next step in my life.'

'You should be. You have so much to enjoy.' She patted her on the shoulder. 'Let me just get some water.'

'Thank you. For everything, Edie.'

Edie smiled kindly at her. Turning to go into the kitchen, she felt another stir of excitement as she thought about gathering everyone close to her and being with her friends on Christmas Day. Somehow she had a feeling that everything would be okay.

CHAPTER SIXTY-FIVE

Fergus sat in the window seat in the darkness as lights twinkled around him. The ceilidh was tomorrow and he really couldn't face it. He never normally bothered with Christmas decorations but had strung up some fairy lights this year just in case . . . But who was he kidding? He never invited anyone into his flat other than the man who read the electricity meter. What a mess. How could his life have become so complicated in the space of a few weeks? Why had he been so stupid to fall for someone? After everything that had happened with Ellen, he should have known better. His heart was too fragile.

But Amelia still managed to dominate his thoughts. He wished they were able to sweep the drama of Kelly and Declan turning up aside, and go back to the night of the fair before things had gone downhill. How he longed to turn the clock back. He was delighted she was back and here to stay, yet miserable about the awkwardness between them. He had almost sent her a text on several occasions over the past couple of weeks to suggest a swim. Then had stopped himself. What if she said no? Or just ignored him altogether? He hadn't seen her walking on the beach or at the café either. Mind you, he had been keeping a low profile too, busying himself with work and spending as much time away in Brodick as possible.

When the sky began to lighten, he got dressed and walked along the high street, inhaling the freezing air. Rejuvenated by the cold and the tangy scent of salt and seaweed, he stopped at Cèic for a coffee. They were opening up and the scent of vanilla and cinnamon hung in the air, with the familiar sound of the coffee grinder whirring in the background.

'Morning, my friend,' called Cano. 'You're early this morning.'

'Couldn't sleep and thought one of your coffees would be perfect.' He knelt down when he realised a lace on his trainer had come loose.

'Come on,' called Cano, through to the back. 'Here is your first customer. See how it goes.'

Fergus stood up and came face to face with Amelia, behind the counter and wearing an apron. She gave him a subdued smile.

'Oh . . . hello. I didn't expect you to be here.' He shrugged helplessly.

'I'm learning the ropes as I'm helping Cano out in the New Year, you know, when Naza goes to Glasgow. You're my first customer . . . what can I get you?'

'Just a coffee, please.'

'A latte?'

He nodded.

'Okay. Bear with me.'

He tried not to stare but couldn't peel his eyes away from her as she busied herself at the coffee machine. He could tell she felt flustered from the way she kept biting her bottom lip.

Her face flushed as she put the cup down on the counter and he was surprised that she seemed to be so nervous.

'Smells great,' he said. 'Thank you.' Then he looked around wordlessly with no idea what to say.

'Enjoy.' She gave a slight smile but wouldn't fully meet his eyes.

Fergus thought about the times they'd spent together. The walks, the freezing swims, nights at the pub, and the nights they had spent at the cabin just talking. And those kisses too. How he missed all of it. He wished he could tell her, but of course he couldn't. He pulled out his bank card and tapped it against the machine. He thanked her for the coffee and began to walk away. 'See you later.'

'Yes . . . oh, hello there, Ed,' she said, as the elderly man walked in with his newspaper.

'Hello, my dear.' He smiled brightly at her. 'Hello, Fergus. Not seen you for a while. Where have you been?'

'Ah, you know, Ed. Keeping busy with work.'

'All work and no play? My Daphne said life was too short to be all work. She was right. I wish I had listened to her at the time.'

Fergus touched his arm. 'Nice to see you, Ed. Take care and enjoy your coffee. Amelia makes a fantastic one.'

Ed chuckled. 'Yes, and I can tell she's got a soft spot for you.'

Fergus's eyes widened.

'Trust me,' Ed said. 'I know these things. My Daphne always did say I had an instinct for spotting true love.' Off he sauntered towards the counter, with his newspaper rolled up and tucked under his arm.

Fergus didn't dare look back.

CHAPTER SIXTY-SIX

Amelia turned away, her face red, when she heard Ed talking to Fergus. He had said the same thing to her not so long ago. She grabbed a cloth and busied herself wiping down the coffee machine and checking the pastry display. She was still trembling from her encounter with Fergus. Trust him to be her first customer and to be so nice about it too.

Rob from the hotel came in and asked for his usual skinny latte in a takeaway cup. 'Are you looking forward to the ceilidh?'

Amelia smiled nervously. No, she wasn't looking forward to the bloody ceilidh at all. 'Of course. Should be fun.' She twiddled with the ties on her apron. 'Can I offer you anything else?'

'Just one of your lemon-and-poppyseed muffins, please.'

'No problem at all.' She always thought it was amusing that there was no need for upselling in this place. No *would you like a pastry with that?* Or *would you like a fresh croissant to go with your coffee?* Cano's goodies sold quite easily all by themselves. She picked up the tongs and reached to pluck one of the fat, crumbly muffins from the plate on the counter. It did look delicious, and she was tempted to bite into the crispy, sugary top. They used to be her speciality and the treat she would bake to take into staff meetings at work. The thought of baking a muffin, never mind anything else, now felt totally alien.

'Earth to Amelia.' Rob laughed. 'You're miles away this morning.'

'Sorry, I am, you're right. I need to focus or Cano will be giving me my marching orders before I've even worked a full day for him.'

'Not at all,' said Cano, who appeared from the kitchen. 'Naza would not forgive me! She doesn't trust me to manage on my own. I need you here, Amelia.'

Rob smiled. 'Well, good luck. Hope the rest of your day goes well, Amelia.'

'Thank you. Enjoy your coffee.'

'Bye, guys. See you tomorrow at the ceilidh.'

'Sure will,' said Cano, bidding him farewell. He turned to Amelia. 'I hope you are coming to the ceilidh tomorrow?'

She nodded, although she really just wanted a quiet Christmas Eve, curled up in the tub chair at the hut, with a large cup of tea and a good book.

She managed to busy herself for the rest of the day, making hot drinks, washing dishes, cleaning the coffee machines and replenishing the bakery's counters as and when they ran sparse. The smell of roasted cinnamon and coffee beans was one she loved, and she found the sound of the coffee-bean grinder rather comforting. All too quickly, Cano shut the door and turned the sign round to say 'Closed'.

'Well done, Miss Amelia. What a good day.'

She pushed her hair out of her eyes, lost for words. 'I loved it! I mean, I am tired now but that was utterly amazing. Thank you for letting me have a go.'

Naza joined Cano and she smiled. 'This means so much. I can visit my daughter now and not worry about him.' She patted Cano on the arm, her eyes dancing in amusement.

Cano laughed, then rolled his eyes. 'We will be okay, won't we, Amelia?'

'We sure will. It will all be fine. We will have everything running like clockwork. I promise, Naza.'

'Thank you, Amelia,' she said. 'But now you should go home and rest.' She gestured towards the door. 'You have worked hard today and must be desperate to sit down.'

Amelia nodded. 'Thank you. And just let me know when you need me next.'

'We will,' said Naza. 'But look out for us at the ceilidh and then at Miss Edie's on Christmas Day.'

Amelia's heart sank. She had forgotten about the large group gathering at Edie's house. She smiled. 'Thanks, Naza, I am looking forward to it.'

The light had faded, but Amelia knew the walk home well now. She wandered slowly along the beach, the wind whipping her hair around her face. What a lovely day. She had really enjoyed her stint at Cèic but she was tired now and would be relieved to get inside the cabin and change into her pyjamas. The thought of socializing at the ceilidh wasn't a good one. She'd much rather stay in, snug and cosy in the cabin tomorrow night. However, she couldn't let Edie down, no matter how anti-social she was feeling. She just had to put a smile on her face and get on with it.

CHAPTER SIXTY-SEVEN

Although snow had been forecast, Christmas Eve brought bright sunshine and a chilly breeze. It was a glorious morning and everything seemed to sparkle in the frost. The trees in Edie's garden looked as though they were scattered with diamonds. The sea was a dazzling blue and Amelia, cocooned in the cosy confines of the cabin, thought she could be on a Greek island in the middle of July, rather than an island off the west coast of Scotland in winter.

Later that morning, she and Edie walked to the village hall together to check if they could do anything to help with the preparations for the ceilidh later on. Grant was there with some of the lifeboat crew who were setting everything up.

Amelia immediately scanned the room for Fergus but there was no sign of him, and she couldn't help but feel disappointed.

'Can we do anything?' asked Edie.

'Everything is under control. The ceilidh committee have been very organised and made sure we were here first thing. But thank you. Just enjoy your day, ladies, and go put your glad rags on. I hope you're ready for some dancing later on, Amelia?' Grant grinned. 'There will be lots of men in kilts, and you know what they say about a true Scotsman . . .'

Amelia laughed but then panicked as she wondered what on earth she would wear. She only had her usual jeans and sweaters. Normally she wouldn't let that bother her. It was the prospect of seeing Fergus . . . or not. She wondered if he would even turn up.

She looked around at the amazing job the crew had done of decorating the hall with streamers, gold-sprayed pine cones, fairy lights and mistletoe strategically hung in several places. The band and kids from the local school were setting up and having a run through of their playlist.

'Looks grand,' said Edie. 'We will see you later.'

As they walked back towards the cottage together, Edie glanced over at Amelia in concern. 'You're awfully quiet today, my dear. Is everything okay?'

She sighed. 'Sorry, Edie, I'm not quite sure what's wrong with me. I'm just a bit nervous about later. And I don't have anything to wear.'

'Well, it just so happens I have the answer.'

'You do?'

'Yes. I have a beautiful dress, which I found tucked away the other day.'

Amelia wasn't sure what to say. It was kind of Edie to offer, however Amelia was also aware that some of Edie's clothes were a bit too outrageous for her taste.

'You'll love it,' she said, evidently noticing Amelia's hesitation. 'I promise.'

When they got back to Coorie Cottage, Edie told Amelia to wait in the lounge while she fetched it. She came downstairs holding an elegant red silk-chiffon dress by its hanger.

'That looks pretty.'

'Do you want to try it on?'

Amelia nodded. 'Sure.'

'Just take it up to the spare room and see what you think.'

Amelia slipped the dress over her head, admiring her reflection in the mirror. The dress cascaded perfectly to a handkerchief midi hem and there were feminine ruffles at the cuffs. She felt wonderful and ran downstairs to show Edie.

'Oh my.' Edie clasped her hands together. 'You look radiant. Just beautiful.'

Amelia swirled around and the material moved gently with her. 'It's stunning, Edie.'

'One of my vintage numbers,' she said, laughing.

'You don't think the dress is too fancy?'

'Not at all. People like getting all dressed up on Christmas Eve.'

'The only thing is, I don't have any shoes . . .'

Edie beamed. 'I do. Wait here.'

Amelia couldn't bear the thought of forcing her feet into stilettos or court shoes and once again worried about how to tell Edie.

'Here you are.' Edie handed her a gift-wrapped box. 'Just a wee thing from me to you. We said we wouldn't do presents but, well, I spotted them and couldn't resist.'

'Can I open this now?'

'Of course.'

Amelia tugged off the gold ribbon and slipped a finger under the red paper to reveal a shoebox. She pulled off the lid and a slow smile crept across her face. 'Edie, I don't know what to say. They're perfect.' Inside was a pair of trainers covered in tiny silver sequins.

'I didn't think you'd appreciate a pair of high heels.'

'You're so right.' She slipped them on and twirled around. 'What do you think?'

'Perfect! And ideal for all the dancing you're going to be doing.'

Amelia smiled at her. 'How will I ever be able to thank you for what you've done? I never thought coming here would be like this. I expected to be lonely and feeling sorry for myself. But the opposite is true.'

'Well, the same could be said for me. You helped me so much with Christine. Without you I would have been a morose mess.' Edie blinked away tears. 'But having you here has been the best gift ever.'

'I wanted to try and find the moment to give you this and, well, this seems like the perfect time.' Amelia went to her handbag and pulled out a small package.

'Oh, thank you. I am intrigued.'

This time Edie laughed when she opened the parcel. She pulled out a red silk scarf covered in tiny robins. 'It's beautiful, and look at the little Johnnys!'

'I know! I saw it at the airport and couldn't resist. I thought of you and Johnny the resident robin.'

'And this is ideal for tonight.' Edie leaned forward and hugged Amelia tightly. 'Right,' she said. 'We had better get our skates on if we are to be ready in time for the ball.'

Amelia walked down to the cabin with the dress across her arm and her new trainers, and this time had a spring in her step. She had no responsibilities, no pressing work commitments, and she lived in the most beautiful place in the world. As she listed all the positives in her life, she thought of that morning's journal prompt: *List all the things in life you are grateful for.* Today she was thankful for so much. She just had to make a point of reminding herself of that, rather than worrying about things that were out of her control.

CHAPTER SIXTY-EIGHT

'You look amazing,' said Thea, as Amelia and Edie walked into the hall. Thea had texted to say she would be going a bit earlier and would save them a table.

'Thanks to Edie. I've borrowed her dress.'

'Wow, Edie. Let me know next time you're doing one of your wardrobe clear-outs and I'll come round.'

Edie laughed. 'I'll be with you in a moment, girls. I just need a word with Naza, before I forget.'

Thea wore a navy-blue jumpsuit, with a stunning red necklace, and her eyes were as smiley as always. 'So good to see you, Amelia. It feels like ages.'

'Yes,' she agreed. 'It's been a strange couple of weeks. Sorry I've not been about.'

'That's okay. And you don't need to tell me any of the details. All I know is that Fergus was pretty cut up about things when you left . . .'

'But . . .' she started to say, then shrugged. 'I didn't leave for long, and it was all a bit unexpected. It was never my intention to go, but my ex-husband turned up, which totally threw me. Especially after events at the fair.'

Thea rolled her eyes. 'I know. But that was all a misunderstanding, wasn't it?'

'Yes, and I have chatted to Fergus . . . but, well, it's not really the same.'

Amelia looked around the hall to see most of the men wore kilts in a variety of tartans.

Thea rolled her eyes. 'Any excuse to get their skirts on and their legs out.'

'Well,' said Amelia. 'They look very smart. Though I don't see Grant. Where is he?'

'Ah, well, his pager went off earlier. They've been called out on a shout.'

'Oh.' Amelia wanted to ask if Fergus had gone as well, but was worried it might appear needy.

'Fergus is with them, in case you were wondering.' Thea smiled at her kindly.

'What happened?'

'It sounds like a fishing vessel in trouble.'

'I hope everything is okay. It must be such a worry.' Amelia could feel a knot start to form in her stomach. What if something happened to Fergus? Would she forgive herself for not making amends and leaving things unfinished?

Thea shrugged. 'Weather's been still today, and hopefully they're just having to tow it to safety. The tidal conditions are good so they shouldn't be much longer.' Her smile widened. 'In fact, talk of the devil.'

'Here you go, ladies.' It was Grant, holding a bottle of prosecco and some glasses. He leaned down to kiss Thea on the cheek.

'I thought you would be a while,' she said, smiling up at him.

'No, we got the boat in quicker than we thought, which is just as well as I didn't want to miss this.' Laughing, he poured the drinks and passed a glass to Amelia. 'Here you go. And can I just say how lovely you look tonight?'

'Thanks, Grant. You don't look too bad yourself. I love your kilt.' She forced a smile but couldn't help scanning the room for Fergus.

He curtsied, swishing the red tartan. 'Thank you.'

Amelia looked back at him. 'I'm glad everything is okay and you made it.'

Grant shrugged. 'Cheers.'

Amelia took a sip and tried to enjoy the feeling of the bubbles on her tongue. Then Grant wandered off to high-five a friend who had just arrived.

'He'll be here soon. Don't worry.'

'Who?'

'Fergus. I know you're wondering where he is . . .'

Amelia didn't reply.

'I think he's fallen for you.'

'Who?'

'Fergus,' she said, rolling her eyes. 'His eyes light up when you come into the room. I've never seen him like that with anyone else . . . well, apart from Molly.'

Amelia didn't look convinced. 'He is full of charisma and charm. It's hard not to be taken in by him.'

'So have *you* been taken in by him?'

Amelia laughed. 'He is clearly the sort of guy who makes every woman in his sights feel like the centre of his world.'

'And how do you feel about him?'

Amelia didn't answer. 'I'm looking forward to the ceilidh . . . I've never been to one before.'

'Trust me, you will love it. Once you get the hang of the moves then you will be fine, and let's just say it can be quite boisterous and energetic.'

Amelia waved at Cano and Naza as they walked past the table. 'Ladies, you both look splendid tonight,' Cano remarked. He looked so different in his kilt and white shirt compared to his usual café uniform of black jeans, T-shirt and apron. Naza's turquoise shift dress suited her beautifully and lit up her eyes.

'Aw, so do you. Isn't this so lovely?' said Amelia, gesturing around the hall.

Naza nodded. 'We are looking forward to tomorrow with you all too. It's so kind of Edie to have us.'

'It will be great fun,' said Thea.

Amelia just hoped that things wouldn't be awkward with Fergus and was glad there was safety in numbers.

'Save me a dance,' said Cano, and they walked on towards the bar.

Thea smiled kindly. 'Look, I'm sorry if I'm speaking out of turn but I just think it's a shame if you two let whatever happened mess things up. You clearly adore each other.'

'Okay . . . thank you, Thea.' Amelia desperately needed to change the subject and felt awkward as she had no idea what to say. She stood suddenly. 'I'll be back in a minute. I need to go and powder my nose.'

CHAPTER SIXTY-NINE

When she walked out into the corridor in search of the toilets, she froze when she saw Fergus. The mere sight of him made her gulp and her breath started to quicken. Tonight, he wore a kilt, which made him look even sexier. Oh God, she was going to have to hide in the ladies all night if this was the effect he was having on her. Then he looked up and clocked her, his eyes widening as he took in her appearance.

For a moment, they were both locked in their own world as they stared at each other. She mouthed, 'Hello,' and his liquid brown eyes danced as he started to move towards her.

'Hey, Fergus, I need you for a minute, please,' said Doris, who appeared from nowhere. She was clearly a woman on a mission. She pulled him away and he looked over his shoulder helplessly as he was ushered into the hall. 'I need you to demonstrate some of the moves.'

Amelia went into the loos and took a minute to compose herself. When she looked at her reflection in the mirror, she saw her cheeks were smudged with colour, her eyes bright, and she looked so different to the woman she had been just a couple of months ago.

'Hi, dear, are you having a good time?' Edie came and stood next to her at the sink, applying a fresh coat of lipstick.

'Yes, thanks. What a lovely atmosphere.' Amelia couldn't help but feel glad that Edie had arrived at that moment. She had such a warm and comforting way about her.

'And the lifeboat boys made it too. It would have been a shame if they'd missed it.' She gave Amelia a knowing look. 'Mind you, poor Fergus has been dragged off by Doris. He's probably desperate for a beer and she's got him teed up to demonstrate the Gay Gordons. I think it's just an excuse to get up close and personal with him.'

Amelia burst out laughing. 'Well, you can hardly blame her.'

The fiddle group had been playing all evening and they now heard Doris on the microphone.

'Oh God. They'll never get her off that thing. Once she starts that will be her for the duration. The band may as well call it a night. I swear she should have been a holiday rep or something. She does love a microphone.'

Amelia chuckled at the thought. Edie was *so* right. Doris should have been leading a coach tour around the Highlands and islands.

'Come on, dear.' Edie's tone was warm and soft. 'Let's go and dance.'

Anxiety nipped at Amelia's stomach as she and Edie weaved their way back through the party and into the crowd. They stood together at the side, watching the demonstration for the Gay Gordons. Doris grabbed Fergus's hand and set off determinedly.

Amelia watched in fascination as Doris issued instructions on how to do the dance in her usual abrupt manner. 'Forward, two, three, four. Reverse, two, three, four. Forward, two, three, four. Reverse, two, three, four. Now, pivot, pivot and polka, polka. Again!'

Fergus was an obedient and obliging partner, though pulled a few faces, which sent ripples of laughter through the crowd. He caught Amelia's eye again as he danced past with Doris, who was clearly enjoying being the centre of attention.

Amelia followed everyone else's lead and clapped along, smiling and watching until Doris decided that she'd had enough. She clapped her hands briskly and dipped into a quick curtsy. 'Okay everyone. Without further ado, take your partner for the Gay Gordons.'

'Oh-oh,' said Edie. 'Watch out. I think someone wants to dance.' Her voice was mischievous and she gave Amelia a reassuring smile.

A sense of panic started to close in as Fergus made his way towards her. 'Fancy a dance?' he said, his eyes twinkling in delight.

Her heart raced and her insides turned to liquid as she casually replied, 'Sure.' His hand was on her back and she trembled as she felt his touch through the silk, and every nerve ending tingled.

CHAPTER SEVENTY

Fergus took both her hands.

'I've never done this before.' She cringed. What on earth was she saying?

'Well, I wouldn't have necessarily expected you to.' He smiled and winked. 'Just follow my lead and I'll keep you right.' They joined hands over Amelia's shoulder and Fergus put his arm behind her back. 'Forward, two, three, four, reverse, two, three, four . . .'

'Doris would be proud,' she said, stifling a giggle.

'Bravo, Amelia.' Doris was now speeding past with Grant, whose expression spoke volumes.

'Well, thank you.' Amelia's words were lost though, as she was now making her way back to the stage.

Then Thea and Cano danced past. Thea threw her a knowing look.

Amelia soon got the gist of it and as they danced together, her dress flowing behind, she couldn't help but laugh.

'Having fun?' Fergus asked.

'The best. I can't remember the last time I danced . . .' Then it dawned on her. Oops. The last time she'd danced was at her wedding. 'Well, actually I can . . . but this is much more fun.' She meant every word.

'Just wait until we do Strip the Willow.' He raised an eyebrow. 'That is quite boisterous. And the Eightsome Reel.'

'Sounds great. I'm so glad I wore my trainers.' The accordion player played the last bars of the tune and they pulled apart, breathless.

'You look very beautiful, Amelia. And, yes, good move with the trainers.'

'A present from Edie,' she said. 'Shall I grab some drinks?'

'Oh, that's a great idea. I'm desperate for a beer.'

They walked towards the bar, Fergus's hand gentle on her back. 'You were called out with the crew?'

'Yes. I couldn't believe it when the pagers went off. I was just finishing up at the centre and about to head home to get ready . . . and then it started beeping. It was a fishing vessel that needed to be towed to safety. Fortunately the tides were in our favour otherwise we could have been there a while. Anyway, at least it all ended well and we managed to come.'

'Do you ever get scared when you're out there?'

He shrugged. 'You don't have much time to think about it. You're just there to do a job and bring whoever's in trouble home safely.'

Amelia's heart skipped a beat as she realised she couldn't bear it if anything happened to him. She reached up and touched his cheek. 'I'm glad you're okay.' What if something had happened to him and she hadn't told him how she really felt? All sorts of possibilities raced through her mind.

'Fergus . . . I'm sorry for the way things worked out . . .'

He reached for her hand and squeezed it. 'Me too.'

'Can we go back to being friends again?' She didn't know what else to say. But she needed to be honest and open with him.

He nodded, a mixture of curiosity and humour in his eyes. His tone was soft as he spoke. 'Friends, or more than that?'

Amelia couldn't take her eyes off him as she wondered what to say next. She willed herself not to say anything stupid.

'What would you like?' The barman, looking flustered, clicked his fingers as he waited for their reply.

'Amelia, what would you like?'

'Erm, just a beer is fine, thanks.'

'Make that two.'

The moment was lost as Thea and Grant arrived behind them and Fergus ordered more drinks.

'What do you think of the ceilidh then?' said Grant.

'Brilliant fun and also exhausting,' Amelia said, laughing. 'It's like a workout at the gym!'

'I know,' said Grant, raising an eyebrow. 'I hope he warned you how tough it is? Will you join us for the Eightsome Reel? We need another couple.'

Fergus hesitated. 'Sure.' He took a gulp of beer and leaned down to Amelia to whisper in her ear. 'To be continued.'

She almost spat out the beer she was drinking. That wasn't what she was expecting him to say at all, and she felt a delicious sense of anticipation building. The scent of his aftershave lingered and she wanted to reach out and grab him.

'Okay,' shouted Doris. 'Take your place for the Eightsome Reel.'

Amelia tried to focus on the instructions, but all she could think about was Fergus and the way he was gripping her hand. She didn't dare to look at him as she didn't trust herself not to kiss him in front of everyone.

'Don't worry. I'll keep you right.'

Amelia felt as though she was put through her paces, being twirled, stamping her feet, clapping and birling around the floor. The dancing was such fun, and so infectious it was tricky not to laugh and smile at everyone, all clearly having as good a time as she was. This time when the band finished playing, she was sweating and thirsty for some more beer.

'I need to go . . .' she said over her shoulder.

Fergus was right behind her and confusion flitted across his face.

'For some fresh air.' She reached behind and tugged his hand.

'Yes, it's hot in here.' His voice was gruff. 'Let's go outside.'

CHAPTER SEVENTY-ONE

Outside the hall, Amelia gulped in the cold air and giggled as they walked towards the bench, looking out into the darkness of the bay.

Fergus offered her his hand and she clasped it, letting him draw her in close. 'Is this fresh enough?' The cold air was invigorating, and he draped his jacket over her shoulders and pulled her towards him as they sat together in companionable silence. 'Are you glad you came back?'

She pulled her head away from his shoulder and looked up. 'Yes. I love this place. Even leaving it for a night was hard enough . . .' She shivered. 'I realised that the simple things keep me happy. As soon as I got off the ferry it was like I had come home.'

'The place kind of pulls you in, doesn't it?'

'I can't imagine a life now where I can't walk on the beach every day or gaze out at the sea. Or smell the seaweed.' She wrinkled up her nose and laughed.

He sighed loudly. 'I know what you mean. There is something calming and grounding about it.'

'It's funny to think that I came here to start afresh where nobody knew me. And now I'm in a place I love with wonderful friends.' She wondered if she should just take charge and say something. Could she be really honest and just say what was on her mind? 'What if—'

Fergus interrupted her. 'Amelia, the thing is . . . when you left, it was awful. I mean, I made a mess of things with the whole Kelly situation. I should have been clearer with her from the start, and then I should have been honest with you.'

She shook her head. 'You don't need to apologise. I shouldn't have run off with Declan without telling you. I don't know what I was thinking . . .'

Fergus leaned towards her, lifted her chin and pressed his warm lips against hers. When he pulled back, he cupped her face in his hands. 'Please don't go again.'

Amelia blushed, moving slightly away but reaching to hold his hand. 'I don't intend to. I belong here . . . and I can't thank you enough, Fergus, for being such a good friend to me. I wouldn't have got through these past couple of months if it hadn't been for you.' Her eyes glistened as she realised that what she was saying was absolutely true. Fergus had been a rock of support to her when she'd needed it most. As she started to relax, she realised how safe and accepted she was here, and much of that was down to him.'

'So, friends?' He tilted his head to one side.

'Mmm, okay.' Her eyes were smiling as she looked at him. 'Does that mean we can start our morning dips again soon?'

'I thought you'd never ask.'

'Should we go back inside?'

He shifted uncomfortably. 'The thing is, Amelia, I don't know if I can be just your friend . . .' He rubbed his thumb over the back of her hand. 'If I'm honest, I haven't felt like this for a long time.'

She held her breath, her heart tightening as she waited for what he was going to say next.

'I think I'm falling for you, Amelia. You're one of the most special people I've ever met and I don't want to be without you.'

Amelia reached over and held him tightly, then kissed him gently on the lips.

'Much as I'd like to stay out here with you, I'm freezing now. Do you fancy a dance?'

He nodded and touched her face, kissing her again and again.

They could hear Doris from the hall and giggled as they walked back inside, their arms wrapped around each other.

'Wait a second,' she said, pausing at the door and pointing up. 'Look what's there.' She rested a hand on his chest.

'Mistletoe. Are you trying to tell me that you'd like another kiss?'

She grinned. 'Yes, please.'

CHAPTER SEVENTY-TWO

At sunrise on Christmas Day, after a restful night's sleep, Amelia lay in bed listening to the soothing lull of the waves, which brought tears of happiness to her eyes. She was rested and content and happy. She reached over to the bedside table for her journal. The prompt for the day was: *Describe yourself in ten words*. She quickly started to scribble.

Happy, fulfilled, sunny, open, forgiving, brave, courageous, inspired, energised, trusting, hopeful, ready to take a chance . . .

Amelia stopped writing and closed her notebook. She could describe herself in far more than just ten words. When she flicked back to the start of the notebook and compared the words to the ones she had written there, she smiled. She had come so far. The journal had helped her to work out who she was and what she wanted from life. It had helped her to clarify so many things, to focus on what was important in her life, and had helped heal her broken heart. She closed it and placed it back in the drawer, then quickly pulled on her swimming things.

She smiled when she saw Fergus standing at the gate, waving at her. They were starting the day with a quick dip. As she walked down the path towards him, he pointed to the sky. A whisper of snowflakes fell towards her and brushed against her face. This really was going to be a Christmas Day to remember. For Amelia, it would always be the Christmas that everything changed.

THE END

ACKNOWLEDGEMENTS

I would like to thank the Choc Lit and Joffe Books team for their support and encouragement. I feel very lucky to have you as my publisher. I would like to extend a special thanks to Lyn Vernham and Lu Taylor for their belief in me as a writer with this book in particular.

Thank you to my incredible editor, Sarah Pursey, whose incredible eye for details helped to strengthen and shape this book. Thank you for getting my writing! And for your sense of humour and encouragement. I have learned so much from working with you. Thanks also to Jasper Joffe, Emma Grundy Haigh, Jasmine Callaghan, Abbie Dodson-Shanks, Alice Latchford and Rachel Malig for help and support.

Thank you to the wonderful Choc Lit family for their ongoing support and in particular, Morton S. Gray, for reaching out at the right time.

Thank you to the very talented book cover designer — Jarmila Takač — for the gorgeous cover!

Thank you to the Tasting Panel who said 'yes' to the manuscript and made publication possible: Aileen M, Alma H, Brigette H, Fran S, Hilary B, Janet A, Jenny K, Jenny M, Kate A, Laura S, Margaret M, Marie W, Michele R and Sallie D.

Thanks also to Frankie Greenwood and Frances Wells for support and encouragement and reading early drafts of this book, and to everyone else who shared their positive feedback and reviews of *A Summer Wedding on Arran*! Your support has encouraged me to keep writing.

I must also extend a big thanks to the lovely people of Arran who always make me so welcome every time I visit. Although the café and pub that feature in this book are the products of my imagination, there are many wonderful coffee shops, bars and restaurants worth a visit if you do go to the island.

Thank you to Colin Smeeton at the *Arran Banner* for featuring an article about my first Arran book. Thanks also to Dougie, Claudia and Grace for happily visiting Arran with me many, many times! I couldn't do any of this without your love and support.

THANK YOU

I would like to thank you, the reader, for choosing to read *A Christmas Escape to Arran* I hope you enjoyed the story of Amelia, Fergus and Edie as much as I enjoyed writing it. The island of Arran has a really special place in my heart and I hope I have done it justice and inspired you to visit!

If you enjoyed *A Christmas Escape to Arran*, then please do leave a review on the website where you bought the book. Every review really does help a new author like me.

You can find me on Twitter, Facebook and Instagram (details on the 'About the Author' page next).

Please do get in touch for all the latest news. I look forward to chatting with you.

Huge thanks again, Ellie x

THE CHOC LIT STORY

Established in 2009, Choc Lit is an independent, award-winning publisher dedicated to creating a delicious selection of quality women's fiction.

We have won 18 awards, including Publisher of the Year and the Romantic Novel of the Year, and have been shortlisted for countless others.

All our novels are selected by genuine readers. We are proud to publish talented first-time authors, as well as established writers whose books we love introducing to a new generation of readers.

In 2023, we became a Joffe Books company. Best known for publishing a wide range of commercial fiction, Joffe Books has its roots in women's fiction. Today it is one of the largest independent publishers in the UK.

We love to hear from you, so please email us about absolutely anything bookish at choc-lit@joffebooks.com

If you want to hear about all our bargain new releases, join our mailing list: www.choc-lit.com

ALSO BY ELLIE HENDERSON

SCOTTISH ROMANCES
Book 1: A SUMMER WEDDING ON ARRAN
Book 2: A CHRISTMAS ESCAPE TO ARRAN

Milton Keynes UK
Ingram Content Group UK Ltd.
UKHW010725151123
432615UK00004B/246